C.S. KENDALL

The Killing Cure: Redeem

First edition

ISBN: 978-1-7342562-2-2

This book was professionally typeset on Reedsy.
Find out more at reedsy.com

To Ryland and Arayna, forever and always my inspiration and why I do everything I do.

Contents

Acknowledgement

I would like to thank Shari Ryan for her amazing cover art and Jacy Mackin for her editorial services. You guys have been great members of my team!

Thank you to my early reader team who are wonderful and encouraging! A special thanks to Kristy Towery and Laura Dickey, who kept after me to finish this series. A special shout out to Janet Grant, who suggested the name "Darius" for one of the characters in this book. And it's such a fitting name!

To my husband, who expresses support and belief in me almost on the daily. I couldn't do this without you! To my parents, inlaws, sisters and brother-in-law who have all encouraged this process and me personally. Thank you.

To all my readers, thank you for your time and investment in this series!

One

Julia and Charlie

"*H*ey you! Pretty lady! Hand me that screwdriver, would ya?" Charlie pointed to the toolbox lying open a few feet from where he worked. Sprawled on the floor, he fidgeted with the bottom of the dining room chair—the one that had collapsed on Julia as she ate breakfast.

Julia dropped the towel she used to dry the dishes and scampered over to Charlie's toolbox. She rifled through his tools for a few seconds before she found the one he requested. "You know, this'd go a lot faster if you'd just use that electric drill I bought you."

"Baby steps, my love. Baby steps. I'm shaving with that highly technological shaver now, aren't I? And I think I can say with confidence that I'm getting the hang of that cellular phone."

"Welll….'getting the hang' might be a bit of a stretch. But you can make a call on it, so that's progress, I suppose." She thrust the screwdriver toward him, only to withdraw her hand playfully when Charlie reached for the tool. Julia threw her head back, bursting into

1

laughter. "Okay, okay, here you go."

When she handed the screwdriver forward this time, their fingers brushed as the tool transferred from Julia's hand to Charlie's, sending a mutual stir through both of them. Julia jerked her hand away, the sensation surprising her. "Three months alone on this island together and your touch still sends shock waves through me."

Charlie cleared his throat. "Yeah?"

But he didn't put the tool into action. His gaze locked on Julia, who stood immobilized too. Waiting, maybe?

Charlie abandoned the screwdriver and jumped to his feet, taking her in his arms. Clutching the nape of her neck, he tipped her head and caressed her throat with the tip of his nose, breathing her in. He inhaled the whole of her. His lips met her skin, just beneath her earlobe, unleashing a torrent of goosebumps down her spine and other sensations through her body.

The touches continued until his lips found her mouth. Both of them trembled as this kiss—long overdue and still wrought with a hundred years of pent-up longing and missions, sacrifice and deceit—threatened to undo them both. They'd shared many before this very one and still. Every time their lips met, Julia's head spun with dizziness. She gripped Charlie to keep from melting to the floor since her legs seemed to forget how to hold her weight when he kissed her. Weak from exhilaration, his touch and his kisses made her heart race and her cheeks burn, just like they had the first time. After a century apart, they were finding their way to each other again, and it was almost more than either of them could stand sometimes.

Charlie stumbled backward, stabilizing himself on one of the kitchen chairs. His arms wrapped around Julia, their bodies crushed together as their kisses deepened, transporting them to the dawn of their romance. Julia pushed away from Charlie, only to direct him onto the table. She climbed atop of him, and they became lost in each other, in their revived love, in the passion that no amount of time could quell.

When they found completion, Charlie held her in his arms, running his fingers through her hair and kissing her temple. Their fingers interlocked across Charlie's chest, and Julia caressed each of his digits, unbelieving of the fact he was there. That she touched him and tasted him. These <u>moments</u> made everything feel okay.

"I wonder," Charlie whispered in her ear. "Will there ever come a time you won't undo me?"

"Mmm," Julia cooed in absolute agreement as a wave of sleepiness crept over her.

Surrendering to encroaching slumber, Julia drifted off. But the rest was anything but tranquil. Faces flew through her mind in rapid succession, bloodstained and screaming. All those whose lives she'd ended haunted her during her brief and fitful rest, one by one, as they had many a night since returning to the island. And, as always, Caroline's face tormented her while she slept. Last of all, Julia saw Rose's wide eyes flood with tears and then go still, life leaving her.

Over and over and over again.

She gasped, shooting upright on the table next to Charlie.

Nausea swirled in her belly, and her heart thrummed rapid beats against her ribs.

"You okay?" Charlie pushed her hair out of her face, attempting to peer into her eyes.

Julia glanced up at Charlie and tried for a reassuring smile. But then she flew off the table and tore through the front door, arriving outside just in time to vomit all over the grass.

Charlie ran to her side and wrapped a fleece robe around her body. "Jul—"

Julia raised her hand into the air to stop him. "Please, give me a moment."

He rubbed her back. "Anything you need."

And Charlie disappeared inside.

Still bent at the waist, Julia wiped her chin on the sleeve of her robe and took a few deep breaths. Standing, she marched over to the Fountain, removed the loose rock, and cupped her hands. She lowered her palms and splashed some of the cursed water onto her face and into her mouth. The taste was sweet, refreshing, and satisfaction whispered through the whole of her. Her eyes fell shut, and she leaned against the rock barrier surrounding the water, finding tranquility in the spring's company.

When she opened her eyes, her gaze fell on Rose's grave. She approached the burial pit and took a seat in the dirt, next to her dead friend's resting place.

"What would you say if you knew what a mess your death has made me, Rose?"

Of course, silence answered her, but she persisted. "I mean, really. It's stupid, right? It's what you wanted all along. To die. Still..." She drifted, her eyes welling. "I'm sorry, Rose. I know I keep saying it, but I don't have better words."

A cool breeze blew, causing Julia's deep red locks to dance. "Turns out the quiet life is not so quiet. Not in my head anyway. And this place, the solitude I thought I wanted—it just brings everything rushing in. What should I do, Rose? I can't very well tell Charlie—"

"—Tell me what?"

Her back to the cottage, Julia hadn't heard Charlie approach. She jumped at the interruption. A smile was on her lips before she turned to face him. "Just how much I love you."

Charlie approached her and kneeled to her level. "Jul, just because I'm a tad...behind the times...does not make me a fool." He met her reluctant gaze. "I tell you what. I'll let you off the hook this time. But only if you come inside with me and help me make that stew we were talking about earlier."

"Deal." She allowed Charlie to pull her to her feet, and they returned to the cottage. Moments later, Julia reveled in the simple joy of chopping potatoes next to Charlie. This confused her, too. Such agony one moment and total peace the next. The duality was enough to make her head spin.

"Ready to put those in the pot?" Charlie elbowed her as she chopped.

"Careful, Charlie! I'll cut myself."

"We wouldn't want that. I mean, it's not like you could spontaneously heal or anything." Charlie winked at her and turned to scoop the carrots he chopped into boiling water. The kitchen space was so tiny, the two stood back to back with barely an inch between them. Charlie dumped carrots into the pot as Julia finished the last potato.

"Here, I'm ready," she said, turning with a sudden motion. Charlie had pivoted toward her at the same time, his knife still in hand. The tip of the blade penetrated Julia's shoulder as they collided.

A searing pain infiltrated her shoulder, causing Julia to abandon her task and drop the cutting board full of chopped potatoes she held. "Ouch!" Her hand flew up to cover the newborn wound, blood staining through her shirt and covering her trembling fingers.

"Oh no, Julia! I'm so sorry!" Charlie grabbed a towel from the counter and applied pressure. Pulling it away, he asked, "Any better?"

"No! I should have healed by now, but it burns." She touched the puncture. "And it won't stop bleeding."

Charlie gasped. "It's because I did it! It was an accident, of course, but I'm immortal and you're immortal. I'm the only one who can inflict a wound that refuses to heal. Or...or kill you, for that matter."

"Ugh, that's right."

"Good thing there's a miracle worker in your midst." Charlie winked at her and guided her to a rocking chair.

Julia lowered, wincing in pain, and Charlie fell to his knees in front of her. "Don't be crazy, Charlie. I'm fine. It's not fatal, merely a flesh wound."

"*You* don't be crazy. I'm going to heal you now."

Julia lifted her palm to stop him. "No. Please. Don't you think you've endured enough suffering for one lifetime?"

"Maybe. But I'm going to live countless lifetimes, so it follows that I should be able to endure a mere 'flesh wound'. Especially if it means I can both alleviate pain my beloved feels and rectify the fact that this is my fault anyway. You always try to educate me on knife safety."

"Yes, and to this point, you are failing."

"Maybe I can earn some extra credit then." Charlie extended his hand to Julia's shoulder.

But Julia shook her head. "I don't know, Charlie. I don't feel good about that."

"Please, Jul, I *want* to show you what I can do. By this time tomorrow, I'll be good as new."

Julia conceded. "Fine."

She nestled against the back of the rocker and took a deep breath.

Charlie covered Julia's wound and closed his eyes. Julia felt her skin pull together as the wound closed. A momentary shockwave of energy echoed through her and then vanished.

"Oy, that smarts!" Charlie grabbed his own shoulder, his head falling to Julia's lap.

"Trade me spots." Julia lifted herself from the rocker and helped Charlie take her place. She retrieved the first aid kit from the bathroom, opened his shirt, and covered the knife wound with gauze and tape. "That should hold you until you're better."

Charlie covered her hand with his. "Thanks, my love." He flashed a feeble smile.

"What does it feel like when you take others' ailments?"

"Like...magic. It's like all my focus goes straight to whatever ails the person. And when I will my healing abilities toward that place, it feels...unlike anything. Amazing, such power. The moment I'm able to pinpoint what it is I'm absorbing, a burst of ecstasy shoots through me. And sometimes...it's almost like looking into the person herself. Like I see them fully for whom they are for just a brief moment. Their entire lives flash and then all the energy and focus centers on whatever it is I'm trying to heal."

"And what did you see in me?"

"Only, ever and always the woman I love."

Julia blushed, words failing her. Not because he stole her composure, but because she felt less and less worthy of such expressions. She cleared her throat. "Want to eat some boiled carrots?"

"I guess our menu is limited to them tonight." Charlie leaned his head against the rocker.

"You rest, and I'll dish us up."

Bowls of boiled carrots emptied, the two sat in front of the fire Julia brought to life. She stared into the flames, lost in her own thoughts, that joy she felt while preparing their meal together now replaced again with other preoccupations.

"You okay?" Charlie's question startled Julia, and she jumped. "Sorry. Didn't mean to scare you. You were deep in thought there, weren't you?"

"Uh yeah...sorry."

"A penny for your thoughts?" The corner of his mouth turned up in a smirk.

"Everything keeps flashing through my mind. My time with Rose, her murder, my brief and strange encounter with Amara, how weak and helpless you looked."

"But I'm good as new now."

"I know. But what they put you through, Charlie."

He reached for her and took her hand in his. "Why don't you let me worry about what happened back there. The important thing is that we're both safe now and we're together."

That's what he kept saying. And he was right, of course. This—minus the small inconvenience of the wound they'd traded—was what she'd wanted more than anything, what she fought for all those years. And yet, time changed things. And there was a tiny part of her that refused to settle. An impulse to flee out the door struck her, but she closed her eyes and squeezed Charlie's hand, finding solace in his touch.

Everything was okay.

Except, she knew, that wasn't entirely true. Besides the decades of murder gnawing at Julia, another thing bothered her. Amara had an agenda—one Julia didn't trust—and it involved Charlie. They lived under the illusion of freedom while Charlie remained Amara's slave. Perhaps it was this that prevented Julia from finding contentment in just being with him.

"You know I love you now more than ever, right?"

She looked up into his eyes, appreciating his assurances, even if she wasn't sure she deserved them. "I do. I love you, too, Charlie."

He released a big breath. "I should get some rest. That always helps with the healing."

Julia helped him ascend the ladder and settle on the mattress in the loft. She stayed with him until his breaths became slow and rhythmic, but sleep eluded her.

As quietly as she could, she descended the ladder, wrapped herself in a warm blanket, and ventured outside. The island air was cool, the smell reminiscent and sweet. She approached the stone barrier surrounding the water and traced the mortar with her fingertips. Her mind had a difficult time reconciling the tranquility she felt near the water to the havoc it wreaked inside of people. Inside of her, once.

As she was just about to pull out the loose stone from the wall so she could touch the water, she heard a strange sound. Weeping. Wailing. Her head snapped back toward the cabin as her heart split in two. The sounds came from inside. Dashing across the lawn, tripping over the bushes they'd recently planted, she tore through the door. Julia flew up the ladder to the loft and found Charlie with his face buried in his palms. His cry was deep and mournful, like nothing she'd ever heard come out of him.

"Charlie?" She reached for him then froze.

Charlie stayed hidden behind his hands. From his palms, his words came out muffled. "She's dead."

"What?"

"Why didn't you tell me? I must have forgotten. How could I have forgotten?"

Julia grabbed Charlie's head, cradling him against her chest. She soothed, "Shhh, it's okay. Whatever it is you've just remembered, it's going to be okay."

"How could I forget a thing like that? I'm a terrible brother." He broke into sobs, his entire body quaking.

"Wait—what? Brother? What are you talking about?"

Charlie peeked out from his hands with red-rimmed eyes. "My sister. Don't tell me you've forgotten too."

"Your sis—..." She turned her head from him and bit her lip, as confused as Charlie seemed. "What do you think happened?"

"She's dead. She died. How could I forget?"

A fresh wave of sobs racked through his body. When he was able to catch his breath, Julia took both sides of his face in her hands.

"You have to listen to me."

He peered back at her, tears staining the whole of his blotchy face, eyes swollen from them.

Julia gulped. "Charlie, you had a brother named Jethro; your mom, Eleanor; and your father, Charles Senior. You never had a sister."

Betrayal registered on his face and then morphed to anger. He pushed her arms from around his body and stood. "How dare you?

How dare you, Julia!" He wrapped himself in a blanket, climbed down the ladder in an angry huff, and burst out the door.

Julia remained, stunned. What just happened? The look on Charlie's face was pure grief, as if he truly had lost someone he loved. She'd never seen anything like that from him before, and this scared her. Leaving the loft, she ran out the front door which still stood open. Finding Charlie next to the wall surrounding the spring, she crouched to his level. He sat in a squatted position, running his fingers over the petals of the antidotal flower.

He sucked in a shaky breath. "If I had this leaf, I could have saved you, and I could have saved her."

"Charlie." Julia rested her hand on his shoulder and massaged his upper back. "There's nothing you could have done to change anything that has happened. We're just here, and we have to do our best to make the most of our time together now."

His gaze snapped to hers. "Easy for you to say. You didn't just remember you sister's tragic death like it was yesterday."

Julia angled her body toward Charlie and sat down on the ground with crisscrossed legs, studying him and trying to riddle out what was happening. His eyebrows creased with worry—grief even—and his cheeks flushed fuchsia. Moist red eyes matched his rosy nose. For him, however false this memory, it was his reality. She had to tread carefully, ensure not to shut him down and send him running for the hills again. "Tell me what you remembered."

"Her illness first. She was already sick, and then it happened. She thought she was going to die anyway—was losing her mind, and so she...she..." He trailed, a fresh set of tears on his cheeks.

Julia wrapped her arms around him, and he didn't resist her embrace. "It's okay, love. It's okay. You can tell me."

"Don't you remember?" He snapped in a bitter tone. "She killed herself. Strung herself up and hung there like some common criminal of old."

A start went through Julia's heart. What a crushing memory, even if it wasn't his own. "I'm sorry. Please indulge me. What was her name, Charlie? Your sister?"

"Adelaide," he answered without missing a beat. "Addy, we called her. And she had such a bright future. How could she do that to herself? How could she?" He buried his head in Julia's chest, his sobs shaking against her skin.

"Charlie, do you remember anything else about her? Your childhood growing up or some other detail?"

He stared at the rock wall, and his focus steeled to determination. And then confusion. Suddenly, he was sobbing again. "No. Isn't that awful?"

"Try, Charlie. Nothing at all?"

He composed himself and wiped his face on the blanket. Gazing into the darkening distance, he shook his head. "Nothing. I can't remember a single event from our history other than the fact she died. And it's like I just found out for the first time."

"Did you wake up with the memory?"

"Yes. Just woke all the sudden and it was like I walked in and found her corpse again. I'm the one who...who...found her when it happened."

"Oh, Charlie...." She caressed his hand in hers as she worked to formulate the words. This didn't make any sense, but whatever this was, it was very real to Charlie. "I want to say something to you, but I need you to listen, and I don't want you to become angry with me."

He sniffed, looking at her out of the corner of his eye. "Okay..."

"You grew up in Iowa on a rural farm with your mother, your father, and your brother. We've known each other since we were five, and we were best friends until we became more at nineteen. I think you remember everything from there. Besides your time serving in the

Great War, the only dead people you ever saw were Caroline, whom I murdered, and Rose. I'm worried...I'm worried you may confusing the details of all that has happened. But even so, neither of those girls was hanged."

He threw a rock, and it hit the wall surrounding the water. "No." He plucked a second stone from the ground and wound up to throw that one, too. Anger filled his gaze as he turned it on Julia. "I had a sister. Adelaide. Addy. She killed herself. I found her. Why don't you believe me?"

He said the words through gritted teeth and with great conviction.

"Charlie, I believe you. I believe you think this is real, but it's not. It's not real."

He tore himself from her grip and stormed back to the cabin. One good thing about having returned to the island was that there wasn't far for him to go. She gave him a moment, but more than that, she needed to take one to figure out what was happening.

Why did Charlie suddenly believe he had a sister whom he'd traumatically witnessed kill herself? There wasn't even a story from their past that she could align with this sudden and strange memory. She took her time by the rock wall, allowing the water to soothe her, soaking in the clarity it brought. Whatever was happening to Charlie had to be the result of what they did to him at Eden Pharma. Or a result of whatever he had become here on the island when he woke up.

Julia shuddered, worried about what all this could mean for Charlie. But she shook off her fears and resolved to go support him. Walking through the door, she found him on the floor fixing the chair she'd now long ago handed him a tool for.

"I'm sorry," she said.

"For what?" The vigor with which he turned the tool told of his anger, his grief.

"I didn't mean to discount your grief."

"But you think I'm mad?"

"Not for a second."

She knelt, stopping his arm with her hand. He looked into her eyes, his anger melting at her touch.

"I love you, Charlie, and I'm sorry for the grief you're feeling. Can I make you anything?"

He sat up and dropped the screwdriver to the floor. "I'm okay, thank you. It's so awful. I can't even sit around and talk about all my memories of her because there's only one that rings clear in my mind."

"That must be terrible. When people lose someone, it's nice to recall happy memories. I'm sorry you don't have that opportunity. But I'm sure Addy was a dear."

"Why don't you remember her?"

She dropped her gaze, turning her fingers in her lap. "The bigger question, Charlie, is why do *you*?"

She braced herself for his anger again, for another storm off. But this time, he shrugged.

"I guess I have no clue. But I'll tell you what helped me through my grief when you were so sick. It was working on that fort back home. Will you help?"

"Of course." Julia stood and resumed her previous task of staining the chairs that were not wobbly as Charlie tightened the ones that were. They worked in silence deep into the night until the entire dining set was complete, now sturdy as ever and stained a deep walnut.

Two

Julia and Charlie

*T*he few hours of attempted sleep were fitful for both Charlie and Julia until finally they gave up. Now morning, they sat on the porch in chairs Charlie had built, sipping coffee. The spring sun rose over the water.

"I can never get enough of these sunrises." Julia counted the number of colors featured in the morning sun's show, trying to push away the thoughts that refused to leave her mind. "How are you feeling?"

"Tired." Charlie yawned and then took a long sip from his cup of coffee.

"And how's your shoulder?"

Gazed fixed ahead, Charlie tapped the site of the wound he'd taken from Julia. "Almost there. I kinda forgot about it in all the madness that was last night."

Julia didn't respond, didn't know how to.

"I don't get it, Julia. That memory feels more distant now, but I still can't deny how *real* it was in the moment."

"And that's never happened before?"

"Not at all. But it leaves me feeling...clouded in my mind. Makes it harder to discern what's real and what's not."

Julia placed her hand on Charlie's and gave it a squeeze. "This is real. You're real. Let's just get to work and try to forget about it for now, okay?"

Coffees finished, they took to doing their chores. Now that spring arrived, they worked hard to grow their garden and fix up the place. It was coming along nicely. Charlie had nearly restored everything to how he had it before he was kidnapped, and Julia had suggested a few touches to make it homier. They had only planned to stay a little while, until they got their bearings and Charlie was comfortable heading out into the new world. But the days melted into weeks and then months.

Julia watched Charlie attack the soil with a pick and couldn't help but admire the strength in his bare arms, the way his muscles flexed with his movements. He glanced up from his work, a streak of dirt across his face, and smirked at her. The dimples sunk into his cheeks and sent her heart skittering inside her chest. How could a one hundred-year-old romance still produce butterflies for her? His effect on her was a mystery, but one she was happy to let go unsolved.

"Whatchu staring at, beautiful?" He lifted his arms and twirled around. "Take a nice, long look. It's all yours whenever you want it."

"I want it now." She ran to him, jumping as she reached him. He caught her. Legs straddling his waist, she kissed him with a sweaty, muddy kiss.

He pulled away. "Should we take this inside?"

"No, here." Julia dropped her feet to the ground and crushed herself against Charlie, sensations surging through her body as his hands roamed. She ran her fingers underneath his tank top and felt his stomach, reaching around and feeling the strength in his back. He squeezed her, holding her close to him, their bodies nearly melding into one.

"Ah!" He pulled away, drawing his hands to either side of his head. "No!"

Bending at the waist, he grimaced.

"What's wrong?" She smacked her lips and placed her hand on his shoulder, bending to match his posture.

"I remember something. But this time it was like the memory jumped into my head, and it hurt."

"That's odd. What was it?"

"Did I ever rob a bank? Me and a buddy I grew up with—Snakes."

"Snakes?"

"His nickname. The robbery was his idea, and I let him pull me into it. But he got shot."

"Oh no."

"He didn't die, but that's all I remember." He stood up straight and exhaled a long breath.

"You okay?"

Shaking his body out limb by limb, he nodded. "I think so. That one was less painful...emotionally anyway. But now I just feel worried for Snakes. I don't know what happened to him."

"But, Charlie, you don't actually know Snakes."

"It feels like I do!" He shouted but lifted his hand to cover his mouth as soon as he did. "I'm so sorry. I don't mean to yell at you. Come here." He pulled Julia to him and kissed her on the head. "I think I need to lie down now. I'm feeling exhausted."

"Okay, you go ahead. I'll keep working out here."

He stumbled into the cottage as worry rose up inside of Julia. That made two memories, both in the space of twenty-four hours. At least, this time, he seemed able to separate it from reality, but still...what had *she* done to him? Both times one of these incidents occurred, Julia's mind took the natural progression to Amara, to that place they kept

Charlie, to his decrepit form in the bed. Part of Julia wanted to track her down, to demand answers of her. But at this point, she wasn't even sure what the questions were. This was all very bizarre, and Julia couldn't help but wonder if they'd done more to him than she realized.

And then there was Amara's immortality. That nagging fact made Julia itch with desire to go on the road again, to figure out who Amara was and how she'd had a drink.

No, she told herself.

It didn't matter anyway. She had enough to contend with without welcoming that mystery. Charlie's strange memories-that-were-not-his-own provided enough for Julia to solve. And she alone was capable of helping him sort through reality and delusion.

Time passed quickly as she finished the work in the garden and quietly crept inside to take a shower. Stepping out, she found Charlie awake in the kitchen, staring at the stove.

With a brush tangled in her hair, she stopped short and watched him. "Everything okay?"

"I think so. I just can't seem to remember how to use this thing." He gestured toward the cook top.

"Oh, I can help you. This is pretty new to you, so maybe it just slipped your mind." She lit the fire under the plate. "There you go. Are you hungry? Want me to make something?"

"I was thinking...eggs."

"Really? You don't usually like eggs."

"I don't?" He looked toward the ice box, and confusion lived in his gaze.

"Are you feeling okay?"

He shook himself out of his daze and gave a smile that Julia knew was meant to reassure her. But it succeeded only in worrying her further. "I'm fine. I guess I'm not too hungry after all. I'm going to get to work on repairing the siding out back of the house that the windstorm pulled up."

"Okay. I'll check on you in a little bit." Julia pulled her clothes on and brushed her teeth. After she grabbed a bite to eat, she decided to pay Rose a visit. Dragging a chair to the grave, she sat down.

"I'm worried about Charlie," Julia told the ground. "I know, I know. That's my M-O, isn't it? But I fear he's in real danger, Rose." She leaned toward the grave and lowered her voice. "He's having delusions. Memories not his own. I suspect it has something to do with Amara. Do you think I should find her?"

Julia paused, as if giving Rose a chance to answer. "Yes, old me probably would have wanted to hunt her down and kill her. She fits the criteria, and she hurt those I love…" Julia trailed as Rose's big, empty eyes stared lifelessly at her in her mind. "Anyway, I've been thinking a lot about that, about the fact I've *killed* people. Sure, I had a hundred years to think about what I was doing, but it wasn't like that. I was always on to the next thing, always distracting myself from the horrible things I did because I had to do them. Had to get Charlie back. Remember how I told you I wasn't sure the quiet was good for me? In the moments of rest, it's *all* I think about. And especially now that it seems I'm losing Charlie in another way, I have to wonder: was it worth it? How am I any better than those I've killed?

"And yes, Rose, I know you are far better than me in that regard. So is Caroline. Neither of you deserved what you got…. yeah, yeah, I know I can't change it, but I also am having increasing trouble shaking all that I've done…"

"Who are you talking to?"

Julia turned to find Charlie, a look of desperation on his face.

"Just Rose. What's wrong?" She sprang to her feet and rushed to his side.

"I'm so sad."

"Did you remember something else?"

"Yes."

"What is it?"

"Was I married before you?"

She huffed a laugh. "No, Charlie."

"Well, did we get married?"

"I guess we're still engaged, but there's never been an official ceremony. We've been a touch busy. I'd say technically we're as good as married, though. I think we've proven our commitment is more than lifelong."

Charlie wasn't amused. "Then....did we have a child?"

"Oh no." She took the hammer out of his hand and steered him to a nearby stump. Pushing gently, she directed him to take a seat on the old tree. Julia kneeled in front of him and took his hands in hers. "You always wanted children, but I got sick before we could get married and then became this before any of those dreams had a chance."

"So we didn't lose a baby?"

"No, Charlie."

He dropped his face to his palms and puffed out an exasperated sigh. "It feels so real. I can't separate."

"What does? What did you remember?"

"You or someone—my wife is faceless in the memory—had a baby boy named Edgar. But he died within a week of his birth. We waited for him for so long, and he looked perfect when he came out. But then he was gone." Tears welled in Charlie's eyes, and he sighed a deep, woeful sigh.

"I'm so sorry this is happening to you."

"Why can't I have a memory that's happy or at least neutral? My heart feels so heavy. If you could gain weight in your chest, I've done it." He paused, glancing around the island. "At least being here is helpful. It's familiar to me, and I spent most of life years here, really. And the water...the water brings calm."

"Come on."

Julia pulled him to his feet and led him to the spring. Jiggling the loose rock, she dipped her hand in and submerged her palm into the water. Her hand tingled, the water alive on her skin. Lifting her hand to Charlie's face, she wiped the moisture onto his skin. His eyes closed. He allowed the soothing properties of the water in until a smile reached his lips.

"That's better," he whispered.

Keeping his eyes shut, he took four long inhales and exhales. Then he opened them. "Thank you. The island helps, but you help most of all. You keep me centered, Julia. You have always done that for me. While I was away at war, I believe even as I was unconscious all those years, you are and always have been my constant. And because of that, I will never leave you."

"Leave me? Why would you say that?"

"Well, despite the fact I'm losing my mind, I still see you. I've watched you these past few months we've been here, and I know you have a lot on your mind. You don't think I know you're having dreams about what you've done. I do. Sometimes I pull you close to me when I can see it happening. And I've heard some of your conversations with Rose—not that I've eavesdropped," he was quick to add when Julia raised her eyebrows. "Look, whatever it is that is burdening you, you can talk to me. I'm here for you."

"Yeah, yeah, Rose."

Charlie squished his face in confusion.

"Sometimes dead Rose talks to me. Not like in a hallucinatory sort of way. But you know how a debate can rage in your mind sometimes—the reasonable voice often sounds like hers. She was reminding me how silly I am to keep things from you."

Charlie sat against the stone wall and pulled Julia onto his lap. "Tell me what's on your mind."

A heavy sigh left Julia's lungs. "I don't know. So much. Now that I'm still I can't stop thinking about those I've killed. And I'm scared because...what if I have to do it again?"

"What? Kill someone?"

"Yeah."

"One: No one ever *has* to kill anyone. In fact, I'd venture to guess that most don't! Two: Who would you kill?"

Julia gave him a look like the answer should be obvious.

"Amara?"

"I just—there's something about her, Charlie. And I worry she's evil and out to get you, and if it comes down to you or her, the choice is easy. But I don't want to be in a position of having to make it. I never wanted to be a murderer."

Charlie laughed. "Yeah, I doubt few children aspire to such a thing."

Julia huffed. "I was *made* a murderer. I'm not compelled by the water any longer, but what if something else forces my hand. I just—I'm not sure I could do it. And then what?"

"Julia, I don't know anyone stronger than you. Most of all, your mind is strong. You get to decide these things. Besides, it's been months, and we haven't heard anything from Mara."

"Still, she practically promised we'd see her again. That concerns me."

"It seems you are carrying many concerns. But I want you to know something. There's nothing you have done or will do that will make me stop loving you. Or that will cause me to leave you. I promise you this. Whatever is ahead, whatever comes up, including my very strange and sudden insanity, I have faith in us, Julia. We can figure anything out. If nothing else, we've proven that our love not only survives the test of time, but that it can't be driven away by anything."

"You're right. I know you're right."

Still, the uneasiness refused to abate in Julia's mind.

21

"If I had to, I'd die for you, Julia."

"Well, you don't have to worry about that. You're kiiiiind of immortal."

"I suppose I am. Good thing you are too." He braced the back of her neck and pulled her mouth to his, kissing her. "I love you," he whispered again, tilting his forehead against Julia's.

"I'm hungry. Let's make dinner." She hopped up from his lap and pulled him to his feet. "I will say I kind of got used to the convenience of grabbing food. That'll be nice again once we can move to some city somewhere."

"Like, you just walked into a place and grabbed it?" he asked.

"Like I went to a restaurant, ordered it, paid for it, and then they handed it to me."

"Oh. You will have to orient me to all of that. But for now, there are still some steaks in the freezer from our last run. Let's cook those up with potatoes."

The night waned, and with full bellies, Charlie and Julia climbed the loft and drifted into an easy sleep.

"Stop!" Charlie sat upright, his scream echoing through the loft.

Julia stirred, disoriented. "Wha—what is it?" She sat up with him.

"She—she's a killer."

"Who, Charlie?" She fought grumpiness as she struggled to wake up.

"Ginny. She killed Mrs. Lingman. Just took her mask off and watched her suffocate."

"What?"

"I stood there and watched her. I wanted to do something to help, but I also had to make sure. See her carry out her act. Sad as it was, Mrs. Lingman was a goner either way. But I should have stopped her."

"Charlie, how do you know about Ginny? Or about Mrs. Lingman?"

"I remember."

"That's impossible."

"Ugh, it's happened again! But why do you say it's impossible?"

"Because that memory is not yours. It's mine."

Three

Darius and Amara: Many, Many Years Ago

She giggled as he chased her, long locks of dark hair trailing behind her as she ran. His arms wrapped around her waist and drew her body to his. Holding on, his fingers found her ribs, tickling her sides, and a fit of laughter erupted from the two of them. They fell to the ground together, the soft grass cushioning the pair, even as the blades caught against their skin. On the ground, he fingered a strand of her hair, tucking it behind her ear. Looking into her deep, dark eyes, a sigh echoed through him as he thought about his love for this woman.

"Darius."

The sound of her voice soothed him, bringing an immediate calm over his demeanor. He closed his eyes as the smooth melody of his name rolled off her tongue. When he opened his eyes, she watched him with a playful smile on her lips. Thinking of her lips stirred something in him, and he had to taste them.

Immediately.

His hand already poised on the base of her neck, Darius drew her to him and found her lips with an eager kiss. She pecked his lips playfully several times in succession. This was her game, and she knew it drove him crazy. Then, like always, she let his kiss in, parting those perfect, beautiful lips so he could taste her tongue. As their kiss deepened in the grass and the sun blazed overhead, beating warmth on the two of them, a sweet breeze rustled the grass against his skin. Darius considered that this was the most perfect moment of his life. All the perfect ones before this one could not be topped. Not until now.

And he couldn't wait for next perfect moment, the one that would outdo this one he reveled in. That's how it went for Darius. Each new day topped the one before, as one perfect moment stacked onto the next.

When he retreated from their kiss, he ran the tip of his finger down the length of her cheek. "Amara, you are the most beautiful woman my eyes have ever beheld."

"And you, my love, are this earth's most handsome man."

His lips twitched into a grin at her return compliment. But really, he was lost in her beauty. Her flawless, olive skin paired with her almost black hair and matching eyes. The fine point of her nose, the cleft in her chin, the height of her cheekbones. All contributed to his beautiful one, his wife. Every single day, he considered himself the luckiest man alive.

"Father! Mother!"

Darius tipped his forehead against Amara's as their daughter's voice sounded through the field they hid in. "'It seems our moment of solitude has ended much too quickly."

"There's always tonight," she whispered in his ear before licking his earlobe, which sent a torrent of chills down the whole of his body.

"You devil woman. That is not fair!" He went to tickle her again, but she caught his hand, laying a kiss across his knuckles.

"I'll make sure you'll get your fair dues tonight, my love."

"There you are! What are you doing out here?" Their daughter, as lovely a sight as her mother, jogged up to them just then. She adjusted the strap on her white tunic before planting her hands on her hips. "I've been looking everywhere for you."

"And now you've found us, my dear." Darius stood and pulled Amara to her feet with him. He grabbed his daughter's head between his palms and kissed her forehead. "My beautiful girl, my dove. Are your chores finished?"

"All but preparations for the feast. But I thought you might want me to seek your guidance for that."

"Clever girl. Mother and I shall accompany you home so we may begin." He reached for her hand, lacing her smaller fingers through his own. "My lovely girl," he said, more to himself than to her. She was growing far too quickly, so close to becoming a woman. Her childhood slipped away before his eyes. Darius studied her for a moment, memorizing her every detail. Hair like her mother's fell to her waist. Dark eyes mirrored hers, too, but with a fleck of gold in them. She stood only a few inches shorter than Amara now.

Darius wrapped his arms around Elora, his precious daughter, and his other around Amara, his beloved wife. With both ladies in his grip, they strode back toward the village, toward their dwelling.

"Tell me, daughter, how were studies today?" Amara peeked over her husband, directing her question to Elora.

"Oh, they were delightful! Today we continued our lessons about caring for the animals. I fed a tiger and swam with a sea giant and watched a nest of baby birds be born. It was so exhilarating! Father, when's the last time you swam in the sea?"

"Just last week, my girl."

"Yes, but have you ever done so alongside a sea giant? Gray and magnificent and frightening?"

"I suppose it's been some time since I've done that."

"We should do so this weekend! You and me and mother. We should experience this together."

Darius and Amara exchanged an amused look. "Your mother fears the giants of the sea."

Darius squeezed Amara's shoulder.

"Mother, say that isn't true?" Elora stopped short on their stroll and tore out of her father's embrace. She blocked her mother's path. "We shall overcome this fear for you. But first—you must learn to swim!"

"My daughter," Amara began.

"No! No excuses. There's nothing to fear. They are big, but they are gentle. Just like the tigers and the buffalo and the large ones with noses as long as my legs!" She skipped ahead, lost in her delight over the animals.

Darius couldn't help the joy bubbling inside of him. Because he'd found it. His next happiest moment. First his wife, now his daughter, the two loves of his life. Nothing on earth matched their beauty, no force in existence could separate them from his love. He supposed all men felt this way—lucky. But he had to be the luckiest among them.

Elora skipped back to her father's side, taking his hand in hers and laying her head on his shoulder as they walked. "I shall like to work with the animals when I grow responsible."

"That would be a good job for you. You have always been a caring girl, and you have always had a fascination with animals. Such a job would suit you. If you like, we can speak with the Great Guardian and see if that might be a task assigned to you."

"Would you, Father? Mother?" Elora jumped up and down at his suggestion.

Amara squeezed his arm. "Darius, do you fear it is too soon?"

"For what, Mother? I do love the animals so."

27

"You are only thirteen. If you should change your mind?"

Elora's face sobered. "I never would."

Amara gave a gentle nod of her head. "Then let it be so."

Elora released her father's hand and ran to his other side, where she tackled Amara to the ground and kissed her all over her cheeks. "Thank you, Mother! Thank you! You will not regret making this request on my behalf."

Amara giggled, pinned beneath her daughter. Darius jumped on top of both of them, tickling his two ladies until they could hardly catch a breath.

"Please, please, Father! Enough!" Elora sputtered.

Darius relented, falling to the ground beside Amara. He gazed at her and watched her for a brief second. Her lips turned up into a joyful smile, her eyes crinkled with laughter. She gave Elora a playful nudge and then was tackled by the girl a second time as she wrapped her arms around her mother and nestled her head in the crook of her neck. Amara smiled, a soft groan of contentment escaping her lips.

She was happy, too. Darius could see it on her face—perfect serenity, complete contentment. Life had no more to offer than this.

Amara's dark eyes opened, her gaze falling on Darius. She winked at him, and he squeezed her hand as they found themselves returned to the ground. For a brief second, Darius forgot the duties calling them at home.

He looked up to the sky, the clear blue almost an exact match to his own eyes. He closed his eyes as the sun warmed the surface of his skin and the breeze rustled his hair. The grass itched beneath him on his bare back , but he endured the scratchiness as he enjoyed this moment.

Opening his eyes, a red berry caught in his line of vision. He reached his hand forward, his fingers landing on the fruit. When he plucked it from the vine, it made a "pop," and he drew it to his nose, inhaling the scent. The berry smelled sweet, carrying with it the aromas sent by the wind. Darius opened his mouth and tossed the berry in, the sweet essence of the fruit bursting on his tongue as his teeth penetrated the berry. When he'd swallowed, he gazed around him, trying to locate where the fruit had come from. And then he spotted the bush.

Just a few feet from where the berry was—from where he now lay—was a lovely plant, vibrant red and bursting with color against green leaves. He'd never tasted this particular berry before, which surprised him as he thought he knew all the land had to offer before now. With a sudden motion, Darius sat up, and in the next moment, he was on his feet. He approached the bush and plucked a second berry, studying it. It was knobby with bumps all around and the most brilliant red he'd ever seen. As if this berry should have something different to offer, Darius smelled the fruit, and then he ate it.

"What are you doing?"

He turned with a sudden jerk at the sound of Amara's voice, and when he did so, he slammed smack into her. "I'm sorry, my love." He caught her arm to stabilize her. "I didn't hear you approach."

"I am very stealthy, "she teased, giving him a kiss on the cheek. "What have you found?"

"It seems in all our foraging of the land we have never stumbled across such a berry as this." He plucked a third one from the brush where it grew and lifted the berry for Amara to see.

She took it from him, turning it over as she studied it. "It's beautiful."

"Take a taste."

She looked from the berry to Darius, as if she wasn't sure if this was a test or not. Then, apparently deciding she would pass, she bit the fruit. Her expression went from skeptical to amazed. Her eyes lit up and then fell shut as the succulent flavor of the berry overcame her.

"Delicious, isn't it?"

"The most delicious."

"We shall use these in the feast tonight."

In response, Amara gathered up her tunic, making a basket of her garment. Darius picked as many berries as would fit in their make-shift bowl, and together with Elora, they took them home.

An hour later, the family worked together preparing their contribution to the evening feast, with the berries as the centerpiece of the dish. As dusk fell over the land, Darius and his family put the finishing touches on their dish and their appearances.

"Ready, my ladies?" Darius waved his hand in front of himself in invitation for his wife and daughter to lead the way.

"Always," answered Amara, and Elora dipped into a curtsy.

The three walked out of their home, each carrying a part of the dish, and into the village courtyard. There a table spread the length of the garden area, as far as they could see, as it did every night. In keeping with the nightly custom, Darius and his family chose different spots than they'd sat in at the previous night's feast. They would keep different company tonight than they did at their last meal.

"Philip! Eve! How is your family this fine evening?" Darius sat back against his seat with an arm around each of his girls.

Philip and Eve sat opposite Darius' family and began to scoop up some greens onto their plates. "We are well. Thank you, Darius. What did your family make? You always have the best offerings at the feasts."

"Here." Darius passed his dish across the table, and the other couple ogled it.

"What is it?"

"A berry treat. Try it."

Philip served himself a generous portion and plopped a serving onto his wife's plate as well. Neither hesitated to dig in, and their eyes mutually fluttered as the flavors of the dish melded on their tongues.

"My friend, you have done it again!" Philip took a second bite and then a third, and those were all the words they got out of him for the moment.

Soon china dinged around them, and the Great Guardian stood from the head of the table. "My esteemed guests...my family. As I am every night, I am honored you have all joined me at this table to feast. Remember, everything is acceptable to eat. Nothing is off-limits. Eat until your stomachs are full and your hearts are the same. As you well know, we share the bounty of this land and thank the heavens for the plentiful harvest that grows. Our only restriction is the Fountain."

"Here we go..." Darius poked his daughter, who rolled her eyes in response.

The Guardian continued. "The Fountain looks beautiful with fresh, clear waters flowing from it. But we mustn't be fooled by the beauty. Drinking from it unleashes a danger to us all..."

With his words, the sky above seemed to darken and a small rumble sounded in the distance.

"But! We mustn't worry of such things. For tonight, we eat! We drink! And we celebrate!" He lifted his glass, and this gesture elicited a loud cheer from the table of people. The cheering ceased as everyone drank at once.

Music followed the feast and, with it, dancing. Darius took turns twirling Amara and his daughter around the courtyard as other families did the same. He replaced his previous best moment with this new one, dancing and laughing with a full stomach and a happy heart. As the night wound down and the music faded, Darius took Amara and Elora by the hand and walked home. As was the nightly custom, he tucked his daughter into her bed.

"Father, why does the Great Guardian remind us nightly of the Fountain?"

"It is his job. You wish to take care of animals. He watches the water."

"Is it really so bad?"

"If he says it is so, then it is so. We each are good at our jobs because we are made to do them. If he says there's danger, then there's danger.

31

Why so many questions tonight?"

Elora lifted her shoulder in a slight shrug. "Just wondered."

"Do you find yourself tempted to drink?"

In response to her father's question, Elora burst into laughter. "No, Father. Not in the least. I do not want to bring danger to our people. Besides, we have everything we need and could ever want here." She grabbed her father's hand with both of hers and kissed his knuckles. "There is always food, drink, and joy. Friends to run with, family to love. We need nothing else."

Darius couldn't help the grin overtaking his face. His daughter had just articulated his sentiment. "I could not agree with you more, my dove." He kissed Elora on the forehead. "Now, rest well. Tomorrow we have another day."

"Do you think he'll really assign me to care for the animals?"

"My daughter, you were born for such a task. Sleep now."

"Good night, Father." With those words, Elora closed her eyes. Darius watched her, his hand still clutched tight in both of hers. He waited until her breathing evened into slow inhales and exhales before he slipped his fingers from between hers.

Tiptoeing to the other side of the small dwelling, he found Amara in bed waiting for him. The moonlight streamed in through the open window, illuminating her soft skin and accentuating the curves of her body. Warm arm blew in through the screen, carrying the sounds of nature's nightlife, the scents of flowers in bloom, and the tang of salt from the sea. Desire for his wife engulfed him, and he remembered the promise she'd earlier made.

"Come, my love. I have my word to keep," she crooned.

As he climbed into bed next to his beautiful wife, Darius found his perfect moment topped again. This. Here. With his daughter sleeping a peaceful rest one room over, his tantalizing wife with her invitations, and the promise of a new day just one night's rest away...these made now—this moment—the most unblemished of them all.

Four

Julia and Charlie

⚜

Julia rubbed her eyes and consulted her wristwatch. 5:12 a.m. "I'll make a pot of coffee."

In a groggy stupor, she left Charlie alone in the loft and started the process of brewing a pot of liquid caffeine. As it dripped, the smell of coffee filled her nostrils and thoughts swirled in her mind. This could only mean one thing.

Charlie's bare feet scuffed on the wood floor as he approached her from behind. Warm arms wrapped around Julia and clasped together at her waist. "I still don't get it. You're telling me that what I described of Mrs. Lingman was what happened to you? As if I was seeing the memory through your eyes."

"Yup. I never told you about Ginny or about her victim. Charlie, I think I know what's going on here."

"Please, pray tell."

She turned to face him. "I think, for some reason, you're seeing the memories of people you've healed. As real as the dead sister seems

34

to you, I promise you did not grow up with one. And as familiar as the scene with Ginny is in your mind, you didn't see that. You were still here, on the island, when all that happened. Actually, you were probably already *there*. At Eden Pharma."

"But...why? Why would I be seeing these things?"

"You got me there. Obviously, it has to do with healing people. You healed me most recently. Maybe that's why my memory was one of the first. I just wish I knew what this meant."

"You and me both."

The coffee finished dripping, and Julia poured two mugs in silence. She turned to face Charlie, handing him one of the mugs. "We need to figure out what's happening here."

"You don't have to convince me. As distressing as it is to take on the painful memories of others, I guess I shouldn't be surprised that being a miracle worker comes with side effects."

Julia laughed. "Stop calling yourself that."

"What? Miracle worker? What would you call me?"

She stared at him for a moment, but nothing clever came to mind. "I got nothing."

"Then don't judge!"

Julia sobered. "But why? Why side effects? You do the world a favor! As far as Amara's concerned, you're some kind of freaking Savior or something. Why should you suffer?"

"Why should anyone? What makes me less entitled to my share of suffering?"

"This isn't your share. This is other peoples' share."

"I don't know...there's always balance, right? The Fountain of Youth heals you, but it makes a killer of you. The antidote spares you from such a fate, but you'll be sick or mortal again. Everything has a cost. A counterweight."

"I suppose. Still—"

35

Charlie set his coffee on the small spread of counter and wrapped his arms around Julia. He pierced her gaze with his chocolate eyes.

"Can you just enjoy the moments I'm sane?" Pushing a tendril of hair out of her face, he laid a kiss on her forehead. "I have an idea. We're up early. How about we try to catch the sunrise?"

"I think that's an excellent idea."

Hand in hand, they retreated to the porch. Julia draped herself across Charlie's lap, and they sat in quiet content, waiting for the sun to take its first glimpse over the horizon.

"Ah, this is what I always imagined." Charlie's eyes were closed, his arms wrapped around Julia as he held her close to his body.

"These are the perfect moments," Julia agreed. "When I was out on the road hunting down all those who had a drink from the Fountain, I would often wonder what a quiet morning would be like with you. Or an uneventful evening. Sometimes I felt so far from the girl I was, I wondered if I'd be able to enjoy something normal like this with you."

"And can you?"

"So far, so good."

She kissed Charlie's nose.

Charlie tipped Julia's chin with his finger, lifting her gaze to meet his. "This is all I ever wanted. You, me, the quiet…." he trailed, a certain sadness shadowing his expression.

"And children. You always wanted children."

She tousled her fingers through his hair and kissed him on the cheek, with the wish in her heart that she could give him what he'd always longed for.

"I did. But I've come to terms with the fact that that dream had to go with everything else. But I'm happy to find a new dream, as long as you're by my side."

"Nothing could tear me away."

They held each other as the sun started ascending over the clouds.

When it poked half-way over the horizon, Julia asked, "Do you miss your family?"

Charlie didn't answer right away. And before he uttered one word a shaky sigh rattled through him. "I haven't thought about them in a little while. But when I first woke up here and had to face a future without you, that was painful enough. Then I found out not too long after that I'd slept for nearly a century. It makes me sad we never got to see our parents again, know how they died. I hate the fact that they probably grieved us and never had any answers to our disappearance."

"I hate that fact too. I can tell you a few things if you want to know."

"What do you mean?"

"Charlie, I checked in on our families over the years. I had to know. I hoped I hadn't destroyed my mother by disappearing. She was always so scared of losing me."

Charlie grimaced and closed his eyes. "That's right. Poor lady."

"Yeah. She was okay. Met a man a town over and remarried. I like to think she found happiness again. And your parents—"

Charlie opened his eyes, his attention snapped to. "What about them?"

"They both lived long lives, Charlie. Your dad died in 1949 of natural causes, and your mom five years later. Neither suffered. For a long time our parents ran a search committee to try to find us, but they had to give that up after several years of coming up empty-handed. Your brother, Jethro, married the girl he was with, and they had five children."

"Five?! That means—that means I have family out there somewhere." Excitement danced in Charlie's expression.

"Yes, that's right."

"We should find them."

"And say what?"

"We don't have to say anything. Just find them, get to know them.

I would like that. It'd feel good to know family again, even if I could never tell them we were related."

"Well, Charlie, if that's something you'd like to do, then we can once we feel ready to go."

"I would like that." He leaned against the rocker.

"Have you had any other memories besides the ones you've told me?"

Charlie's brow furrowed. "Just one."

"What was it?"

He blew out a long breath. "I remembered my grandfather dying. When did that happen?"

"Your mother's father or your father's father?"

Charlie squinted his eyes, like he was trying to see something in the distance. "I guess I'm not sure. In my memory, it's not clear. But I loved him, and his death was a great loss."

Despite his words, Charlie's eyes were dry, his expression indifferent.

"You don't seem so traumatized by this one."

"I woke up in the middle of the night, and it struck me. So the Ginny memory was the second one that came in the night. I didn't want to wake you, so I got up for a little bit and did my grieving in silence."

"Oh, Charlie, you could have woken me up."

"I know, but I want to be strong for you. All those years you were strong for me while I lie sleeping. I need to start carrying some of that weight."

"You don't have to 'be strong' for me, Charlie. You were my strength all while I was sick. You were what kept me going, kept me believing. Your continued hope that I would get well is the only reason I didn't tell you how serious my case was while there and the ultimate reason I took that drink."

Charlie sobered. "Ah, yes, the drink."

"No, that's not what I meant. We're not going to revisit an old blame game. What happened happened. And now everything is okay."

She squeezed him in her grasp, securing her arms around him. She was almost convinced her statement was true, and she needed to say those words as much as they both needed to hear them. Hope against hope, she whispered a silent prayer that her words would prove true.

When the sun was fully risen, they began their work around the island for the day. Charlie picked up his work of repairing the shingles on the house. Julia painted the ones he'd already restored next to him. She hummed a song as he pulled up the last piece of siding.

"Ah!" Charlie dropped to his knees, grasping his head.

"Are you okay?" Julia massaged his shoulders. "What is it this time?"

"You—you're sick again, aren't you? Why didn't you tell me?"

"What—no, Charlie. Look at me." His gaze met hers as she worked to reassure him. "I'm still just me. I can't get sick, remember?"

"It feels so real. I remember the diagnosis. The doctor brought us in, told us you had cancer. I know cancer. I took many forms of it at Eden Pharma. Oh, Julia, you weren't supposed to ever become sick again!"

"Look at me!" Julia commanded.

When his sad eyes snapped to her face, she continued. "Can you see my face in the memory?"

His gaze dropped to the ground as he thought about her question. "No, I guess I can't. I can see mine and the doctor's, but you're just a blur."

"Because it's not your memory. And I'm not the one who received the diagnosis."

Charlie fell to his knees, a flash of emotion striking him. Bringing his hands to his face, he cried. "I just can't tell. I want to believe you, but the memory is so compelling. I can't sort it out."

"But you did this morning, Charlie. Remember—it was a new

memory, so you knew it couldn't have been real. This one just occurred to you, too, so the same thing applies. Think about it."

"I'm trying. Really, I am." He wept openly. "All I can think about was the possibility of losing you again to some other disease. You have to remember that my memories of you on your deathbed are only two years old. This most recent memory is too close to what I experienced then."

"I'm okay, Charlie. And so are you," Julia soothed.

"Am I?" Charlie heaved a heavy sigh. "I want to believe you," he whispered. "But maybe you're not telling me because you don't want to hurt me or because you think I can't handle it right now because of what's happening to me."

His voice raised and he stood, forcing Julia off his lap. "I can handle it, Julia! I took the last near-death experience of yours like a champ, didn't I?"

He was pacing now with balled fists and gritted teeth.

"Why are you angry at me?"

"Because! You're lying to me!" He snapped.

"No, I'm not! Think about this. It makes no sense. I know it feels real, like you can't separate truth, but I'm immortal. Unless cancer can turn into a physical tool and you, as another immortal, strikes me with it, I can't get it."

"No," he said, his voice coming out in a whisper. His eyes roved over the island. "It's like the more mental energy I give my confusion, the more complex the web of doubt grows. I can't make sense of anything. Everything—all these new memories that feel so real—just swarm in my brain in a jumbled mess, converging details of my former life with these newer, vivid memories. I can't—I just can't tell it all apart." He stopped, breathless and squatted to the ground with his head between his hands.

"Charlie." Julia lifted his face so their eyes could meet. "You can trust me. Remember? You told me I am your constant. Try something. Try just pushing those thoughts away."

"I am trying, but they're persistent as hell."

"Try picturing a room with a door. Think about shoving all the thoughts in there and locking the door."

"Yeah, they're just pounding from behind the door, begging to be let out."

"Oh, Charlie."

He met her gaze, worry and grief rolled into his expression. "I don't want to worry you." He motioned in the air like he was locking a door, and then he tossed the imaginary key away. "I'm locking them away, I'm drowning out the pounding, and I just threw away the key." When his words met with an uncertain expression from Julia, he added, "I'm okay. Thank you. You do help me. You keep me sane."

"You don't need me for sanity. If that's the case, we're both in trouble." She laughed, and some of the weight of the moment lifted. "Why don't you go lie down? Maybe you'll feel better after some rest."

He nodded, and Julia walked him into the cottage. Before he climbed the ladder, she squeezed his hand and gave him a kiss. "I love you, Charlie. Come get me if you need me."

Charlie gave her a kiss on the top of her head and climbed the ladder.

* * *

Sleep proved good for Charlie and gave Julia a chance to be alone with her thoughts. As had become her daily ritual, she consulted Rose at the site of her burial.

"I mean, the new memories just keep coming, Rose. And I'm getting really worried. Do you think we should seek our Amara? Is that wise?"

She paused and tossed a stone toward the lopsided cross marking Rose's grave.

"You're probably right. It's probably not a good idea, but I'm not sure how to help him. He tried drinking more of the Fountain's water, just to see. Nothing happened, as expected. I feel incapable here. All this is going on, and it's kind of caused the constant onslaught of regret and horror that runs through my head to cease. So that's something. But I know it's still there, in the back of my mind. I know because I dream about it. Every night. I don't tell Charlie, because he has enough to deal with. But I can tell you, can't I, Rose?

"I probably should get him off this island, though. I just don't know where to go. I can't take him to a hospital, and I don't want to seek out Amara...I know, I know. She could probably help make sense of it. But I don't trust her. That's the long and short of it. I just *don't* trust her.

"I can't say this has been particularly enlightening, Rose. You're off your game today." Julia huffed a small, amused smile at her own joke. "But thanks for listening anyway."

She patted the earth and stood.

Inside, she found Charlie with messy hair and heavy eyelids. "How was your nap?"

He checked his wristwatch. "Three hours and I still feel terrible."

"Maybe some food will snap you out of it."

Without another word, they started preparing a meal together. Julia sautéed onion in butter and listened to the rhythmic chop-chop of the blade Charlie cut vegetables with. Back to back in the small space they worked in tandem.

The chopping sound stopped, and the only enduring noise was the sizzle of the onions.

Charlie held the knife he used out in front of him with a look of utter confusion on his face. Turning it over and over in his hands, he watched the light catch the shimmer of the blade, touched the tip to his finger, poking himself.

"Ouch!" he shouted. A drop of blood came from the wound, and he grabbed a towel to catch the single droplet, the pinprick puncture closing up in an instant.

"Did you cut yourself?" Julia turned, and leaned over Charlie, examining the now healed puncture on his fingertip.

"I guess so. I was using this thing on the vegetables, and then I just didn't know what it was."

"What do you mean?"

"What is this called?" He held the knife in the air by the handle, dangling it in front of Julia.

"A knife, Charlie. You literally stabbed me with one the other day."

"Knife. Nnnn—iiiiiii—fffff. Knife. Okay."

Julia raised her eyebrows at him. "Doesn't that sound familiar to you?"

Catching her worried gaze, he dropped the utensil on the counter. "Oh yeah, of course. A knife. Just forgot for a sec." Charlie turned around and chopped veggies as if nothing had happened.

Julia faced the onions again, stirring with her spatula as they sizzled in the pan. Now he'd forgotten a common knife? Something wasn't right with Charlie. She chose to choke down her concern and focused on finishing the meal. But alarm bells screamed inside her brain.

Once they were asleep for the night, Charlie awoke like he had the night before, screaming. This time he remembered a tornado hit his home, and he'd lost everything. And on this went for days, which then melted into weeks. Every night he had at least one new memory and a couple hit him each day. But the most alarming thing to Julia was the rate at which he forgot everything else. It had started with forgetting how to use the stovetop and then what a knife was, but before long, he couldn't remember how to tie his shoe or brush his teeth.

Julia tried not to let him see her alarm—the ways he was scaring her, but sometimes it was impossible to shield from her expression.

"What's wrong?" Charlie asked one evening as he fixed the window.

He'd just finished caulking it and was tightening up the nails around the frame.

"Nothing. I'm fine."

"Then why are you watching me?"

He hammered three times and then stopped. Julia watched him drop his hand to his side, the hammer dangling from his fingertips.

"Why'd you stop?"

"No reason." His voice was quiet, his body motionless.

"Look at me!" she screamed.

Charlie turned, alarm in his eyes. "I—I don't know how to use this." He lifted the hammer in the air. "One moment I was pounding away, and the next..."

"Charlie, something is wrong. I've been telling you for weeks, but you have to acknowledge it. We need to get help."

He nodded, helplessness written on his face. Placing the hammer on the table, he pulled the chair out and sat down. "What is happening to me?"

"I don't know."

"Julia, I'm scared."

She crossed the room to him and sat on his lap. Running her fingers through his black hair, she faced the fear coursing through her. "Me too."

"Maybe we should—"

"I know. But going to Amara is the last resort."

"I think we may be out of options."

They nestled their foreheads together. "Okay. In the morning, let's fuel up. We'll go to Eden Pharma and figure out how to get in touch with her."

"Okay," Charlie answered, his eyes closed. "I'm so sorry, Julia."

"Look at me." She raised his chin with her finger. "You have nothing to apologize for. This is something that is *happening* to you, okay?

And tomorrow, we'll see if can get some answers."

Five

Julia and Charlie

*J*ulia had been trying for almost an hour to read a book on the porch while Charlie slept, but her mind refused to focus. Distracting her was the notion of how different reality was turning out to be from what she'd imagined. She'd thought that once she and Charlie were reunited and they had a chance to be alone, they could just relax, build a life together, and leave everything else behind. But complications from the drink just seemed to keep following them, and part of her wondered if she'd ever be free from the curse of the water.

Her thoughts dangerously progressed to what it could mean that Amara was also immortal, her assurances they'd meet again, and her request for their help. Had she known Charlie would lose his mind? Had she caused this?

The latter question brought flaming heat to Julia's cheeks. *If Amara is to blame*...and then she remembered the other part of her psyche, the one filled with regret and eager to shed murderous compulsions

46

of all kinds. Squeezing her eyes hard, she slammed the book shut, frustrated that she couldn't seem to get her thoughts off the hamster wheel. Round and round they went, circling in her brain. Answerless questions persisting in an endless tangle.

THUD.

The sound was thunderous and harrowing, and it came from inside the cottage. It was followed by Charlie yelling, and Julia sprang to her feet and burst through the front door. She found him at the foot of the ladder holding his leg.

"Help!" he cried.

"Did you fall down the ladder?" She bent to examine him, just in time to see his broken bones set back into place. Rubbing his leg with her hands, she massaged the remainder of discomfort out of his leg.

The moment his leg was restored, Charlie jumped away from her, fear in his eyes. He looked around the place like a scared little bird, eyes darting to each corner of the cottage as if he were lost. He pulled his knees into his chest and hugged the wall with his body.

"Charlie, it's okay."

Julia's heart raced. Terror swept through her as she regarded him. This seemed like yet another progression to whatever was happening to him.

"Get away from me…" Charlie murmured as his foot began to bounce, and his fingers tapped wildly on his leg. "Where—where am I?"

"Charlie!" Julia didn't mean to yell at him, but fear made her voice rise.

"Don't…." He closed his eyes and put his finger in the air, as if to stop her. Opening his eyes, he sucked in a deep breath and narrowed his gaze at her. With a steady voice, he spoke slow words. "Tell me right now. Where am I, and *who* are you?"

A pang of hurt shot Julia in the chest. "Charlie, it's me. Julia."

He drew away from her, scampering across the room and huddling on the floor. "No. I don't know you. Leave me alone."

Her heart pounded; her stomach filled with nausea. "Charlie—"

He put his hands up, as if to shield himself from Julia.

Julia's body trembled as she turned and ran out of the cabin. She ran the entire length of the island until she reached the river's edge. By the time she got there, her breaths were hard to come by. She bent at the waist, stabilizing herself against a tree as she tried to breathe. She gasped for air, and her lungs weren't working. On top of that, sprinting from the cabin had stirred the nausea in her stomach, and she puked into a nearby bush.

"Get yourself together." Closing her eyes, she inhaled, counted to five, and exhaled to the same count. Charlie didn't know her anymore. The grief of that reality struck her heart, and the next thing she knew, she sobbed. With a glance toward the cabin, she wondered what he was doing in there. The look of terror on his face told her his words were sincere.

She was a stranger to him.

Circling Rose's grave, she worked to gather herself. "Do you see what's happening, Rose? He doesn't know me! I need to get him out of here, but I fear I've waited too long. How am I going to convince him to go with me?" She paced back and forth until she made up her mind. "It can't wait. We have to go now."

Julia rubbed her face on the sleeve of her shirt and released a trembling sigh. Clearing her throat, she squared her shoulders and made the return walk to the cottage. The door squeaked open with a slow crawl, and there was Charlie, sitting in one of the two chairs in front of the fireplace. Face buried in his palms, the sounds of the door did not disturb him.

"Ch—Charlie?" Julia called as her voice cracked with uncertainty.

He turned just enough to glance over his shoulder. "Jul…"

48

Flooded with relief, she ran to him, throwing her arms around his shoulders. "You know me?"

"I—I don't know what happened. It's like I went away for a minute."

"The only thing that matters is that you're here now." She grabbed his hands and pulled him to his feet. "We can't wait. I can't risk you forgetting me again. We're leaving now."

"It's the middle of the night."

"I don't care! I'm fueling up the boat. You pack a bag."

The topic was not up for debate, and Julia stormed outside and headed straight for the speedboat. She kissed her hand and transferred the kiss to the cross sticking out of Rose's grave as she passed by.

"We're leaving, Rose. See you sometime."

She froze in her steps. Turning around, she pulled the cross from the ground. Charlie's axe stuck into a nearby tree stub, and she plucked it with one vigorous motion. With the cross lying on the ground, Julia used the axe to lob off a corner. Returning both the axe to the tree stub and the cross upright in the ground, she gave the grave one last, lingering glance.

Julia shook the shard of wood in her palm and then pocketed the memento. Moving purposefully, she fueled the boat and prepared the vessel for departure. Moments later, Charlie arrived with two bags. No words passed between them as they packed up the boat, untied the rope holding it against the island, and set off into the black night.

They'd only been on the water a few minutes when the clouds opened and dumped buckets of rain on them.

"Perfect! Visibility is already limited!" Julia yelled over the down-pour.

She'd paid attention when they were here the couple of times before, and she knew exactly how to follow the compass over the water, even in the dark night and pouring rain. The rain glued her hair to her face and soaked through her articles of clothing. Shivering, she forged ahead, determination driving her on. Every few seconds she spared a glance at Charlie, but he gave no indication of losing his mind. The entire trip was over in about forty-five minutes, and the small boat idled up to Eden Pharmaceuticals. Dripping wet and frozen to the bone, Julia and Charlie approached the front entrance. They buzzed in.

"State your name and—"

"—Julia Franklin and Charlie Harris. We need Amara. Now." Julia interrupted.

A pause followed her demand. The silence stretched longer than it seemed it should, so Julia buzzed a second time.

Another pause and then the door clicked open. Julia shoved her way through and was met on the other side by security. "Where's Amara?"

The security guard blocked her path. "I'm to find out the nature of your visit."

Julia shoved the guard aside and stormed deeper into the lobby.

"Where is she?" Her voice echoed off the stone walls. "We need to see her. Now."

Julia spared a glance at Charlie in time to see him reach for his head.

"Ow," he cried, doubling over.

Julia shot the guard a nasty look and crossed to Charlie. Bending at her waist, she touched him on the shoulder. "You okay?"

But Charlie didn't answer.

Julia stood and hammered her finger into the guard's chest. "Tell Amara that Charlie is in trouble. Tell her we need her help."

The guard clashed his gaze against Julia's for a moment before whipping a cell from his belt. He hit one number and placed the receiver to his ear. "Yes, ma'am. They're on the premises...Okay, ma'am. I can ask." He covered the receiver with his hand. "She wants to send a chopper for you."

"And take us where?"

He spoke into the phone again. "She'd like to know where to..." And then his hand covered the receiver again. "Her estate. She wants you to be her guests."

"This isn't a social call!"

"Yes, ma'am. She says it's not a social visit. Yes, okay." And he hit the end call button and fastened the phone to his belt. "Sit tight."

He turned and disappeared through the revolving doors.

"Hey!" Julia hollered after him.

She'd hoped Amara would be here, that she could tell her what was going on without having to wait. They needed help now. They needed answers now.

Returning to Charlie, she patted his back. In moments, she heard the rotation of the revolving door and looked up to see Amara approaching them.

"There you are!" Julia stormed up to the other woman. "Always with the drama, Amara. You couldn't have just told the guard you'd be here in a second?" A cutting wave of irritation rumbled through her.

"It's wonderful to see you two. You must be cold."

Only then did Julia see the blankets in her arms. She extended them to Julia, who took them.

First, she wrapped one around Charlie, and then she covered her shivering frame.

"Hello, Charlie," Amara called, but he didn't spare a glance toward her. Amara frowned, alarm in her gaze. "Is he okay?"

"He's not okay. That's why we're here."

"Come, let me get you set up in a room so you're more comfortable. You can tell me what's been going on."

"Oh, no. Not a chance. I'm not giving you or your...cronies here the opportunity to lock us up again. Not happening."

"Well, you weren't keen on my invitation to my estate, so I figured you might be more comfortable here."

"I'm not comfortable at all, to be honest with you." Defeat threatened to overcome Julia. "I guess if you're giving me the choice, I'd rather not be here. This place does not hold the best of memories for Charlie. Plus, I'm ready for some fast food."

"Whatever you'd like. They're fueling the chopper now—" she smiled at Julia's confused expression. "—I assumed you'd be more comfortable elsewhere." Amara crossed to Charlie and placed her hand on his shoulder.

Finally, he looked at her. A sigh of relief echoed through him. "Hello Mara. Thank you."

"It's my pleasure." A warm smile spread across her face.

"What is that? Why does your touch help so much?" Julia snapped.

"There are many questions I'm sure you have, and for each one, I have an answer. I'll tell you anything you want to know, Julia. Okay? But first let's get you dry and comfortable."

Her own phone vibrated, and Amara lifted it to answer. "Yes?...Thank you." And then to Julia and Charlie, "Chopper's ready. Are you?"

Julia wished there was another option, but she could think of none. "Let's go."

Six

Julia, Charlie, and Amara

~~~~~

The chopper thundered over the headphones they all wore. Amara sat across from Julia with a soft smile. The spinning blades roared overhead and Amara talked into the microphone attached to her headset. "Do you want to talk about why you've come?"

"I hardly think this is the appropriate time or setting to get into all of that."

Julia turned her gaze to the dark sky outside. The chopper's flashing lights cut through the black of night with rhythmic beats.

Charlie grasped one of his covered ears and hissed. Julia turned with an abrupt motion and settled her hand on his elbow.

"Another one?" Julia murmured.

"This one is real. It's a war memory. My brother came with me, and I saw him get shot."

"No, he didn't. Jethro was off studying to be a lawyer when you went to war. I'm sure it feels like you lost him, though. It's been a long time since you've seen him."

"No!" he shouted into his own microphone. "I feel it. I know this one is real."

Julia cut Amara a look. "Or we can get into it now."

"What's happening with him?"

"He's been having tragic memories that aren't his own. Only, he can't separate what are his true memories and what are not."

Something occurred in Amara's expression, and Julia didn't miss it. "Do you know what's wrong with him?"

"I may have an inkling. It's good you are coming with me. Listen, I have a guest house at my estate, and I want you two to stay there. We'll make Charlie comfortable. I'll have my best doctors and researchers on it."

"'Make him comfortable?' You talk as though he's dying."

A subtle smile lifted Amara's lips. "A poor choice of words on my part then. Will you stay with me? Let me help you get to the bottom of this?"

Julia sat in silence for a moment, allowing the question to linger. She glanced at Charlie, whose own gaze was lost in space. She was reminded of their limited options.

"That's why we came, Amara. I'm hoping you can help us. I'd take him to a hospital, but that would never work. If you can get doctors on his case who can be discreet about his...special qualities, that would be greatly appreciated."

"Of course. Why do you think I started my company in the first place? It's always my hope to help."

Julia refused an answer, as she had her doubts about Amara's claim. Being helpful seemed her furthest motive when she took part in holding Charlie captive.

Charlie managed to hold it together without any additional memories until they were able to land on a helicopter pad. Stepping out of the chopper, Julia's eyes fell on a massive mansion not far from the helipad where she stood. White and pristine, large jutting pillars flanked the home. Beautiful, rolling landscape surrounded them with bushes cut into intricate designs and an outdoor entertainment area, complete with a pool, hot tub, outdoor living room, table tennis, loungers, a bar...more luxury than Julia had seen in a very long time. The scene froze her in her tracks.

Amara paused beside her. "I've done well for myself," she said in response to Julia's gaping expression.

"I'll say."

Charlie stepped out and opened his mouth for the first time. He let out a low whistle. "You have been holding out on me, Mara. I have to tell you, for the next time you kidnap someone, these would be preferable accommodations."

Julia smiled beside him. "You've been so quiet. It's good to see you joking around."

He gave her a smile that did not reach his eyes, which failed to reassure her.

"Come," said Amara. "Let's settle inside while my staff prepares the guest house for you." She turned from them and issued a few commands into her cell phone before she started toward the mansion. "Follow me."

The pair did as told, and they entered through the back of the home into a vast, open kitchen. Marble and mahogany stretched from floor to ceiling. Julia counted four ovens.

"You're both still wet, and I'm sure you're cold. Would the two of you like to shower first?"

Julia looked to Charlie, and he shrugged.

"I have a bathroom for each of you. Follow me upstairs."

Still without a word, they followed Amara. Julia was eager to talk to Amara about what was happening with Charlie, but she also craved warmth and dryness. She could see the discomfort in Charlie's posture too. He stood with his arms crossed close to his body, shivering. Yes, hot showers and a change of clothes would do nicely.

The two bathrooms were next door to each other and attached to two bedrooms. "Are you sure you're okay alone?" Julia asked Charlie. "Should I stay with you?"

He nodded, a coy grin curling up the corners of his mouth. "You should definitely shower with me, you know, just to make sure I'm okay."

"I know you're joking around, Charlie, but in all seriousness, I would be more comfortable."

Normally, a shower together would inevitably lead to a deeper expression of intimacy, but despite Charlie's jokes, the somber mood hanging over their circumstances dictated a quiet and serious approach to their washing. The shower they stood in had a rain nozzle overhead, pouring down a steady stream of hot water onto them. Each side of the stall had another head that blasted each of them in the back. Steam filled the bathroom, and Charlie and Julia held each other's gaze, facing each other as they washed.

"Are you okay? You barely said a word the whole ride here."

"I'm fine. Just trying to stay grounded in the moment, focus on something, anything, so my mind doesn't get away from me."

"What did you focus on?"

"The sound of the chopper blades. I tried to shut everything else out, and still..."

Julia caressed Charlie's arm. "We're going to figure this out. Okay?"

"And if we can't?"

Julia allowed the question to hang in the air; she had no answer, and the reality of that terrified her. She pushed her fear down, and pouring a quarter-sized amount of shampoo into her palm, she lathered it into her damp hair.

"How do you feel about being here?" Julia asked him as she scrubbed her hair.

"It's a bit fancy for this Iowa farmer's son."

"Not the house. About being here. With Amara?"

"We talked about this. What choice do we have? I just hope she has an idea what's happening."

"Did her touch really help you that much when we saw her again?"

Charlie smiled and traced a wet finger down Julia's cheek. "Yes, but it doesn't mean anything. It's like she's a bandage for a wound."

His words stung a little, even though Julia knew what he meant. She tipped her hair into the stream of water behind her. The heat covered her head and trailed down her body, warming her icy skin. She should leave it alone but she couldn't deny the wave of jealousy rippling through her. "I'd like to be your bandage."

"Jul, you're so much more than that. Please, don't worry about her, okay? Never seen this before. What is it for?" Charlie held up a bottle of body wash.

"Ha! All I do is worry about her. It's body wash. Like soap. You use it to wash your body."

Julia opened the bottle and squeezed some of the contents into Charlie's palm. Scents of coconut and vanilla filled their nostrils.

"That smells amazing!"

Charlie lathered and scrubbed.

Both done washing, they stood there, gazes locked, hot water pelting them from above and behind as steam collected in a thick cover.

"I don't want to get out. This feels good. And when we do, we have to talk to her, and what if I don't like what she has to say?" Charlie mused, worry creasing between his eyes.

Julia took his hand and gave him a reassuring squeeze. "Whatever she has to say, whatever we have to face, we'll do so together. Okay? You ready to get out now?"

Charlie nodded, and Julia turned the handles to the off position.

Hair wrapped in a towel and dressed in dry fatigues, Julia led Charlie down the stairs.

Amara waited for them in a room at the foot of the stairs, the room she'd previously regarded as 'the parlor.'

"I trust you're warm now. I hope you're more comfortable," Amara said as they entered the room.

"Thanks, yes," Julia answered.

Julia and Charlie sunk into a fancy green love seat across from where Amara sat cross-legged in an ivory chair.

Julia's gaze traveled over their surroundings. Wooden pillars stretched between marble floors and the ceiling. She knew from the exterior that the place would be huge, but nothing could have prepared her for the twelve-foot ceilings or the seemingly unending and open six thousand square feet. Everything about the place had modern appeal, from the sharp lines in the furniture to the cold, white walls to the funky lights overhead. Perched in her high-backed seat, Amara's form appeared tiny next to the marble statue of a Greek god behind her.

A green—the same color as the couch the couple sat on—and black Persian rug covered the floor of the room they sat in. Bookcases lined the wall behind Amara, next to the statue towering over her. A coffee table separated them and a teapot with three mugs sat on a tray with a plate of cookies.

"Ah yes." Amara's gaze followed Julia's to the coffee table. "Would you like some tea?"

Julia's stomach gave an involuntary rumble.

"No, thank you," she said, ignoring the emptiness of her stomach.

She regarded the other woman across the room. Amara remained a mystery to Julia, sitting there dressed in black pants, a soft blue button-down top, and heels. Her inverted bob was teased, giving it volume, and her face was made up. All this in the middle of the night, as if she knew they'd come for her help when they did. Julia thought about how exquisite Amara's beauty was but also how different she appeared from the first time she met her at Eden Pharma which reminded Julia that Amara had played a role at her research facility. This thought sent an uneasy wave through Julia's belly, and for a split second, she worried they'd made a mistake in seeking her out.

Amara cleared her throat. "I know this must be odd for you given how we met. Charlie, again, I'm so sorry for what we subjected you to. It is so good to see you again."

Neither Julia nor Charlie responded.

After a moment, Amara continued. "What happened on the chopper—I assume that wasn't the first time?"

"No, far from it, and it's been progressing. Charlie—" Julia gave him a side-long glance and then took his hand. "The worst one was when Charlie forgot me altogether. He didn't know me from...from anyone."

Julia spared a glance Charlie's direction and found him gazing at her, with a million apologies in his eyes.

"I know," she assured him. Then she turned her attention to Amara. "I suspect he is having memories of the people he healed. In fact, I know he had one of mine."

"He healed you?" Amara cocked her head.

Julia chuckled. "Yeah. After trying to run me through with a blade." She elbowed Charlie, who gave her weak smile.

"He remembered one of my most recent memories before we were reunited—something I never told him about."

"But he regards the memories as his own? Charlie, you feel like these things have happened to you?"

Charlie lifted his gaze to Amara. "I can't tell the difference between my own, true memories and the ones I'm acquiring. And they keep coming, popping into my brain with sudden force and... they overcome me."

"Hmm," Amara said, drumming her chin with her forefinger. "I have some thoughts."

Charlie groaned, grasping his temples and closing his eyes. His chest began to heave, and his breathing accelerated. "No," he cried. "Not Mama too."

Julia rested her hand on his arm. "Charlie, it's okay. Is this a new memory?"

"Has to be, with how real and intense it feels." he replied, head still grasped tight between his palms.

"Then you know it isn't yours, that it's not true," she soothed, rubbing his back.

"There's knowing and there's feeling, and I can't convince the feeling despite the knowing."

His breaths quickened until he was panting. Standing up straight, his face turned a blotchy crimson, and his gaze held panic.

"I can't breathe. I can't—" He braced himself against the wall and fanned his burning skin with frantic waving motions.

Julia took his face in her hands and forced his eyes to meet hers. "Listen to me. You're having a panic attack."

"I don't know—I don't—what—"

"It means your anxiety has taken over your body. You can't breathe because you think you can't breathe, and your heart is racing because you're freaking out. Look me in the eyes, and focus your breaths. In..."—she guided him as they both took a breath in—"...and out."

They breathed out together, and Charlie struggled to keep his breaths in sync with Julia's. She walked him through the same exercise until his lungs expanded again and his heart slowed the erratic beats down.

Charlie nodded at her and stood up straight. "I thought I was dying."

"It can feel that way." She massaged his shoulders. "You okay?"

"For now. Except for what I just remembered about my mother."

"Charlie." Julia grabbed his face again. "Your beautiful mother was named Lorraine Harris. She had brown hair and blue eyes and a heart of gold. She died in June of 1954 of natural causes at eighty-one years of age. She was celebrated, grieved, and remembered well by those who survived her. Your mother didn't suffer in the end, and she loved you thoroughly."

Tears welled anyway and spilled down Charlie's cheeks. "I didn't get to say goodbye."

"I know you didn't, and I'm sorry. I'm sorry, Charlie…"

Amara stood. "How would you feel about getting some rest, Charlie? The guest house should be ready by now."

Charlie kept his eyes trained on Julia's face and gave her a subtle nod.

"That would be great, thank you," said Julia. "Where do we go?"

"Actually, Julia, if Charlie is okay with it, I'd love if you stay and talk with me."

"I really should stay with Charlie. In case he has another incident."

"I'll tell you what. I have cameras everywhere; I promise, when the two of you stay there, I will disable the ones in the guest house. But for the time being, I can pull it up on my tablet. If we see anything concerning, you're thirty seconds away."

Julia cast a glance at Charlie, asking with her eyes how he felt about this.

"It's okay, Jul. I'll be okay. Stay."

Julia sighed deeply. "Okay, Amara, let's get Charlie tucked away for the night, and then you and I will talk."

Seven

Darius and Amara: Many, Many Years Ago

mara stretched, the morning light beckoning her awake as it streamed in through the window of their dwelling. Darius lay fast asleep next to her, the even rise and fall of his chest signifying the depth of his slumber. As he slept, she watched him.

How handsome he was. How deep her love for him. A pink blush covered his dark complexion, and his almost black hair stood tousled from sleep. She traced his fingers with one of her own, feeling the softness of his skin, the length of each digit. Crawling closer to him, she angled her body against his, snuggling him as she woke up the rest of the way.

Darius stirred, and when he noted her next to him, he opened his arms and scooped her into them. This was their morning routine, and Amara loved starting her day this way—safe within his arms. Indeed, she could think of no safer place—nothing more secure than his embrace.

"Good morning, my love," she greeted.

His first response was a big yawn, which made it impossible for him to answer her. But once that was complete, he kissed her head. "Morning. Did you sleep well?"

"Yes. I always do next to you."

He squeezed her close and stroked her shoulder with a gentle caress.

"Mother! Father! Are you awake?" Elora parted the curtain to their room, and Amara looked up at her precious daughter with a smile.

"We are, my sweet. Come, give me a hug."

Elora jumped onto the bed, and with a tackle, she squeezed each of her parents tight, laying kisses on their cheeks. "I'm starved," she giggled. "Father, come prepare something?"

"Of course, my dove." Darius swung his legs over the side of the bed as Elora hopped to her feet.

She reached for his hand, tugging on his arm to make him stand. "I want more of those berries!"

"We'll have to gather some later. We're all out here at home."

"Uggh." Elora reveled in her disappointment for a mere second and then broke into a smile. "Then I'll have some delicious honey and fruit from the garden."

"I shall help you gather them."

Darius stood, stretched, and followed his daughter outside where they plucked a few juicy pieces of fruit. Once their breakfast was gathered, they met Amara at their table, feasting on fruit and honey.

With breakfast done, the family dressed and prepared for the day. Amara brushed her daughter's hair, the smooth dark locks waving just slightly at the ends. "Are you excited to continue your work with animal care today?"

"Oh yes. Will you talk to the Great Guardian about this? Please?"

"Today?"

"I don't want to wait a moment longer than I must, Mother. If you get his blessing today, I can begin training soon."

"And you are sure you don't want another job? You could prepare the food like your father or help care for the garden as I do."

"Of all the jobs, Mother, nothing calls to me so clearly as the animals do."

Amara stopped brushing, resting a hand on Elora's shoulder. "Then, my darling girl, I shall talk to the Guardian today."

Elora jumped from the stool and into her mother's arms. "Oh, thank you! Thank you, Mother!"

"I haven't gotten the blessing yet, my daughter. Let us not forget that. Come, I'll walk you to meet the others."

On her way to the door, Amara kissed Darius. She meant for it to be a simple good-bye peck on the lips, but he scooped her up into her arms, dipped her, and kissed her like it was their last.

When she was swung upright, Amara giggled. "I will see you shortly."

"It is too long to be away from you," Darius called after them.

When she looked back, he blew her a kiss.

Once she'd dropped Elora to group under the care of their instructor, Amara returned to the center of the village to begin her day's tasks. She pruned the hedges and watered the flowers.

"Good morning, Amara."

At the sound of his voice, she jumped. Turning, she faced the Great Guardian. She'd been lost in her thoughts and hadn't realized how close she'd ventured to the Fountain. With her hand to her heart, she blew out a deep breath. "You startled me. Good morning."

"Forgive me. I did not mean to. How is your family this morning?"

"We are well, thank you Guardian. And how are you?"

"Rested from my night's sleep."

"May I ask you a question?"

"Of course, anything."

Amara's gaze wandered to the Fountain, the small spring in the center of the garden. "Who watches it while you sleep?"

The Guardian followed her gaze. "Ah yes. Wonderful question. Even in my sleep, I have a sense of the water. I always know when someone is near."

"But...how?"

"Are you thinking of sneaking off with some in the night?" His voice held jest, but his gaze was leery.

"No! Of course not. I'm just curious." Amara busied herself with a nearby bush, trimming some of the pieces.

"Of course. Curious. I just know, dear one. It is my job as it is your job to care for the plants. We all have one."

"Yours seems a bit weightier than the rest of ours."

"I suppose it is."

Amara paused, and with a step back, she examined her work. Satisfied, she moved down the line.

"Each job is important, though. Each one keeps the balance here—ensures all are fed, all are happy. And we have it pretty good. Would you disagree?"

She agreed. And yet...she wondered. "Yes, Guardian. I never want for anything, and in that way, life is very, very good."

"In that way?"

Amara's cheeks filled with heat. She didn't like having her motives examined by the Guardian. She needed to change the subject, and remembering her conversation with Elora, she had the perfect topic. "Guardian, Elora thinks she knows what she would like her assignment to be."

"Let me guess. Animals?"

Amara stopped in her tracks. "How did you know?"

"I have seen her with them. She lights up in their presence and takes great pride in them."

"Is it too early to establish her future job?"

The Guardian scratched his chin. "Some have a good awareness early of what they would be most fulfilled by. It seems Elora is one of them."

Amara smiled. "She will be so delighted! I cannot wait to tell her."

"Why wait? Go tell her now." A warm smile touched the Guardian's lips.

Amara stood on her tiptoes and gave him a kiss on the cheek. "Thank you, Guardian."

She ran off toward the sea, toward her daughter with the news. Within minutes, she reached the shoreline, and she didn't hesitate to wade out into the waters toward Elora and her class.

"Elora!"

Amara forged deeper into the water before she had a chance to absorb what she was doing. The water reached her waist and then her shoulders.

"Daughter!" she called, but the class was out too far swimming, petting the belly of one of the sea giants.

And then, all the sudden, Amara couldn't touch the bottom. It was a curious thing—the fear of being unable to control her body, even if she was immortal. Even if dying at sea was an impossibility. She knew all these facts, and yet panic set in. She flailed her arms and legs, trying to keep her head above water, but she couldn't fight the waves. They swept over her head, pushing her below the surface again and again. She gasped when she came up for air, but water filled her lungs, the salt burning her from the inside out.

"Elora!" she gargled, but her cries were lost amidst the crashing of the waves and the laughter of the children.

Amara sunk below the surface, forced down by another wave. Eyes opened, she gazed around the underwater world. Just as she lost consciousness, she marveled at the beauty under the water. Her mind grew foggy, and her head felt as light as her body floating through the water. Panic over, she closed her eyes and gave into the sleep of suffocation.

Amara drowned.

And she dreamed. Of their village. Her family. The Fountain. In her dream, she approached the forbidden waters, dipped her hand in, and lifted her finger to her lips, just to taste a drop.

Bam! She became vaguely aware of pressure on her chest, of force. Her body endured a second blow.

Someone hit her.

Hard.

Amara sprang to a seated position, gasping for air as if she'd been devoid of oxygen for a long time. And then it all came flooding back, and she realized that much time had passed since she took a breath of air.

"Are you okay?" Elora's voice echoed inside Amara's head.

Light above blinded her, and the sand rubbed against her skin. Amara scratched her head, orienting herself. Breathing took less effort now, and her breaths evened out as she inhaled. Exhaled. Inhaled. Exhaled.

"Mother?"

Amara looked to her daughter's face, and it waved in and out of focus until she could center her eyes and adjust them. "My daughter."

"What were you doing out there? I pulled you to shore."

"You did?"

"I saw you floating in the waves. I do not know how long you were there."

"I do not know, either."

"Why were you there?" she asked again, concern written all over her angelic features.

Amara's heart crumbled at the worry creasing between her daughter's eyes. Worry put there by her.

"I am sorry, my darling." She caressed Elora's cheek with the back of her hand. "I came to find you. In my excitement, I forged into the sea before I thought about what I was doing."

"And why were you so excited?"

"I...the Great Guardian has granted your wish. Once you're fully grown, you will care for the animals. That shall be your task."

Elora dove onto her mother, crushing her with her hug. "Oh, thank you, thank you, thank you! I am so happy, Mother!" She jumped to her feet. "Come. We must go tell Father!"

Amara's gaze scanned the sandy shores. Elora's class sat a distance away, listening to their instructor.

"Is it okay if you leave?"

"Oh, yes. He told me to make sure to care for you. Come on!"

She jumped up and down and yanked Amara to her feet. Unsteady, she stumbled.

Elora grabbed onto her, stabilizing her by wrapping her arms around her mother's waist. "Are you okay?"

After she took a breath and a beat, she answered. "Yes, I believe I am."

Elora helped her mother back to the village, but Darius was nowhere to be found. After asking around, they discovered he'd forged outside of the village in search of more of yesterday's berries. So the two women followed the path to the fields outside, to where they'd gone the day before.

"Father!" Elora forgot the task of aiding her mother along, abandoning her to run to her father at the first sight of him.

But Amara had regained all her strength by now, as if the incident in the sea had never happened. When she reached Darius and Elora, she gave a weak smile.

"You drowned at sea?" Darius' tone filled with alarm.

"I see our daughter has caught you up."

"Why were you out there?"

He braced her by the shoulders now, looking her over, as if he'd find some kind of physical evidence of her drowning.

"Ah, I see she hasn't told you everything. I am fine, love. You know we are always fine." She crossed her arm to the opposite shoulder and covered her husband's hand.

"Yes, but still…" He trailed, unconvinced.

"You worry so over such silly things. I am okay. Elora, tell him your news."

The girl nearly burst with excitement as she spilled to her father that her task had been assigned.

* * *

Following the evening feast, hours later, Amara lay in bed alongside Darius. He held her in his arms, their nightly lovemaking long complete. Running his fingers through her hair, Darius's expression darkened.

"What are you thinking of, my love?"

He didn't answer for a moment, the shadow refusing to leave his face. Gulping, he looked into her eyes. "If I ever lost you…"

Amara sat up. "Darius, what a ridiculous notion! We are immortal, and we will live this way together. Forever. There's nothing to fear."

"I know. I know. I just have…"

"…What?"

"A feeling. It's been nagging me. I set it aside each time it occurs, because this life here—with you and Elora—is perfection. And each day for me is happier than the last."

Amara lay down, nuzzling into the crook of Darius' arm. "For me too."

"I can't imagine life without either of you in it."

69

"You don't have to, love. Elora will reach maturity soon, and then she'll be frozen in age as we are. To live her immortal days alongside us in this village, this garden, this paradise. There's nothing to fear."

Darius kissed the top of Amara's head. "You're right, my love. I shall push the silly feeling aside."

They rested in quiet bliss for a moment as the evening breeze kissed their bare skin through the window above their bed.

"Do you ever wonder...?" Amara started and stopped, gnawing on her bottom lip as she thought about how to pose the question.

"Wonder what, my love?"

"What it would be like if things were different?"

"Different how? You just got done telling me they shall always be this grand. That it is unchanging."

"It is. And that is part of where my question comes from. This life, in all its perfection and joy, what if one aspect were different? What if we had to work to make the fruit and honey grow? Or what if the giant animals turned on us? Or the ones with teeth? What if mankind was not at peace?"

"Then that would not be the world we know." Darius' fingers found Amara's hair and sifted through her dark locks.

"I suppose that is true."

Darius dipped his head to see Amara's face. Tilting her chin with his finger, he drew her gaze to his. "Do you want things to change?"

Her answer followed a pause—a much too long pause. "No. I just wonder..."

"My darling." He held her closer to his body. "Quiet those thoughts within your head. There is nothing to wonder about. Life is perfection, and this shall be our eternity. Can you not be content with that?"

"Yes! I am. It is just...why do you think the Great Guardian gets the most important job? And is it even the most important?"

"Guarding the Fountain?"

"Yes."

"Everyone knows that drinking from it will unleash danger onto our world. Is that the change you seek?"

"I seek no change. But what do we know of this supposed danger? What is it that looms over us by one drink of that water?"

"What has you so deep in thought about the Fountain?"

Amara sighed deeply, calling to mind her drowning. "When I drowned, I had a vision. In the vision, I touched the water and lifted it to my lips. But I awoke before I could taste it."

Darius drew back, releasing Amara from his hold, and sat up on his elbows. "You must promise me to forget that dream. To quiet the curiosity inside of you. It is forbidden, Amara. It matters not what kind of danger the water will bring. Only that it would be disruption to this world. This life we have. And this...you and Elora...are enough for me. Are we enough for you?"

Amara didn't hesitate this time. She grasped each side of Darius' face with her palms and pulled him into a kiss. "Of course you are. You and our daughter *are* my world."

"Then let us be content with that." He wrapped his arms around her.

As they drifted off to sleep, Amara pledged just that—to quiet the questions within and let contentment fill the curious corners of her heart.

Eight

Julia and Charlie

*J*ulia walked through the back door of Amara's sprawling mansion into the kitchen. She found the other woman there, stirring milk into a mug. Sandwiches and an assortment of raw vegetables and fruits lined the kitchen island in front of where Amara stood.

"I thought you might be hungry."

Julia took a seat on one of the island stools. As promised, a tablet propped up on the center island, displaying the image of Charlie, settling into bed for the night. Julia checked in with her body.

"Actually, I am." She helped herself to a sandwich and some grapes. Mouth full, she said, "It's nice that I didn't have to cook this."

Amara smiled. "I'm happy to provide the food for you."

Julia swallowed a bite. "Why are you being so nice to us? And why did you want to talk to me alone?"

"Charlie appears so fragile. I thought it best we discuss his care out of his earshot, and then, once you decide how you'd like to proceed,

I'll leave it up to you to communicate to him." Amara plucked a grape and tossed it into her mouth. "As for my kindness, well, that's just the kind of gal I am."

Julia narrowed her gaze at the other woman. "Oh yeah? What I saw back at your research facility might suggest otherwise. I have to say I'm kind of traumatized by all that went on there—by the condition Charlie was in, by the ease with which you just snapped that doctor's neck, by Rose's unnecessary death..."

She trailed off, emotion threatening to choke her. No way would she let herself cry in front of this woman.

"Truly, I am sorry for all of that. You are so right—your friend Rose should not have died. Dr. Monroe's actions seemed to deserve a swift and exacting punishment."

"That's a pretty permanent form of discipline. Not sure how he's supposed to learn from his mistakes."

Amara huffed a small laugh but ignored Julia's statement. "I want to know more about you, Julia. Charlie told me how he loved you and some of the story of your courtship, but I want to know how you came to be...as you are."

"I have the same question for you." Julia narrowed her eyes and tilted her head.

Amara took a long swig from her mug. "And I will be happy to tell you my story. In time. But first, tell me how you came to drink from the Fountain."

Julia cleared her throat. She wanted to trust Amara but there were too many red flags warning her. Still, with Rose gone and Charlie out of his mind half the time, Julia had no one to talk to about her immortality and all the questions surrounding Charlie's strange and sudden decline. And she could not deny the warmth she felt in Amara's presence, strange though it was. Never had she felt anything like it with any other immortal person she'd encountered over the years.

Amara interrupted her thoughts. "Listen, I understand your hesitancies when it comes to me. I do. I regret the way I went about my work with Charlie. I didn't see another way, though."

"You could have just gone to the island and talked to him. Help him understand why he is how he is and ask for his help."

Amara dropped her gaze to her hands. "As I said, I didn't see another way at the time."

"Did you do this to him? Did you experiment on him or inject him with something that is resulting in what's happening?"

"No, I promise you we only had him heal and studied his abilities and the outcomes. I assure you."

Julia leaned against the stool. "I was sick."

Amara hunched over the kitchen's center island, interested.

"It was 1919, and Charlie and I had just started our relationship. I got horribly ill with tuberculosis—consumption, as it we called it then. I went away to a sanitorium and only deteriorated while there. Charlie had the water. He'd gotten it from a war buddy who had traveled to the island and stolen some of it. And along with that, Rose's innocent and lonely heart..."

Julia's thoughts wandered to Rose, and she realized she'd never gotten the full story on what had happened between her and Arnold. And now she'd never be able to ask her.

"So the two of you hadn't been to the island yourselves?"

"No, not until after my drink. Charlie brought me this little vial of water. All his hopes hinged on me taking a sip. He was desperate—he knew I was dying and didn't want to face a future without me."

A soft smile reached Julia's lips. "I thought it was stupid. Water is water, right? Knowing what I know now, I likely ingested more bacteria that should have made me sicker...but I took the drink. The *only* reason I drank the water was for Charlie.

"But next morning, I woke up, good as new. Overnight, my frame put on the thirty-some pounds I'd lost during the course of my illness. I never felt better."

"What took you to the island?"

Julia gulped. "My first murder. I killed a girl who wanted Charlie. She wouldn't leave us alone, and it just got the better of me...I couldn't live with myself after what I'd done. But Charlie didn't give up on me. He probably should have. I think most people would walk away if their fiancé murdered someone in cold blood. That's generally a deal breaker, right? But not Charlie. He loved me through what I'd done. He believed in the better parts of who I am.

"When there seemed no answer to change what I'd become, Charlie drank the water too. You were right back at your lab that he drank of selfless motives. He drank the water to save me. Once we found out that I was sentenced to murder forever unless I could kill an immortal, he was prepared to do anything necessary to free me from the curse of the water, even if it meant one of us had to die." Saying the words out loud sent a start through her and a small smile etched the corners of her mouth as she was struck with gratitude for the lengths Charlie was willing to go for her. Her insides warmed as she reflected on the depth of his love, then and now.

"And that's why I have to figure out what's happening to him. That's why I must help him hold on to the better parts of himself too. The crazy thing is, we just continue to be robbed of our chance to be together. Something always gets in the way. And it makes me wonder if love is enough to save us. If it's enough to redeem what each of us has done and who we are."

A sudden wave of discomfort washed over Julia. She was a stranger to such vulnerability, and she shuffled in discomfort on her stool. "I don't know why I'm telling you all of this."

"I appreciate you entrusting your story to me. But where did you go all those years Charlie was on the island?"

"Oh, that. Rose—who was guardian at the time decided she would task me with bringing an end to the curse of the water—stabbed Charlie, and only she knew how to save him. In exchange for killing the ten others who had gotten away with a drink, she would keep him alive. Only it took a whole lot longer than I expected. So that's where I was. Murdering murderers. Doesn't make me much better than them, does it?"

Amara leaned deeper over the kitchen island. "Fascinating. As far as you're aware, it's just you and Charlie left?"

"Well, and you." Julia tilted her head back and laughed.

"What?" Amara listed her head with a curious smile on her face.

"It's just funny the way I can talk about murdering others with you. But I guess watching you do the same in cold blood kind of ensures you won't judge me."

"Oh, I don't judge you. I'd have done the same." Amara stood tall and slurped from her mug. "You know, you called the water a curse. I see it differently."

"How? It makes killers of those who drink it."

"Temporarily, yes."

"Not temporarily. Eternally."

Amara traced the rim of her mug with her finger. "Depends. *You* are no longer inclined to kill."

"No, but that's because I've killed immortals. You know how all this works, don't you?"

"Oh yes, I know how it all works intimately. I suspect you might agree that your time spent killing killers proves that not everyone deserves this life, no less an immortal one."

"I don't know. Why should I get to decide that? How am I any more deserving having done what I've done?"

"You had good reasons. And think of the countless lives you saved with what you did. All those people would have continued to kill.

Perhaps the lives you saved are more worthy of living than the ones you took."

"But who gets to decide which life has more value than another?"

"Ah, that's the question, isn't it?"

Silence settled between the two women, and their gazes locked. Amara broke off eye contact when she turned to pour herself a second cup of tea.

When she turned back, she said, "I wanted to talk to you alone because I have some suspicions about what is happening to Charlie. You remember I called him my Phoenix?"

"Oh yes, I haven't forgotten something like that. So when you talk about the Phoenix, you do mean the legendary bird, right? The one who burns up every five hundred years or so and reincarnates? Tell me you don't think Charlie is a bird?"

Amara howled. "Clearly he's not a bird."

Julia leaned into the conversation. "Then what did you mean?"

"The Phoenix has been a bird, historically. Always coming to rest on the island where you two were making your home. Always igniting into flames once every five hundred years and being reborn there. It's the bird's birthplace and final resting place. It was told that one day that bird would be reborn into a man. A man who interacted with every aspect of the Fountain—the water itself, the antidote, the flower. A man who drank from the Fountain with pure motives and not for the benefits the water gives. A man who paid the debt to the water with his own life, thus burning up and being reborn to his human form…only enhanced."

"How would that even be possible? You can't kill yourself once you drink the water. So he didn't choose that. Rose stabbed him."

"He doesn't need to be the one to wield the knife, only the one to die before he answered the water's call to kill. He paid the debt with his own life, and he absorbed the abilities of the flowering plant his wounds were dressed with, which ultimately derive from the water itself. He is an agent of the water—all the good found within—and able to heal. Of course, there is a cost to him...the ugly necessity of absorbing whatever ailment he takes for a short time. But he can do all that without the nasty side effect of requiring the recipients of his gift to become murderers and repay the water's life stores."

"You said when we were at Eden Pharma that the water no longer *works* while Charlie is as he is. Why is that?"

"It's a period of rest from the demands of the water. While Charlie is able to do what he does, the water lies dormant. But it's temporary. A time will come, and another cycle will start over. The Fountain will be accessible again, more accessible than it was. Everything is going to come full circle thanks to Charlie."

"That does not sound like a good thing. What do you mean *more* accessible?"

"It won't be so remote," Amara clarified.

"Like it'll move?" Julia propped her chin on her hand.

"Yes. And it has before. The Fountain remains on the island it's on, but every five hundred years, when a new Phoenix cycle begins, the entire island and the water change locations. It moves itself somewhere else in the world."

"Why would it do that?"

"There are reasons." Amara took another slow drawl of her tea.

Julia huffed. Classic cryptic answer. "Care to elaborate?" Her tone dripped with irritation and impatience.

"I want to tell you everything, Julia, but all in due time. For now, you have to understand that Charlie's abilities represent something very exciting ahead. Something I want you to be a part of."

"And Charlie?"

Amara cleared her throat and averted her gaze briefly before answering. "Of course, for as long as he can be."

"What does that mean?"

"As it happens with the Phoenix, he will eventually fulfill his lifespan, and that's another reason I wanted to talk to you alone. I suspect the fact that he can't separate fact from fiction in his head suggests that perhaps he is deteriorating, that he won't last the full five hundred years."

That statement stunned Julia. She sat up against the back of the stool, eyes wide with alarm. "Deteriorating? But...how?"

Amara sighed. "There are many questions. And I don't know for a fact that my suspicions are correct. With your blessing, I'd like to get my team of doctors to examine Charlie, to see what is going on with him and if we can slow the process or make him better altogether."

She waited a moment to let Julia process before continuing. "There's one more thing. I've called an old...friend of mine, and he's on his way. I called him while you were getting Charlie settled in my guest home. He knows just as much about all of this as I do, and I think it'd be good to have him here."

"I don't want to risk too many people knowing about Charlie, and especially with what he can do."

"You can trust Darius." Amara stretched as a big yawn hit her. "He'll be here in the morning. You and I should get some rest, and then we'll dig in tomorrow. Does that sound okay to you?"

Julia glanced at Charlie's sleeping form on the tablet camera. "I don't see what other choice there is. You all know more about this than me, and we need help. I can't stomach the thought of losing Charlie altogether, so whatever we need to do, I'm in."

* * *

Julia tip-toed into the guest house, navigating through the darkness to the bed. Exhaustion made her body feel heavy, and she climbed into bed next to Charlie. He groaned and rolled over. His eyes fluttering open, he smiled at her.

"Hey there, gorgeous."

Julia touched her palm to his cheek. "Hey, love. I'm happy you know me."

"Well, I'm happy to know you." He wrapped his arms around her and drew her close.

"You know what I mean."

He didn't answer, and his breathing indicated that he'd returned to sleep. Julia mulled her conversation with Amara over in her mind. She should sleep; she needed her rest. But she couldn't shake some of the things the other woman had said. That she almost commended Julia for her murdering mission and Amara's assertion that some lives were more valuable than others.

Did Julia's immortality make her more entitled? She didn't believe so, but Amara seemed to hold such an opinion. And had she saved lives? Getting Charlie back and knowing what the Fountain made people into were justification enough. But maybe Amara had a point. Maybe she'd served a purpose after all.

She tried to settle on that thought, but the moment her eyes shut, the faces of her victims flashed through her mind, one right after the other until Rose's cold, dead eyes stared at her. The only thing that freed her mind of that image was the other part of the conversation that Julia struggled to digest.

Charlie was no longer immortal.

At least he wouldn't be forever...and that forever may be shorter than Julia thought. She nestled in closer to him, placing her hand on his chest and watching it rise and fall with his rhythmic breaths.

"I won't lose you," she whispered into the dark.

With that promise on her lips, she drifted off.

Nine

Julia and Charlie

*T*hump! The sound woke Julia from a deep sleep with a start. She sprang upright in bed, her heart racing.

Charlie was on the floor next to the bed, groaning.

"Charlie! Are you okay?"

She hopped down from the bed and knelt to examine him. When he met her gaze, his was empty, and she knew. He'd forgotten her again.

"Who—?" The rest of the question hung in the air as his face filled with panicked alarm.

"Shh, it's okay," Julia cooed. She held her hands in a position of surrender and retreated, giving him space. "Are you okay?"

He hugged his leg and glanced back and forth between the limb and her. "Fine. Where am I?"

There was a tremble in his voice as his gaze swept the room.

"You're in a safe place and with a safe person. Can you trust me when I tell you that?"

A look of confusion, like he was working to make up his mind. "I—I don't know."

"You're Charlie. I'm Julia. And we are completely safe together. I know you're scared, but this will pass. Trust me." She held his gaze, and his face softened.

"I don't know why, but I—" His attention snapped at the sound of knocking on the front door. The same noise had Julia jumping.

"Wait here," she commanded and closed the bedroom door behind her.

Julia tore the door open and found Amara standing there, dressed in a tight fitting black dress that was far too formal for the normal day to day. Her short locks were curled with perfection, her lips painted red, and her eyelashes stretched for miles. Julia privately wondered what the occasion was, but then, she had more pressing matters to sort out.

"Come in. We're in the middle of a crisis." Julia stood aside and held the door open.

"New memory or has he forgotten you again?" Amara pushed passed Julia and came to stand in the center of the living room.

"He forgot me."

Just then the bedroom door opened, and Charlie emerged. "Jul?"

Julia rushed to his side and embraced him. "You're back," she said.

"I am." He looked deep into her eyes. "I'm so sorry."

"You have nothing to apologize for."

Amara cleared her throat. "If everyone is okay, I just wanted to alert you that Darius has arrived. He's at the main house if you'd like to join us for breakfast."

"Who's Darius?" Charlie rubbed his eyes and stretched.

"He's someone I've known for a very long time. And I think he can help us sort through some of what's happening to you."

"I still don't know about involving other people, Amara." Julia stood in front of Charlie like a shield.

"Jul, come on. She thinks this guy can help. Let's at least go meet him."

Amara peered around Julia with a grateful expression. "Thank you, Charlie. I assure you, Julia, he is no one to worry about. You'll figure this out soon enough, but Darius is also…like us." Amara waited for the revelation to land.

"There are *more*?" Julia deflated. "Okay, Amara, you have to tell us: how many people do you know of who have had a drink? Is there a whole society of people like us or something? Have I tricked myself into thinking I was doing the world some kind of favor by killing the ones I knew of who had had a drink? Was it just a waste of my time? A senseless century long errand? Have I become a serial killer for nothing?"

She panted, her cheeks hot. Julia paced the small space between them as her stomach clenched.

"Shh, shh," Amara crossed to her and took Julia's hands into hers.

An instantaneous wave of calm washed over Julia and she closed her eyes, allowing the inexplicable comfort Amara's touch brought soothe her. Her breathing slowed, and her heart rate followed.

"Thaaaat's it," Amara coaxed with a soft voice. "You're okay. Look at me."

Julia opened her eyes.

"Nothing you did was a waste. You did what you had to do to get your beloved back. That is never a waste. And you did spare the world more unneeded death by killing people who were always going to kill others. Now, learning of you and Charlie has been such a lovely surprise to me. You are part of a wonderful family."

Julia wanted to debate that last statement, but doing so warred with the way she felt in Amara's presence.

"Thank you, I feel better. Can you give us a moment to change and we'll meet you inside?"

"Take your time." Amara smiled and left the guest house.

Charlie approached Julia, who hadn't moved. "Try not to worry about what's already happened. She's not wrong—you probably did save a lot of lives doing what you did."

"But I still *did* what I did."

Charlie took her in his arms without another word on the topic.

"Charlie, I have to tell you something before we go to breakfast."

He pulled out of her embrace and stood back so he could look her in the eye.

"Anything."

"Last night when Amara invited me to come talk to her..."

She trailed as a war raged in her. She didn't want to utter the words, but he deserved to know. "I don't know if this is true or quite what it means," she rambled. "But Amara seems to think that, as this Phoenix, you will eventually fulfill a five-hundred-year lifespan and burn up, just like the mythological bird. She says one has reincarnated on the island every five hundred years and you are the fulfillment of something spoken long ago about the water. Charlie, she thinks you are only immortal for as long as the lifespan lasts."

She could not utter the last bit of it—the fact that Amara also believed his strange recent occurrences meant that timeline had somehow shortened.

Charlie took a moment to absorb this information. "This is all so very strange."

He lowered himself to the couch, his gaze lost in the distance.

Julia sat next to him and waited. "You okay?"

"This just keeps getting weirder. Magic water that heals overnight. Murderous compulsions that can't be tamed. And now I'm...I'm some reincarnation of a bird...Don't you have to die to be reincarnated?"

A start struck Julia. "Didn't...didn't Rose tell you?"

"Tell me what?"

"On the island. When I was gone and she was taking care of you, you were okay until one day...you did die. You died and all that was there was a pile of ashes…until you reappeared to her. I don't think Amara is wrong."

* * *

Dressed, Julia and Charlie made the short jaunt from the guest house through the back door to Amara's expansive kitchen. They exchanged a glance when they heard low voices in the adjoining room.

"Hello?" Julia called.

"In here," came Amara's response from the other room.

They followed her voice and walked through the kitchen into the formal dining room. A table ridiculous in size sat as the centerpiece of the room. Amara was at one end and a man at the other, but they both stood when Julia and Charlie entered. The man approached Julia without pause and took her hand in his. His kissed her knuckles and then ran his lips over them.

"My, you are more lovely than Amara let on."

The words were spoken with a deep, buttery voice, and they sent a strange sensation through Julia. The man holding her hand was handsome in the stop-you-in-your-tracks and take-your-breath-away kind of way. His complexion matched Amara's—dark olive—and jet-black hair combed against his head in a clean-cut style. Sideburns graced his strong, angular jawline. Crystal blue eyes looked her up and down, and Julia couldn't help but notice how they contrasted with his dark features. He stood several inches taller than Charlie, and his stature suggested he spent time in the gym.

Julia glanced down at her sweatpants and baggy tee, her hand reaching up to touch the messy tousled bun in her hair. What was this man talking about? She cleared her throat and snatched her hand from his grasp.

"Julia, and this is Charlie."

"Charlie," he greeted, his voice smooth like velvet. Darius's gaze shuffled with momentary politeness to Charlie when he said the other man's name, but then he turned to Julia.

"Let me show you to the table."

He placed his hand on the small of her back and guided her to the enormous dining table.

"Thanks. It'd be kind of hard to miss," she said, taking the seat he'd pulled out for her.

"Charlie, you can sit across from Julia," Amara directed as she and Darius took their places at the two heads of the table.

Amara cut Darius a glare. "Keep it in your pants for once …darling."

Darius let out a low whistle. "Oh, Mar. I do love how jealous you still get after all these years."

"Do not flatter yourself. You are here as a matter of critical importance."

"So you mentioned on the phone."

He helped himself to the stainless pot of coffee, pouring a mug and dropping in two cubes of sugar. Stirring the dissolve the cubes, Darius returned his attention to Julia. "I know almost nothing of you. Tell me, where is it you're from?"

Julia shoved a bite of fruit into her mouth, more to avoid the penetration of this man's stare than anything else. She put her finger in the air and pointed to her mouth to indicate her momentary inability to speak. Stealing a glance at Charlie, she found him glaring at Darius. This was uncomfortable, to say the least.

"Darius, I've told you how special these two are."

"Is your hair naturally that lovely shade of red?" He hadn't taken his eyes off Julia, and he completely ignored Amara.

"Darius!" Always calm and composed, Amara's outburst caught Julia and Charlie by surprise, making both jump.

Darius turned his head until his gaze met Amara's. "Darling, I was simply asking a question, trying to get to know her a bit." He gave Julia a smile of apology before turning back to Amara. "Please do contain yourself. You mustn't always worry so."

"I'm not worried. I simply urge you to focus on the matter at hand. Leave her alone; you're making her uncomfortable."

He returned his gaze on Julia. "I apologize if I've made you uncomfortable. But, Amara,"—he faced the other end of the table now— "you know you hold a special place in my heart reserved just for you." He blew her a kiss.

A subtle pink tinged Amara's cheeks, and a little smile tugged at the corners of her mouth as she moved her food around with her fork.

That actually worked? Julia thought, staring in disbelief at Amara's flustered face.

Amara cleared her throat and regained composure. "Anyway, dear, these two have a problem. As you remember from long ago—"

"Wait." Julia interjected. "I know you've had a drink, too," she directed at Darius. "So how do you know each other, and how have you come to drink like us?"

Darius flashed her a brilliant smile, the white of his teeth contrasting against his dark skin. "Has our lovely hostess left out that little detail?" He listed his head Amara's direction.

"Would you—" Charlie shot up from his chair, only to sink back to seated position. "Jul, I—I'm having another one."

Julia popped up from her seat and crossed to the other side of the table. She kneeled next to Charlie and caressed his arm.

"It's okay, Charlie. I'm here. Whatever it is, it's not real, not your memory. You are Charlie Harris. Your parents were farmers, your brother was a lawyer, and you grew up in a yellow farmhouse in rural Iowa. We've known each other since we were little, and then we fell in love. Those are the facts."

His breathing slowed, and his gaze lifted to meet Julia's. The distress in his appearance faded as he locked his eyes with hers.

"Thank you," he whispered.

She wished she were seated next to him so she could comfort him with her touch during the meal. She hated seeing him so distressed and felt helpless across the unreasonably large table. She gave Charlie's hand a squeeze and went back to her seat.

"Isn't that wonderful?" Darius's hypnotic blue eyes lit with excitement; his white teeth popped against his dark skin with his smile. "You are as kind as you are exquisite."

"This isn't about me!" Julia thundered. She snuck a glance at Amara, who only held an amused expression. "I'm sorry, Amara. I know I'm being rude." She turned toward Darius, trying to avoid the trance his crystal eyes threatened to put her under. "But stop trying to charm me, man. You're here to *help* us."

The smile only widened across Darius's lips, and he leaned against the dining room chair with a finger pointed at Julia. "I like you. You have spunk."

Julia ignored his compliment. "Amara said you know just as much about the water and what it does to people as she does and that you will understand what's happening to Charlie. She seems to think he's the reincarnation of some mythical bird."

Darius slammed his fist on the table with a sobered expression. "The Phoenix?"

This time he was looking at Amara, but there was something in his expression Julia couldn't read. Still, his body had gone rigid, a miniscule sweat broke out in tiny dots on his forehead, and his breaths pulsed with an emotion Julia couldn't quite pinpoint.

"Darius, as I told you, they're special."

"You told me they were like us—the first you'd met in countless years. But you didn't tell me this!" he boomed.

Standing, he approached Charlie, giving little attention to personal space or matters of etiquette. He got right in his face, his own contorted into a mistrustful scowl. "This guy?" he whispered. "He's just a kid."

"He's remarkable." Amara's tone was full of pride, and she clasped her hands to her heart as she spoke them.

"Someone, *please* tell us what is going on." Julia rubbed between her eyes, this whole thing seeming more insane to her by the moment. "You said he could help, Amara. So *help!*"

Darius remained by Charlie, but he stood tall and regarded Amara. "How am I supposed to be helpful?"

"Because," Amara answered, "you were also there when everything happened. Charlie is having some unfortunate side effects. *He* told you more than he told me, and I wondered if perhaps you might have some ideas."

"He told me more because you couldn't be trusted after what you did!" His voice boomed across the room and was followed by a stiff silence.

"*He* who?" Julia tested. Silence only lingered between the other couple as they stared at each other, so she continued. "If Charlie is who you think he is, then you probably know he can heal other people. Recently, he began having memories that aren't his. You just witnessed one a moment ago, and that was mild compared to some of them. He can't differentiate between what's real and what's not, and it's getting worse." She paused, cleared her throat. "He also hasn't recognized me a couple of times."

Darius's eyes narrowed, and Julia thought she saw momentary alarm reach his gaze. But he stood tall and drew in a long breath. "He's not your Phoenix, Amara. Whatever he can do—it doesn't matter. He's not it. You're right. I know more than you do, and he doesn't fit."

He resumed his place at the head of the table as a hush fell over the room. Amara's face had fallen, and words failed her. Julia felt a strange hybrid of relief and disappointment. Relief that Charlie was not who Amara thought he was and disappointment over the fact that Darius couldn't help them. Charlie stared ahead, and Julia imagined he was doing his best just to stay in this moment.

"No!" screamed Amara as she jumped to her feet. "No." Her voice dropped to a whisper. "He *is* the Phoenix. I don't know why you refuse to see it, but he's here. *Finally*. You know how long I've waited, that I've been watching and looking for him. It seems to be happening faster than we thought now that he's arrived. The time is so close, love. So close."

Her chest heaved, and her cheeks flushed as tears filled her eyes.

Darius had returned to his seat, and he chewed a sausage link as Amara made her appeal. "My dear, if you believe so certainly that he is the one—that is the scariest reality of all."

Ten

Darius: Present Day

O nce breakfast was finished and the table cleared, Julia and Charlie returned to Amara's guest home. Darius lingered by the breakfast table with Amara in his shadow. She approached him, running her fingertips across his shoulder blades. "I've missed you, you know."

"I do know, my lovely." He looked up at her, at the desire in her eyes and the invitation in her smile. "I wish I could say the same."

"You're so cruel." She pouted a lip out at him. Still, when he stood, Amara laced her arms around his neck. "He's really the one, you know. It's almost over."

Darius reached behind his head and unlocked Amara's fingertips from around his neck. Drawing her arms down to her side, he kept his body close to hers, his face only inches away. She puckered her lips, and he enjoyed how much she longed for his kiss. Even when he always refused to give her one.

The game was fun, as it always had been, and he loved leading her to believe there was still a chance for them. When it was convenient for him, he allowed her to think he was wrapped around her finger. And then, just to remind her who was in control, he left. Every time. But she always called him back. He never had long to wait before another one of her calls, but this most recent separation had been the longest.

"You scared me, you know." He looked her in the eyes, their noses inches apart. "I haven't heard from you in years."

"You missed me." A sly smile curved up one corner of Amara's mouth. "I knew I wasn't the only one." She went in for a kiss, but Darius turned his face, and her lips landed on his cheek instead of his mouth. "Tsk, such a tease."

Tracing her finger down the length of his cheek, she turned and approached the sofa in the living room. She spread her arms across the back of the couch and crossed her legs. She'd been sure to wear the black dress he loved, the one that showed off how long her legs were.

"I was waiting, my love. I needed to be sure of who he was before I called you. And now I am." Amara crossed her legs, letting the slit in her dress fall and show them off.

"Amara, I know you want that to be true, but I just don't think it is. It's been so long, and I'm not sure what was foretold will ever happen."

"Darius, he is. I don't simply believe it. I know it. He fits all the criteria. There's just one thing."

"His strange amnesia?" He plopped down on the sofa next to her, and she angled her body toward him.

"That's the one."

Even though a sizeable space separated her from Darius, she stretched her fingertips across the top of the sofa to his shoulder and caressed his arm.

"Think about it. He shouldn't be able to get ill. Doesn't that give you pause in thinking he's the Phoenix?"

"Perhaps it should. But, Darius, he can heal and he recovers quickly.

He took his drink for selfless reasons, and he was born of the water and the plant that grows alongside it. He fits the bill to a tee."

"He drank for her, didn't he? That's why she's so devoted?"

"That and she loves him. You remember what it's like to share that kind of love, don't you?" She leaned her body closer to Darius.

But he wasn't fazed. He shifted his gaze away from her. "Hardly. It's been so long."

Amara rolled her eyes and righted her posture.

Darius puffed out a breath. "Did you try making him heal multiple maladies?"

"I tried it all. He can take it, and he's recovered every time."

She slid closer to him on the sofa.

"If he is your Phoenix—"

"Our Phoenix," she corrected.

"If he is your Phoenix, he wouldn't be so fragile. Think about it, Amara."

She persisted. "What did He tell you about the Phoenix's demise? You've held out on me all this time."

"And I shall continue to. It's not for you to know. That's why He told me, not you."

"But the quicker Charlie fulfills his purpose, the quicker I can fix this."

"Mara, even if he is the one (and he's not), we both know the Phoenix lifespan is five hundred years. I think you have some time."

"But what if his mental deterioration means it's not going to take as long. What if it indicates—"

"—don't be ridiculous. Just because you want it to happen faster than the prescribed time doesn't mean it will. You can't force these things. This is your mess, and you are not in control of the clean-up time." He looked at her now, disdain in his gaze. "You haven't changed, Mar. In all these years, you think only of yourself."

"Darius, I think of us." Positioning her body so that no space remained between the two of them, she draped one leg over his lap. "One of my biggest regrets was losing you when I took the drink. And after all this time, I'm going to set it right. I'm going to return everything to the way it was, and you *will* love me again."

He flung her leg off him. "You can't return *everything* to the way it was, now can you?"

Bitterness crept into his tone, and hatred lived in his gaze.

"You still haven't forgiven me?"

Darius sprung to his feet. "*Forgiven* you? She was our daughter! And the fact that you can just discard her as one more casualty in this whole mess you've made confirms to me that we can never reconcile!"

He paced now, his breaths hastened by his anger, his face turning red.

Mara stood too and approached him. With her hand on his shoulder, she soothed. "Darius, don't you think I miss her every day too? I carried her in my body, gave birth to her, watched her grow—"

"Caused her death," Darius interrupted.

"Yes, it was my fault. All of it. And I'm sorry. That's why this is so important to me. I want—I need to right those wrongs."

She closed the gap between them and wrapped her arms around Darius's torso. Inhaling deeply, a smile formed on her lips.

"Your arms are the most secure place there is—they make me feel safe." She slid her hands down the length of his arms and wrapped them around his waist.

This time he didn't resist.

"We share this grief. Let me be there for you, D. Hold me like you used to," she said.

His arms wrapped around her, squeezing her body against his, and she nestled her head in the middle of his chest.

"You smell so good. Your aroma is locked in my memory."

Lifting her gaze to meet his, conflict rested in eyes. Amara licked her lips as she watched him for cues that he was breaking under her touch, her spell. And there it was. A tiny crack in his resistance, a softening of his posture. She used that window to stand on tiptoes and place a kiss on his lips. Just one. To test the waters.

He allowed the kiss, and when she pulled away, he forced her back, holding her body to his, meeting her lips, and allowing his eternal desire for her to overcome him. Amara wrapped her arms around Darius' neck and pressed his body toward the sofa. Pulling out of his embrace, Amara pushed him down onto the couch and climbed on his lap. As she kissed him, she loosened his tie, trailing her kisses onto his neck, his earlobe, to his lips. He groaned, first out of delight then something else.

Throwing her off his lap, Darius jumped from the couch. "No, Amara!" His voice was stern, commanding. "I'll not fall under your spell. One touch from you does not undo the mess those hands made."

And he stormed off, leaving Amara stunned.

* * *

Darius paced the courtyard outside and scolded himself for nearly allowing Amara to undo him. He had to make sure to keep away from her, not allow her to touch him when they were together. The reminder was tough to recall since part of him longed for her hands on his skin. Part of him still craved her, but that part was largely overshadowed by his disdain for her. How could a man's heart be so divided, with love and hatred living side by side? He'd given in far too many times, despising himself afterward. Not because he'd led her on, but because he hadn't stood strong in his resolve. Any other woman, he could have or deny, but Amara held a special power.

He knew coming there was a mistake.

95

The door to the guest house opened, and the red-haired girl stepped out into the courtyard. She'd changed from her scrubby sweats and now donned jeans, tall boots, and a sweater. Her red hair cascaded around her beautiful face, her green eyes contrasting against the black of her sweater and her auburn hair. She was a sight, and Darius found himself intoxicated by her at once, a welcome distraction.

"Well, hello there," he greeted.

She froze where she stood, surprise in her expression. Tucking her hair behind her ear, she crossed her arms and narrowed her eyes.

"Have I offended you?"

She merely cocked her head.

"Sorry if I came on a little strong earlier. It's just…"

She shifted her stance and tensed. "Just what?"

"You are lovely beyond words, and I was overcome. I am always riveted by the beauty of a woman. And you, my dear, are gorgeous."

Pink filled her cheeks, bringing a smile to Darius's lips. "Besides, as you've figured out, we're in the same family."

"Then that just makes you kind of a sicko for coming on to me."

Darius reared his head and laughed. "You are quite charming, aren't you?"

"*That* charmed you?" She raised an eyebrow. "Why are you still here?"

"A girl who cuts to the chase. I like that."

"Is there anything you don't like?" Hand on her hip, she planted her feet to the pavement.

"Oh yes, plenty. Let's see, I abhor public transportation. Brussel sprouts are particularly dreadful. Morning breath—that's something we could all do without, don't you think?"

Julia rolled your eyes. "You were going to tell me why you're here."

"Oh. Right, then. Amara called me. She likes to do that on occasion."

"Neither of you mentioned how you know each other. Clearly,

there's a history there. So…what are you two?"

"Why? Interested?" He smirked and lifted his right eyebrow.

"Only to the extent that you can help us."

"Ah yes, well. I'm afraid I'm of no use to you there." Hands in his pockets, he walked the path through the courtyard.

Julia jogged to catch up. Matching her pace to his, she trailed alongside him through the rows of flowers. "Amara thought you might know what's happening to Charlie."

"I may. But even if I do, well, there's nothing I can do to help him from inevitably fulfilling his role."

"What—this Phoenix? So it's true? Those aren't some ramblings of a mad woman?"

Darius chuckled. "Oh no, Amara is quite mad. But as to the Phoenix, I'm afraid that notion is real."

Julia's posture deflated. "I was really hoping she was just crazy. After all, you generally think of the Phoenix as a bird, and Charlie is a man."

Darius stopped walking, turning his body toward Julia. "You're quite astute, you know that?" His tone held a mixture of humor and sarcasm.

"Shut up."

"In any case, yes, traditionally, the Phoenix is a bird, but only once will he reincarnate into a man. I'm afraid, from the sound of it, your Charlie fits the bill."

"*And?*"

"Sounds weighty, doesn't it?"

"Uh…yeah. What's it mean?"

He paused, drew in a deep breath, and then let it go. "It means enjoy the time you have with your Charlie. His days aren't eternal, as you once thought."

Darius's confirmation struck Julia's heart and riveted through her body, making her stumble backward. Amara had suggested this was true, but Julia had hoped she was wrong.

"You're surprised?"

She gazed into Darius's eyes. He'd stopped walking too. The crystal blue swallowed her up, making it difficult to look away.

"I'm sorry," he said. "But at least you have a chance to say good-bye. And you might do that sooner than later. He's deteriorating, right? The memories happening with greater frequency? Has he forgotten common items?" A sadness shadowed his expression, and Julia wondered what secrets lay beyond his suave exterior.

"Yes," she whispered.

Darius nodded. "Then it has already begun."

"What are you not telling me?"

"Don't trust Amara. She may seem like she's trying to help, but the only person she cares about—has ever cared about—is herself."

Julia dropped her gaze to her hands. "And I should trust what you tell me?"

Darius smiled, and he looked impressed. "You are clever." He watched her a second and then continued, "If you should like a break from it all, either now or when he dies, you're welcome to come with me. I could show you a lovely time. I could show you the world."

Julia sniffed, and recoiled at his invitation. "I've seen it, thanks."

And she turned, storming back toward the guest house.

"Have it your way, then."

Darius continued his now solo stroll through the courtyard. He should just leave. But as he watched Julia disappear into the guest house, he found himself not wanting to.

Eleven

Darius and Amara: Many, Many Years Ago

Morning burst anew, and Amara prepared for her day. She and Darius walked Elora to her lesson, kissed her good-bye, and went hand-in-hand to carry out their daily tasks.

"What do you plan to do with all those berries you collected?" Amara asked her husband. She still couldn't believe how many baskets they'd come back with.

"Eat them, of course!" Darius jabbed her in the ribs and smiled down at her.

"Of course. But do you plan to prepare them in any special way?"

"Today I shall try various ways of eating them. As they were in nature, warmed over fire, and perhaps smashed into a pulp."

"You're going to destroy them?"

"Not destroy them. See if we can make a drink of them. What's in store for you today?"

"More of the same. I shall tend the garden and gather greens for the feast."

Darius made a swift and sudden move, stealing away with Amara into the cover of trees. He maneuvered her against a tall-standing trunk and nuzzled her neck with his nose.

"What's this?" Amara giggled, welcoming the sensations coursing through her.

"Just a little good morning farewell."

He kissed her furiously with arms wrapped around her body and passion in the way his tongue moved in her mouth. When he pushed away from her, his breaths were rapid, as was his heartbeat.

Amara placed her hand on his chest, feeling the thrashing of his heart within. "My, it is racing."

"For you. Eternity is not long enough, Amara. My love far outlasts our immortality. I need you to know that."

"I do."

"I need it to be enough for you."

Amara drew away, locking gazes with Darius. "Is this about last night?"

He could not hold her gaze when he nodded.

"My love, listen." She tilted his chin forcing him to peer into her eyes. "I love you. And there's nothing more I want. Okay?"

Darius nodded, and Amara laid a soft kiss on his lips. She smacked his bottom.

"Now off! There are berries awaiting your touch. I shall see you for lunch."

With one final kiss, Amara turned to go, heading toward the garden. She glanced behind her and found Darius watched her leave as he retreated toward their homestead, to try his hand with the berries.

When she could see him no more, she righted her path toward the garden. But her heart was troubled. As much as her assurances to Darius were truth, something inside of her remained unsettled. She could not confess that to her husband, though, for fear he'd worry.

She did not want to arouse that in him. The unsettled parts would be handled and her troubled mind quieted, as she'd promised.

Approaching the garden, she watched the Great Guardian. He paced back and forth around the perimeter of the Fountain. For just a moment, Amara took in the whole breathtaking scene. Circling the center garden, trees grew in every assortment. Fruit-bearing trees, flowering trees, and green trees made up a medley of every color in the rainbow. Inside the garden, a small walking path carved through flowers and bushes and plants of every kind and color. Brilliant reds mimicked the blush in her daughter's cheeks, yellows shone as bright as the sun, and oranges matched its setting hue. Blues ranged from the clear ocean waters to the deep indigo of its depths. Violets and greens complimented the rest, and the whole scene was brilliant. Too often, she took the beauty for granted, setting to work in tending to the plants. But now, just for a moment, to quiet the troubling thoughts within, she allowed herself to enjoy the view.

Taking a deep breath, she noted all the scents in the air. Fruit and floral and salt and evergreen. Each individual fragrance mixed together into a symphony of aromas which smelled as delicious as the scenery was to her vision. With a deep exhale, Amara allowed contentment in at the sights, the smells, the love, the joy. Truth was, nothing existed that should trouble her. Everything was perfect.

Opening her eyes, her gaze fell on the Fountain. In the center of the garden, with tables running on either side for the evening feasts, it sat. In a circle, flowing with a steady, rhythmic babble. If she strained her ear, she could almost hear it from where she stood. Flowers surrounded the Fountain, and the water looked to be just one more component of the garden. But then she saw the Guardian pacing. Reminding her that it wasn't just one more piece of all the beauty she was surrounded by. A danger lurked among them.

At least, they were told as much.

Part of what troubled Amara was that she did not know if what the Guardian told her was true. His task was to guard the Fountain and, as such, knew only what he was told. Amara squared her shoulders, making up her mind. Marching through the garden and right up to the Fountain, she fixed her hands onto her hips.

"Guardian?" she called.

He jumped, having not heard her approach, and turned. "Ah, morning, Amara. And how are you and your family today?"

"We are well, thank you. May I ask a question? About the Fountain?"

The Guardian froze and tension filled his posture. "I suppose."

His tone dripped with hesitancy, and for a moment, Amara was tempted to retreat.

But she thought better of it. "What danger?"

"Pardon?"

"What dangers live within the waters? Why must we not drink?"

"Amara. You are more curious than the rest, are you not?"

"An answer that is also a question." She stood her ground, her gaze fixed on the Guardian.

He puffed out a laugh. "Yes, well. Not much escapes you, does it? Do you know that no one questions about this? You are the only one."

"I suspected as much. So what dangers, Guardian?"

"Truth be told, I do not know the specifics. Just that the water is a force not to be reckoned with. That drinking from it opens the door, unleashes terrible things we cannot comprehend. These things are impossible to understand because they go against the fiber of our beings...immortals who live in peace. In harmony with everything and everyone around us. To drink disrupts all that."

"But how? How can a drink do that?"

The Guardian shrugged his shoulders and resumed his stroll. "I do not know, but I do not wish to find out, either."

"Very well, Guardian."

His answer was not satisfactory, but there was nothing else to say. She picked up her tools and set about to work as she did every day.

But today was different. She was different. Somehow. Since she'd drowned and come back. Since the vision while she slept. Something stirred within—not just a curiosity.

A desire.

To taste the water.

Come what may.

* * *

The feast was divine, and Darius' experiments paid off with the fruit. As usual, everyone ate to contentment, and the entire village retired to their individual homes for the night. Amara kissed her daughter goodnight and climbed in bed next to Darius. He already had fallen into a deep sleep. His bare chest moved up and down with his steady exhales. Amara laid a palm on his chest and watched her hand move in time with his breaths.

She shouldn't do it.

All day long, she'd entertained the idea.

But she shouldn't.

She'd never get past the Guardian anyway. He'd see her even in his sleep—that was part of the gift he was given in return for his duties. He had told her as much. And yet…

She'd thought of a way to taste the water. Several, in fact. And she couldn't shake the vision. In her dream, she'd almost had the water to her lips and could smell the sweet aroma. Almost had her thirst quenched. Still, the little thought nagged in the back of her mind—what if it did unleash something terrible? What if the Guardian was right?

But what if he wasn't?

What if it was just a silly rule? Amara didn't understand why there would be a need for that. Everyone lived in perfect harmony together. Everyone was happy.

Everyone except her...of late.

"Darius?" She called his name just above a whisper, but he didn't stir. If he had, that would have been her answer. But he snoozed away, deep in slumber.

Amara kissed his cheek, silently slid off the bed and tiptoed to the other side of the curtain dividing their bedroom from the rest of the living quarters. Drumming her chin with her finger, she paced back and forth in the small space. To distract herself, she snuck to her daughter's bedside. Elora lay fast asleep, too, a sweet smile playing at the corners of her lips.

This *was* enough. She didn't need to satisfy her curiosity. Darius, Elora...they made her world—her life—complete.

Then why couldn't she shake the temptation? Why could she not put it out of her mind as Darius had told her to? This was no good. She needed to get some air, clear her head. In absolute silence, she opened the door and stole into the night. She took a stroll to the sea and watched the black waves crash against the sand. The moon overhead shone full in all its glory, lighting up the night sky and painting shadows across the land. Amara walked on, eventually finding herself in the garden.

"Evening, Amara," the Guardian called. "What brings you out this time of night?"

"I did not expect to find you awake. I myself cannot sleep."

"Still mulling over your questions?"

She gulped, her cheeks filling with fire. "How did you know?"

"I was warned."

"By whom?"

He didn't answer, but he joined her in her stroll around the perimeter of the Fountain. "Balance, Amara. This life is all about it. We take care of the plants, and they give us food to eat. We love our families, and they love us back. We all have different jobs—you tend the garden, I guard this water, your daughter will care for the animals, and Darius prepares food. And everyone else who lives among us does the same, according to his or her inborn interest and ability. It is all harmonious, beautiful, balanced. And doing what you are considering will disrupt that. Will throw it all off."

"What I am considering?"

"Do you not wish to taste the water?"

With a glance at the full moon, Amara considered how to answer that. She did, but she also did not. "I am perplexed. I do, and I cannot shake the desire. But there is the question of what that drink will do to us."

"Yes, that is the question. And one I fear the answer to."

"I am not afraid."

But it wasn't until she spoke the words out loud that she realized they were true. This was part of what troubled her. She should fear the outcome, the unknown. But she did not. Instead, she craved it. So strong was her curiosity, the drive, the vision playing on repeat in her mind—that they did away with any fear. She could think only of what the water might taste like, only of learning what would happen if she took a drink.

"The obsession is growing within you. Amara, listen. You must tame it now. Tame it, or you and I both know what decision you will make."

Amara stopped short on the path and grabbed the Guardian's arm. "And if I have already made the choice?"

The Guardian froze, and for a moment, Amara thought he'd stopped breathing. He looked to the moon then to the water then back at Amara. "If your mind is set, I cannot stop you."

A satisfaction crept over Amara's heart, bringing a smile to her face.

"But I can plead with you not to go through with it. There will be consequences. For all of us."

"I do not know what that means."

Her gaze settled on the Fountain now, and it almost seemed to call to her with the promise of satisfying her curiosity, of quenching a thirst like no other drink ever could.

"It means there is a price."

Her gaze snapped to the Guardian. "A price?"

She had no understanding of this either, the word making no more sense to her than did the Guardian's talk of consequences.

She had to try the water.

Had to taste it.

Had to know.

"Guardian, may I?"

He stiffened. "You may, but I beg that you not."

"What is your purpose then, Guardian? If not to stop me?"

"Your will is your own. My job is to protect these waters and warn of the dangers. But you...your will is your own," he repeated.

He remained between Amara and the water, blocking her path.

She peered around him, to the water flowing. Flowing with innocent beauty, just like the rest of the world. Arrayed in splendor, adorned with brilliance, quiet in its elegance. And yet...dangerous? It didn't add up, and she had to know. Had to test the warnings. Had to taste.

"I am sorry, Guardian, but I must know." She went to go around him when he grabbed her arm.

Tears welled in his eyes. "I beg of you. You know enough. Let it rest."

Amara paused, her gaze falling on the hand gripping her arm. Her flesh turned red beneath the tight hold of his fingers. She wanted to squirm out of his grasp, but she also knew she didn't need to. He would let her pass. Her will was her own, as he'd said.

But he was wrong. She did not know enough. No vague warnings about danger and consequences—whatever those were—could keep her from her curiosity. From the need to know, to confirm. She wished she could give the Guardian what he wanted and satisfy her own questions with one decision, but the two were at war. Opposing forces and only one could win.

Amara reached for the Guardian's hand, gently prying one finger at a time off her arm until she was free. "I will let you know how it tastes."

"No!" he cried, but he didn't advance. He stood back, hands lifted to trembling lips, eyes wide.

Still, Amara proceeded, approaching the water. As in her vision, she watched the spring flow and reached her finger down, dipping it into the Fountain. She swirled her finger through the water, and the spring seemed to respond, to sigh, to call, to invite. She lifted her finger to her lips, just as she had in her vision. But this time, she didn't snap awake before she tasted.

A single drop fell from her fingertip to her lips. Her tongue grazed the surface of her mouth, the water's sweet taste taken in by her senses, by the one single droplet. The flavor was divine, and she craved more. Cupping her hands, she filled them and slurped the sacred substance from her palms.

She stood, looked around her, waited. The Guardian watched, his hand trembling, his lips uttering something indiscernible.

"See, Guardian? Nothing."

As if in response to her declaration, the nighttime sky went from deep blue to black. Amara looked up to see the normally clear sky become covered in dark clouds. She had never seen them look so angry or appear so gray. Light cut through the sky in flashes and a loud, low rumble echoed all around her. "What is that sound?"

A furious wind whipped up, swirling around and blowing her plants with its violent breath. A tree cracked with the gale force, branches breaking and flying all around. Birds dove in and out of the sky in strange formations, dogs howled, and something else roared in the deep of the night.

"A disruption, it seems," the Guardian called over the torrential winds.

Amara clung to the side of the Fountain, fear rising up inside of her. What was all this? Certainly, one drink did not cause the world to spin out of orbit. But then...

"Amara?" Darius had come out of their dwelling, holding Elora tight to his side. "What has happened?"

She looked at the worried faces of her family, to the horror living in the Guardian's expression, to the whipping wind and wild trees, to the agitated animals, to the other villagers as they emerged from their homes in a sleepy haze, awakened to madness around them.

"I...I...took a drink," she said.

And the world stood still.

Twelve

Julia and Charlie

Darius and Amara

"There you are. You disappeared on me." Amara emerged from her mansion, her body swaying back and forth as she approached Darius. "Please tell me you aren't planning to leave me so soon after arriving."

She seemed unfazed by his earlier denial of her. He shouldn't have been surprised—he was used to the delusion clouding her world by now.

"I think I've decided I'll stick around. See if you're right." Hands in his pockets, he made his way toward the fountain in the center of the courtyard. "Where did you find these two?"

"You know I have eyes and ears everywhere."

"Sadly, I do."

Darius buried his hands in his pockets and strolled the path around her property.

Amara followed. "Their timeless love and devotion touched me. It's not unlike another eternal love I know of." She raised one eyebrow toward him, waiting for her words to take effect.

They were met with complacency. Darius merely grunted, his gaze fixed on the door he'd watched Julia disappear through moments before as they circled the courtyard.

Amara's eyes followed his and landed on her guest home. "Oh, tell me you don't have your sights set on Julia. I've not said a word as you've gallivanted around the globe seducing women, but that one is off limits."

Her gaze narrowed as it drifted between the guest house door and Darius's face.

Darius side-glanced her. "Off limits? What are you—her mother? Oh wait, I forgot. Your daughter is dead." His cold words were like little daggers of ice let loose in Amara's heart.

After a moment of silence passed, she whispered, "That was not kind."

"I'm not sure you're one to speak of kindness, Amara."

She stopped still in her tracks. "Have I done something to upset you?"

"I'll let you take a stab at that." His answer came out monotone, his tone icy.

"Ahh!" She turned and began walking in reverse in front of Darius so she could face him. "Would you stop?! How long do you plan to punish me for the past? It's always about the next girl or the next adventure or thrill! I've let you roam free, do what you want for all these many years. Now it's time to focus, to come home."

Darius released a heavy, bored sigh. "Mara, this is your big plan. Not mine. How many times must I remind you of this? I want no part of it."

The door of the guest house yanked open, and Julia ran out, hands in her hair, panic in her expression. Laying eyes on the pair, she beelined for them.

"Help me, please!" After issuing her plea, she turned toward the house, running through the door which stood open. Amara and Darius exchanged a glance before advancing toward the house.

When they walked through the door, they found Julia standing helplessly in the living room as Charlie was in the middle of a tantrum in the kitchen. His face flushed and stained with tears, he raked his hands through his hair as he grabbed another glass and threw it against the wall. It shattered on contact, falling to the floor in pieces where three others already lay in a broken mess. Next, he grabbed a plate from the cupboard and cast it into the air like a Frisbee. It spun and hit the wall, finding the same fate as the glasses.

"What's he doing?" Darius asked, bewilderment in his gaze.

"He's losing it. He had two memories not his own, one right after the other. And in the next instant, he didn't know me. Then he didn't know himself, and he started freaking out. I tried everything—reminding him he was safe, what his life consisted of, who I was. Being calm and gentle and patient. But it didn't work. I don't know what else to do!" Her voice shook, and she brought her hands to her mouth.

Amara stepped forward and approached the kitchen. "Charlie." Her voice was soothing. The comfort was meant for Charlie but even Julia calmed at the sound of her voice.

As Amara faced Charlie, Darius came to Julia's side and rubbed her shoulders. She didn't resist.

Charlie paused, plate in mid-throw. He sniffed, wiping his face on his sleeve. "I don't know you. Leave me alone, or I'll break another."

But instead of retreating, Amara took another step toward him. "You don't want to do that. It's okay. We're friends. You're safe."

"I do want to. Can't you people see I don't want you here?" He tossed the plate into the air, allowing it to fall to the ground and shatter.

Amara took another step, broken glass crunching beneath her heels. Extending her arm, she took Charlie's hand in hers. "You're okay.

You're safe. Let's just take a moment."

Alarm filled Charlie's face and then calm washed over it, replacing his angst. His shoulders eased, his posture relaxed. By the touch of her hand, comfort overtook him.

"That's good. Very good. Now come with me."

Amara led him out of the kitchen and into the living room, where she sat him on the couch. Taking a seat next to him, she massaged his hand and waited for him to come back to reality. "Give us a moment, would you?"

Julia's chest tightened, and emotion choked her. Running out the door, she made her way toward the pool. A fountain flowed into the body of water, and she splashed some on her face as she gained her bearings. *What* had just happened?

"Are you alright, my lovely?"

Julia jumped, the smooth voice pulling her out of her own head. Turning, she found Darius standing there with hands in his pockets. She sunk down onto the ledge surrounding the fountain.

"I'm fine." Tracing the rock on which she sat with her fingertip, she amended her answer. "Wait, no, I'm not. I don't know how much more I can take. And what was that? Amara walks in and everything is better? What is it about her?"

Darius strolled to her side, taking a seat next to her and leaving only inches between them. "That was Mara's voo-doo you just witnessed."

"What?" Julia snapped.

"She has the ability to bring calm over...*certain* people. It's her gift."

The implication stung. Like Amara could comfort Charlie in ways Julia couldn't, and she hated his explanation. Hated Darius for being the one who gave it. But then she considered the actual words he's said. "Certain people?"

"You know, special ones. Like us." He nudged her shoulder with his own.

"She has that ability on anyone who has had a drink from the Fountain? Why?"

"Let's just say Amara has a special connection to the water, more than anyone else who has had a drink from it."

"You people love your cryptic answers, don't you?"

Darius raised his shoulders in a shrug. "It's the truth. Don't tell me you haven't experienced it yourself."

"Of course I have." She turned her attention toward the guest home, wondering what was happening behind closed doors. "I should have been able to ground him, to pull him out of whatever was happening."

She kicked the pavement beneath her feet.

"Ah, so that is what's really bothering you. That *you* weren't the one to bring him back."

"Of course that's what's bothering me. Charlie and I have known each other for over one hundred years. We were engaged before—you know—the water took hold. And every time before now, I've been able to return him to reality or at least deescalate him. But today—I've never seen him do anything like that." Her gaze snapped to Darius's face, and surprisingly, she found compassion in his eyes. "To be honest, I'm terrified. I don't know what's happening to him or if I can save him."

"I think I may know what's happening."

He moved a piece of hair out of Julia's face, the gesture far too familiar to her, and it sent a mixture of feelings through her—sweet reminiscence and discomfort. She pushed aside both.

"Tell me. Please."

He stared at her for a beat, intensity in his gaze. "I'm trying to decide how much I should entrust to you."

"Please, tell me whatever you know. Whatever it is that will save Charlie."

His look held pity, and then he said, "I'm sorry, love, but there is no saving your Charlie."

Darius's words felt like a heavy weight dropped on her chest.

"So that's it? How can that be?"

"I'll get to that, but you are going to think me mad."

"I drank from magical water, and it made me kill someone. I can suspend my sense of reality."

He smirked. "Fair point."

He got lost for a moment, flashing Julia his most genuine smile. "A long, long time ago, Amara took her drink. That set into motion a series of events. Charlie's arrival as the Phoenix—and I'm sorry, my dear, but he does fit the bill—means those events have almost come full circle. The only thing left is for Charlie to fulfill his lifespan. The Phoenix has extraordinary power, but he isn't invincible."

"There's no saving Charlie." Julia's gaze searched the distance as she worked to process this, as the weight of that reality beared down on her, threatened to ruin her. "But there has to be a way. Balance, right? The Fountain of Youth gives you eternal life, but then you have to kill others to replenish the stores. You can live with that fate or take the antidote and live with whatever your circumstances were before. There has to be a failsafe here too. I refuse to accept that Charlie is just doomed to die."

"The Phoenix *is* the failsafe." Darius's voice dropped to a somber whisper.

"For what?! It isn't right, isn't fair...after all this time..."

Darius took Julia's hand in his. "I know what it is to love deeply and then lose it all. I know." The compassion had returned to his gaze, and Julia allowed his comfort in. "And you're right. There is balance in all of this, and it dictates that you can't have it all. You can't be immortal and deny the water its demands. You can't be mortal and never die or get ill. The water won't work like it has for millennia as long as the Phoenix is alive."

Julia settled into silence, absorbing Darius's words. "It's just—it all feels like it's been for nothing."

"What has?"

She glanced at Darius. "You're immortal. You've murdered?"

"Please," he answered.

"Okay." Julia exhaled a heavy sigh. "I killed everyone else who has ever had a drink. Well, that is, until I met you and Amara."

"Are you warning me?" Darius winked at her.

"Ha, hardly. My murdering days are behind me. For a long time, I convinced myself that that was my purpose in drinking the water, to rid the world of the killers it made. And I did that because Charlie's life hung in the balance. It was my end of the bargain to get him back. So if I did all of that and Charlie just dies anyway, it's a waste...and I have to live with the fact that I have spent almost a century being a serial killer myself."

Darius let out a slow whistle. "You're pretty badass. You know that?"

Julia huffed a brief smile at his compliment and then sobered. "Yeah, not sure that's something to brag about." A moment of silence passed between them. "How about you? You've killed other people. Do you ever get to a point where you stop seeing their faces every time you close your eyes?"

"Ah," Darius said. "I've had many years to confront the ghosts I've made."

"So...no?"

"Yes. But it's taken a long time. Listen, you can't undo what's been done. And you can't continually reject that aspect of yourself. You are both a savior and a murderer. The two are not mutually exclusive; they can't be. What you've become through your drink of the Fountain has changed you. You will never be the girl you were before you took the drink. I imagine in some ways that's a good thing? Everyone has their reasons for drinking. But sooner you come to terms with the parts of yourself, both who you were and whom you've become, the sooner you'll accept your regrettable actions and have peace."

"You know, you're not just a class-A jerk. I'm thinking there's a little more to you than this suave persona you try to put out there."

"Well, I have been around a while. It's taken me a long time to realize what I've just shared with you."

"Thanks."

"For what?"

"For what you said." Another moment of silence passed, and Julia gazed at the guest house. Still nothing stirred from inside. "Amara suspects Charlie's descent into madness is indication that his lifespan might be shorter than the prescribed five-hundred years. But she acts like maybe there's a solution. Maybe we can slow it down."

"Maybe she can find a way to slow it. If anyone can, it'd be that woman." He paused, a long look lingering on Julia.

"What?"

"Amara is correct."

"About which part?"

"About what Charlie's decline means."

Julia closed her eyes and dropped her face to her palms. The news only got worse. She felt Darius's arm wrap around her shoulders.

"How do you know? Amara said she 'suspected' this was true. How do you *know* it is?"

Darius sat up and cleared his throat. "I have...some information she does not."

Julia slapped his shoulder. "Are you holding out on me?"

"No, no. Just on her. I've confirmed for you that Charlie is the Phoenix, and I've told you he can't be saved. There's really no more to it that you need to know."

Just then, the door to the guest home opened, and Amara poked her head through.

"Charlie's asking for you," she told Julia with a soft smile on her lips.

Seeing her face flashed both relief and uneasiness through Julia's insides. She turned to Darius and pointed her finger at him. "You and I are not done."

She stood and marched toward Amara, but instead of going inside, she paused in the doorway and said, "I want to know what you plan to do with Charlie. This can't continue this way."

"No, of course not. I've already put in calls. I have a team of doctors on the way to him. We're going to get this sorted out, figure out what's going on and how to fix it."

Julia cast a glance back at Darius. "If that's even possible." She turned from Amara and walked into the guest house.

There Charlie sat on the couch where she'd left him, face buried in his hands.

"Charlie?" She kept her tone low and lingered by the door in case he'd forgotten her again.

But he glanced up, and relief covered his expression. "There you are."

Standing, he crossed the room and embraced her. He held on tight, like keeping her in his arms assured his sanity. When he finally did release her, he gazed into her eyes. "I'm so sorry. I don't know what came over me."

"Charlie, something is wrong. It's getting worse, closer together, and you're really scaring me."

He brushed her hair off her face with his fingers. "I know. I know, and I'm sorry. I'm not going to let anything happen to us."

But Julia threw his hands off of her. "How can you say that? You're not in control of your own mind half the time, and you don't know me anymore, and I'm helpless to do anything about it. The only thing that helps is Amara's touch." Her own words struck her heart, and she pushed her fear down, favoring anger instead. Julia paced wildly, letting her fury in. Anger about Charlie's decline. Anger that she was powerless to stop it.

"I—I'm sorry. I don't know what to say."

Julia softened and crossed to Charlie, pulling him down on the couch next to her. "I know. This isn't your fault. I don't mean to take my frustration out on you. Charlie, I don't know how long you're going to stay lucid, but I have to tell you what I know." She paused, not wanting to go any further. "I was talking to Darius outside. He tells me there is nothing we can do to stop what's happening to you."

"But Amara said her doctors are on the way. That they'll figure out an answer. "

Julia smiled and caressed Charlie's arm. "I know. And I hope they do. But, Charlie, if they can't…"

"Haven't we figured out a way every time? Life keeps throwing obstacles in our paths, and we keep decimating them."

"Everything keeps getting in the way. We overcome one, another appears. I can't keep thinking about how everything I did to get you back was pointless. I became the thing I feared just to lose you for good. I thought murdering Caroline would drive you away, but it didn't. You're steadfast, Charlie. You don't deserve this. And I'm not sure…"

Charlie cupped her face. "Not sure of what?"

"I'm not sure I deserve you. Not after what I've become. I can't shake it, and now seeing this happen to you makes me feel worse. Everything that has happened is my fault."

A tear escaped her eye and trailed down her cheek.

"Hey, hey." Charlie swiped her tear with his thumb as he held her face. "Need I remind you who convinced you to drink that water in the first place?"

"Yeah, but Charlie, you can't hold your past self responsible for what you present self now knows."

"And you can't continue to punish yourself because of the choices that led us here."

"Is this such a great place to be?" She gestured her hand back and forth between herself and Charlie. "Me a psycho killer and you demented half out of your mind?"

Charlie laughed. "I hardly doubt a 'psycho killer'"—he used finger quotes—" would be torturing herself the way you are. And as for me—" he sat up tall and haughtily. "—I've never been more sane."

Julia laughed, and the release felt good. "Oh, Charlie." She embraced him and kissed him.

"Whatever has happened, whatever is happening, you and I will find a way. And we can determine our paths from there."

Julia stared into Charlie's deep brown eyes. "I hope you're right."

Thirteen

Julia and Charlie

J ulia and Charlie sat on the sofa of the guest house wrapped up in each other, their only companion silence. What more was there to say after the acknowledgment of Charlie's impending death and Julia's declaration of feeling totally unworthy of his love? Charlie kissed the top of Julia's head as he ran his fingers through the tendrils of her long, red hair.

"This," he said.

"Hmm?"

"This. Can we just stay like this? No more magic, no more amnesia. Just you and me?"

Julia sighed and closed her eyes, enjoying the feeling of his hands in her hair. "If only…"

Charlie sat up suddenly, forcing Julia to do the same. "I've been thinking," he exclaimed, an excitement in his eyes that she hadn't seen in some time. "You said I have some relatives alive, Jethro's descendants."

"That's right."

"Where are they?"

"They live somewhere in Colorado."

"Colorado…" He trailed off, his gaze lost in the distance before snapping to meet hers. "I've never been." He shrugged and pulled her into his embrace, settling against the cushions of the couch. "Once we get this figured out—and we will get this figured out—and I'm healthy again and we can move on and leave all of this behind…I'd like to go to wherever they are. I'd like to set up our lives there and work to get to know them. They're the only connection we have to our past lives besides each other."

Julia's lips lifted to a sad smile. "I think that would be great, Charlie." How she'd love to dream of a future with him, but she feared that not facing the facts of their reality could be dangerous for him. "It's just—I think we have to consider the fact that maybe there won't be a future beyond this."

She saw the impact of her words before Charlie responded. His posture deflated and his face fell.

"Can't I have this, Jul? Can't I focus on what I'd like our life to be rather than on what's happening to me? If I think about *that*, I feel crushed. You've always been able to face your realities, but if I do that, it means I lose hope. And I can't lose hope. I refuse to."

Julia lifted her face so she could see his eyes. "I've always loved that about you. And if I'm honest, you have always brought hope to every dire situation." She laughed, recalling a memory from their childhood. "Do you remember when I had that bunny? He was so small and sickly, and I kept thinking he was going to die. But you—you insisted he was meant for great things. As the runt of the litter, he needed extra care, and I made a schedule to ensure he was checked up on every two hours, even if I wasn't available to do it. And when he got sick, it was you who believed he'd pull through when I was already grieving him."

Charlie smiled and nodded his head, remembering. "And he did!

That crazy bunny refused to die. How old was he when he died? Twelve and a half? And he was robust as ever until his last breath."

A warm smile spread across Julia's face at the memory. "Even then, Charlie, you believed in what felt like the impossible." She scooted up on the couch and trailed her finger down his cheek. "I'm sorry I tried to be a dose of reality for you. Hang on to your hope. It's your superpower."

Charlie kissed her forehead. "It's not that I don't realize what's happening or that I'm in denial. I just refuse to accept it." He scrunched up his face. "That's different, right?"

Julia laughed. "I get what you're saying."

She traced his arm and trailed her fingers until they met his hand, and she squeezed him tightly around her body. And yet, she worried they were facing the final challenge life threw at them, and she wasn't sure they'd survive.

As if he could read her thoughts, he tightened his grip around her. "Think of what you've done. You almost died, overcame sickness, and conquered the water by taking out everyone you knew who has had a drink. You traveled the world, tracked me down, and took on a major pharmaceutical company to get me back. And here we are. I may be losing my mind, but it's never been more made up about you. Please know that. Cling to that truth when I step outside the bounds of sanity, would you?"

His words brought her comfort. She tilted her head towards him, and their lips met in a long, slow kiss.

"Everything I need to know I've found in your kiss." Charlie gave her another. "There is certainty there, familiarity, like coming home."

He kissed her a third time, and this one deepened, unlocking their desire for each other. Julia's hands tangled in Charlie's hair, her fingers running through his black strands and gripping his head. Charlie held her tight, his own fingers digging into her flesh as the intensity of the moment increased.

Knock! Knock! Knock!

Their kiss broke apart, and the two stared at each other, breathless and flushed. They exchanged a smile, and Julia reached up to put Charlie's hair back in place. She stood, pulling at the hem of her shirt to straighten her clothing and exhaled a deep breath.

When she opened the door, she found Amara, Darius, another man, and a woman with them.

"May we come in?" Amara gave her a soft smile.

"Of course." Julia stood aside and let them through.

Darius gave her a coy, suspicious look, and his gaze volleyed between her to Charlie. "Flushed cheeks, tousled hair. Did we interrupt something?"

"Darius, mind yourself," Amara admonished.

He put his hands up in surrender and retreated, not issuing another word.

"Julia, Charlie, these are Drs. Lydia Clark and Joseph Dearborn. They're some of my best, and they're here to examine Charlie. Would you allow them to do so?" Amara glanced from Julia to Charlie.

The two of them exchanged a look, silently agreeing.

"Of course," Julia answered. "As long as Charlie is comfortable with it."

"Yes, please." He stood. and extended his hand and shook each of the doctors'.

The female of the pair, Dr. Clark, smiled warmly at the other three. "If you don't mind, we'd like to examine Charlie alone." She turned her attention to Charlie. "Would that be okay?"

"Yes, that's fine," he answered without pause.

Julia crossed the room and gave him a kiss. "I'll just be right outside if you need me, okay?"

She retreated from the guest house to the courtyard separating the small dwelling from Amara's monstrous one. Both Amara and Darius followed her outside. When the door to the guest house closed, Julia paced.

"I assure you these doctors are brilliant," Amara encouraged. "I've sent them Charlie's files and shown them his blood samples. They know what he can do, and if there is a way to save him, they will figure out what that is."

"Please," said Darius, his tone dripping with sarcasm. He leaned against the guest house with arms crossed and one knee posed on the siding.

Amara turned her attention to him. "Do you have something to say, darling?"

"Only that you know this is a waste of time. He's either not your Phoenix because of his strange side effects or he is and you have to keep waiting."

"Please, Darius. Even if we have to wait five hundred years, wouldn't it be better for him to spend that time lucid? So that he and Julia can enjoy their years together?"

"You know that's not the purpose of the Phoenix. You know his life is no longer his." He stopped short, covering his mouth as though he'd said too much.

The two women regarded him, but Julia spoke first. "What does *that* mean?" Her tone was sharp.

"Yes, Darius, what does that mean?" Amara tilted her head, and a coy smile reached her lips.

"Amara, you need to stop lying to this girl. If he is who you think he is, then you know his purpose in all of this. He is the break, the resting period between having access to the water and not. *You know this.* That's *if* he is the Phoenix. I still say he's not. I'm betting your doctors will confirm my suspicion."

"But you told me—" Julia began.

"—I know what I said," Darius injected, shooting a look of warning at her. "I was wrong."

"Say you weren't. Say he is the Phoenix. Why did you say his life is no longer his?" Julia squared her posture, hands on her hips.

Darius turned his gaze to her, and his eyes held pity. "Think about it. If he is intended to bring the good the water provides, his life is meant for healing. Not for gallivanting around the globe on some five-hundred-year romantic holiday."

He dropped his foot to the ground and punched one hand into the palm of the other. He too began to pace.

"What's it to you if Charlie and I travel the world together?" Julia took a couple of steps toward him. "Haven't we earned that opportunity? Just a few years of peace and quiet would be nice! Why should it be his responsibility to heal the world? He didn't ask for that!"

"He took the drink! You took the drink! It doesn't matter what the reasons were." Darius was in Julia's space now, inches separating their noses. His eyes narrowed into a glare while his tone lowered. "There are consequences for your choices."

"Yes, I agree. But we've had our fair share of those."

"You don't get to choose what they are or when they end."

He turned away from her, but not before she saw the disgust on his face and tension in his posture.

"And, Amara, we'll see what your doctors say, but I think you bear more responsibility for his condition than you admit."

Amara waved her hand like she was bored. "Yes, yes, I know. I caused this whole mess. Blah blah blah."

She rolled her eyes.

"We all know that, but that's not what I meant."

Before either woman could respond, the door to the guest house opened. Dr. Clark walked through and gave the trio an easy smile.

"We've just had an episode. It was helpful to see one happen. In addition to your notes and verbal report, Amara, Charlie explained what's been happening. We conducted a battery of tests, and the episode we saw confirms our suspicions. Now, we'd like to run some updated brain scans on Charlie to rule out other options, but it appears he is suffering from an early onset of his own brand of Alzheimer's." She paused, allowing the words to land. "We've never seen a case in someone so young, but I'm afraid—with a few variations that fit his specialized condition—his symptoms fit to a tee.'"

The doctor paused, making sure everyone followed. "The other thing I need to make you aware of is that this is a very rapidly advancing case. It is a degenerative and progressive disease, but the rate at which he's going…" She trailed off, her gaze dropping. "I know this is hard news. The rate at which he's going indicates to me that his years may be shortened."

"Even with his special abilities?" Amara asked.

"Yes, even then. He responded well to other inflictions. We poked his finger, and he instantly healed. However, from his report and yours, the degeneration of his brain seems only to be progressing."

"Is there nothing we can do?" Julia demanded.

Dr. Clark looked at her with compassionate eyes. "I can prescribe him some medication that can minimize his symptoms, keep him more lucid. But as far as reversing or slowing the progression of the disease, I'm afraid not. Now, there are some experimental treatments we've been working on at Eden Pharma, and with your permission, we could consider Charlie for those. In the meantime, I'd like you to track his episodes so we can get a good idea of a baseline—how frequently they occur, how long they last, that sort of thing."

"We can do that," Amara answered. She sighed and shook her head with slow sad movements. "I suspected this."

"And you're wrong," Darius interjected. "This just proves what I've been telling you—he's not who you think he is. He can't heal from this."

"But, Darius—"

"No. Let them go, Amara. Keep searching. I know you're desperate for your big retribution, but you aren't going to get it through Charlie. You aren't." He glared at her.

Amara cleared her throat and turned her attention to the doctor. "Thank for your time. I'd like you to see him daily, manage his care."

"Of course."

Just them Dr. Dearborn emerged from the guest house. "Charlie is resting now. You can see him when you're ready. I trust Dr. Clark has given her report. Are there any other questions?"

A hush fell over the group, and when it became apparent no one was going to ask any questions, Amara dismissed the doctors and turned to Julia. She took her hand, sending a swath of warmth and comfort over her.

"This is hard news, and I'm sorry. With your blessing, I'd like to keep Charlie here and allow my doctors to follow him. It's the least I can do after what we did to him back at Eden Pharma. We'll look into the experimental treatments, too, see if anything will help. You, of course, are welcome to stay."

Julia considered her offer and concluded she didn't have much choice. Anywhere she went with Charlie, she'd be constantly fighting his episodes. And then she couldn't ignore the fact that Amara's soothing touch was helpful when they happened. She nodded, unable to speak for fear she'd cry.

She had to face facts. No amount of Charlie's superpower hope could change this outcome.

She was going to lose him.

Fourteen

Julia and Charlie

~~~

J ulia stared off over the calm, blue water of the pool. The hard
surface of the chair she rested on dug into her legs, but she
couldn't feel the penetration of the metal and cloth. She gulped
down the insistent lump in her throat as a swallowed sob shuddered
through her body.

Alzheimer's.

The word itself was devastating. Was this something he would
have genetically been prone to anyway? And somehow being the
Phoenix—or whatever—accelerated the condition once he was awake?
It had been over two years since Charlie woke up on the island. Maybe
the disease had ravaged his brain from that moment.

But it didn't explain the memories of others he had. Or maybe it did.
Maybe that was his brain's unique expression of the illness. After all,
Charlie was not exactly your run of the mill Alzheimer's patient.

All the details swirled in Julia's brain. In the end, they mattered
little. The real crisis for Julia was facing an eternal life without Charlie.
This was a prospect she hadn't been forced to imagine since Rose first

struck him down.

Rose.

In all the craziness, Julia hadn't had time to think of the girl. And as she sprung to Julia's mind, the usual wave of grief didn't accompany it. Instead, a strange jealousy rumbled through her. Rose was gone, at peace, and though Charlie's last stretch of time—however long it may be—promised to be tumultuous, he'd soon be at peace too.

And she'd be alone.

"Hello, love." The buttery voice cut through her thoughts.

Julia glanced up into the face of Darius.

"Mind if I join you?"

Her body devoid of energy, she merely gestured to the chair next to her.

"I need to talk to you." The seriousness of his tone grabbed Julia's attention. She raised her eyebrows at him.

"You have to get out of here." Urgency marked his words.

"What?" she asked. "I can't offer him the kind of care Amara can."

"You're not safe here. Or rather, Charlie isn't. He is most definitely the Phoenix, and that means neither of you is safe."

Confusion crossed her expression. "But you just told Amara that this confirms he's *not* her Phoenix."

Darius's gaze darted around, and he went on in a hushed tone. "I haven't been completely forthcoming with what I know about the Phoenix."

Julia rolled her eyes. "Surprise, surprise, you're a liar too."

"I didn't intentionally mislead you. I just didn't disclose everything. Mara, on the other hand…"

"You intentionally misled her?"

"Yes."

"Why?"

"The arrival of the Phoenix presses some cosmic pause button on the power of the Fountain. But once his life span is over, Amara will have access to the water again."

"She talked about it becoming more accessible, but she never let on that she meant accessible to *her*. Wait. Why can't she get to it now?"

"It was one of the...consequences...of her drink."

"But—"

"That doesn't matter right now. What matters is that, once she has access, I have no doubt in my mind she will only make more mistakes where the water is concerned. That can only mean bad, bad things for humanity." He paused and then closed his eyes with a deep breath before continuing. "I'm pretty sure I know why Charlie is deteriorating and why he's having other people's memories."

Julia stiffened. "Because he healed them?"

"Yes. I didn't know quite how this would happen, but I have known that the Phoenix will lose touch with himself. He'll become less and less of who he was as he heals. The reason for this is because the Phoenix will have to be detached from his life and all strings that might keep him tied to it in order to complete his cycle. He can have nothing holding him here or giving him pause because he will have an opportunity—one—to ensure the Fountain isn't restored. That it doesn't create the kind of chaos it has before."

"But how?" Julia sat up straight and angled her body toward Darius.

"That I'm not sure of. What I am certain is that Amara's relentless barrage of sickies she threw at Charlie has something to do with his accelerated loss of self. The whole process could take five hundred years, but it could also take much less time. His healing is a double-edged sword. It's a gift to the recipients, but bestowing that gift accelerates Charlie's demise. The more he heals, the less he's Charlie. The only thing I can't figure out is why it started so suddenly and is now advancing so quickly."

Julia's insides burned, and she was filled with a sudden, angry burst of energy. She sprung to her feet and punched her fist into the opposite palm. "*She* did this to him."

"I don't think she realized. She doesn't know his vulnerability, only that the end of his lifespan means access to the water. Up until this point, she thought she would have another five hundred years before she could lay claim to the Fountain again."

"That's why she let us go."

Julia sunk back to a seated position and stared off into the calm water of the pool, digesting everything Darius was telling her. "She already suspects his deterioration means his life span is shortening—"

"—It'll only be a matter of time before she figures out why...and how to make it go more quickly." He finished the statement for her.

"How do you know and she doesn't? How do you know about the Phoenix losing himself and what that means for Amara?"

Darius leaned against the poolside chair and folded his arms behind his head. "When did you take your drink?"

"About a century ago."

"Ah, yes. That's a long time." His tone had a hint of mockery in it. And then his expression morphed, like he was connecting something in his mind. "And when did you reunite with Charlie?"

"Just a few months ago. I finished with my...task—the one I told you about earlier...and returned for him on the island. Only he wasn't there. Why do you ask?"

Darius sat up straight. "Wait a minute. It took you nearly one hundred years to kill everyone you thought had had a drink? How many were there again? I'm thinking we can mark efficiency off your list of qualities."

Julia's stomach tightened as her defenses rose. "Excuse me. I had a list of names, and that was it. Do you know how many people in the world have the *same* names? I can't begin to tell you how many wild goose chases I went on. There was no internet during most of that time, and I was alone. And even when I thought I'd found each one, it took time to study them, learn their habits, their vulnerabilities. Sometimes I infiltrated myself into their lives, or at least into the lives of their loved ones, so I could gain access. And I ran into my fair share of obstacles that slowed me down too. Those things took time. But guess what? I never gave up. I never quit."

"Fair point." He nodded. "I remember how less connected the world used to be compared to now."

She shot him a look of annoyed disgust. "You were going to tell me how you have all this insider information on the Phoenix."

"Ahh yes. Well, love, the Fountain has been around for much longer than a century."

"I know. Rose's family protected it for generations."

Darius threw his head back and howled. When his over-the-top laughter died, he said, "That's cute."

A hot wave of irritation radiated through Julia, and her face reddened. "Why are you laughing?" she spat.

"Julia, love, the Fountain of Youth has been around since the beginning. Like the beginning beginning. And Amara—she was the first one in all of humanity to take a drink."

Julia absorbed this. "The *first*?" Her gaze traveled out over the pool again and then snapped to Darius. "And you?"

"Among the first." He shrugged a shoulder. "As the first, she is bound to the water in a way no one else is. And there was a Great Guardian, long before your friend Rose's family came onto the scene. He was bound to the Fountain, the protector of it, but Amara's drink made him vulnerable too. In any case, the waters weren't hidden from me like they were from her, and in desperation to undo what Amara had done, I sought him out years later. I found him, and he revealed some of the truths to me. Truths Amara does not know, can't know."

"You reeaally don't trust her, do you?"

A darkness covered his expression. "And you shouldn't, either. And that's why you have to go. If Amara finds out that healing others is what shortens Charlie's lifespan, she will stop at nothing to ensure it ends swiftly."

Julia exhaled a long breath.

"I know she seems like she's on your side."

"Called us family."

"And she is warm and caring...at least parts of her are. But the other parts are so far from the woman I knew long ago. She's gone mad, and I don't know quite what her plan is. She's tried to pull me into it, but.."

He gulped, and something flashed in his gaze. Julia thought for a moment she saw grief there. But it dissipated as quickly as it had appeared. Darius cleared his throat.

"Whatever she intends, it won't be good. A lot of bad things happened when she took her drink, and she has since lived under the delusion that she can make everything right again. But to do so, she needs her Phoenix. And imagine once she discovers that when Charlie heals, it brings her closer to what she wants. Imagine."

Julia sat up with a sudden jerk. "We need to get away from her. But I don't know where to go. Charlie's out of his mind half the time. How can I keep him safe?"

Darius drew in toward Julia and squeezed her knee. "I got you covered."

"So you know, you aren't going to get me into your bed. If that's your motive, you can forget it."

Darius smiled, every handsome feature of his face accentuated. "As lovely as I'm sure that would be, my motive is to keep Amara away from that water. Which means she can't have access to Charlie."

"What do you propose?"

"Well, as I've been around multiple millennia, I have amassed a small fortune. I have a place we can go. Just pack and be ready and meet me here in an hour."

"And Amara?"

"I'll take care of her."

* * *

Julia entered the guest house with caution, unsure what state she might find Charlie in. But he sat up against the bed reading a book and flashed her a bright smile when she emerged through the door.

"Hey there, gorgeous." He put his book down and opened his arms to her. "Come here."

Julia obliged, crawling onto the bed next to him and into his arms. "Charlie, we have to talk."

"I already know. My mind is deteriorating. It is progressive, and there is no cure."

Julia met his gaze and fought the emotion threatening to rise up. She gulped. "There's more than that."

"Hit me." He leaned against the headboard and opened his arms.

"I need you to trust me, okay?"

"With my life." He smiled again, and his dimples came alive.

"We have to leave."

Charlie's forehead furrowed. "But Amara said her doctors are going to follow me, treat this, see if they can slow it down."

"Once Amara knows why this is happening to you and what it means, she won't have any interest in slowing things down."

"Why not? Why is this happening to me?"

Julia took a beat, trying to decide how much to tell him. He could lose his mind again any moment.

"Just... she won't." She sighed, studying his confused expression, and then she made up her mind. "Okay, Charlie. We don't know what caused the onset of your symptoms, but healing makes it worse. The more you heal the quicker you'll lose yourself. No matter what, you cannot use your ability on anyone. It's only a matter of time before Amara tries make you heal again. We are no longer safe here, and we need to go."

"Where to, though, Jul? Back to the island?"

"No. We're going with Darius."

"That fool? He can't keep his eyes off you, and we barely know him!"

"I know, I know. But this is where you have to trust me, okay? He's known Amara for a long time, and he knows about what's happening to you, and we just...we have to go." She stood from the bed then and began throwing their scant belongings into their bags.

"Julia, I don't know..." Charlie approached her and took her hands in his, halting her packing for the moment.

"There's no debate here. It's only a matter of time before she figures it all out, and then you're toast, Charlie. Do you hear me? This is life and death." She snatched his cell phone from the charger and dropped it into his hands. "Keep this in your pocket at all times, okay? It's important we have a line to each other. I don't know what'll happen if we're trying to travel and you go away in your head and wander off."

Charlie nodded and tucked the phone into his pants pocket. But then his eyes emptied of all awareness. He looked at their interlocked fingers and then threw hers from his grasp. He lifted his gaze, and she knew he had checked out. "I—don't know where I am."

Julia closed her eyes and covered her face with her hands. Clearing her throat, she quieted the frustration within. Of all times!

"You're safe. You can trust me," she began.

Charlie backed away from her, a wary expression on his face. He picked a pillow off the sofa and lobbed it at her. "I don't know you!"

The words stung as they had each time before. Choked by emotion, tears fell down Julia's face. "I'm sorry," she said. "I don't know what to do." She turned and haphazardly threw more belongings into her bag as defeat swallowed her.

From behind, Julia felt arms wrap around her. "Jul? Are you crying?"

"I'm not—I..." She wiped her tears with a forceful gesture.

"I did it again, didn't I? I'm so sorry." He tightened his embrace around her. Holding her close, Charlie stroked her hair and kissed her head. "You don't deserve this. After everything...'"

Julia pushed herself away from his chest. "We love each other. And that means taking the bad and the ugly with all the good. But right now, Charlie? Right now we have to GO!"

Surprised by her forceful statement Charlie nodded. "I'll do whatever you ask. I trust you."

"That's all I need to hear."

But then, his eyes went empty again, and he frowned, confusion covering his face. He retreated a second time and ran to the corner of the room, backing himself into it. "Who are you?" he said sharply.

"Oh, Charlie, again?" Never had he had episodes this close together, and that sent a shiver of fright through Julia.

But Charlie only screamed. "Get away from me!" over and over again.

The front door of the guest house burst open, and Amara ran in, alarm on her face. "I heard screaming." She looked from Charlie to Julia. "May I?"

Julia waved her hands toward Charlie.

Amara approached, hands up like she was surrendering. "I'm just going to come close, okay?"

Charlie recoiled.

"You're safe, and all is well." She took several steps toward him as he regarded her with mistrustful eyes. When she reached him, she said, "May I have your hand?"

Charlie didn't reach for her, but he also didn't resist. Amara stretched her hands forward and placed them on Charlie's arm. The comfort her touch brought registered an instantaneous response on Charlie's face.

"There you go. You're safe, and all is well," she repeated. She guided Charlie to the sofa where he took a seat. "Lie down now."

He obeyed, stretching out on the sofa. Amara propped a pillow under his head and covered him with a throw blanket.

"Julia, may I have a word?" She asked the question without sparing a glance in her direction.

Julia planted her feet. "Have your word."

Amara turned to her. "Not here."

There was a severity in her tone, and her face was devoid of her usual warmth. "I'll meet you in my kitchen."

She stood and left the guest home.

Fifteen

Darius and Amara: Many, Many Years Ago

D arius stared at his beloved Amara, disbelief clouding rational thought. She couldn't have…she didn't. After she'd promised they were enough. After she'd sworn her questions were put to rest. He held fast to their daughter as the winds swirled around them, threatening to tear her from his grasp.

"Father, what's happening?" Elora cried, and the fear in her eyes struck Darius' heart.

He had no category for what was happening, leaving him feeling helpless, and he would give anything to keep her from the terror her face told him she felt in that moment.

"It's okay, my dove. I'm here. You'll be safe. Stay close." He shouted over the wind and, with his words, drew her tighter to his body.

At the same time, Amara collapsed to the ground in a heap, and he wanted to run to her. But he had to keep Elora safe, and so he hastened his gait with her in tow until they reached Amara. The wind fought them, making his steps difficult as he resisted the fierce gales

138

thwarting his efforts. Around him, others stood daunted, half of them lingering outside their homes, half in the garden. Confusion swam in each person's eyes as much as Darius' mind tried to register what had just happened.

Reaching Amara, Darius lowered Elora and himself to the ground, attempting to shield his family with his body, his strength. The winds persisted, the angry clouds above rumbled, as the world reacted to what Amara had done.

Beneath Darius' form, she wept openly. "Make it stop!" she screamed. "Make it stop!"

If only that were possible, but he felt as helpless as the rest of them. All he could do was keep his family safe, keep them under the cover of his arms. All of them were immortal. All would survive this. As if the universe begged to differ, a limb snapped from the tree and landed on Darius' shoulder. He yelped in pain as the branch struck him, sending an agony so severe it stirred an immediate nausea in his belly. And it didn't relent. The affliction—a burning inferno—persisted. Darius feared looking at it—seeing what was causing him such agony, but he stole a glance anyway. His shoulder caved in, and it appeared deformed, separated. The sight sent a second wave of nausea, and he almost lost his dinner all over Amara.

"What is it?" she cried beneath him.

"My shoulder. I'm...I'm hurt."

"But how?"

"I don't know..."

He longed for the winds to die, for the universe to finish its tantrum so that he could inspect his shoulder with greater ease. He moved minimally, and that shot a scourge of pain through his shoulder and down his arm. Darius cried out again, the torment almost more than he could take. His head became woozy, and he feared he was losing consciousness. Every last bit of his energy was required to stay awake.

He had to protect his loved ones.

But the unrelenting stabbing in his shoulder, the dizziness it caused—they threatened to subdue him.

Darius fell to the side as consciousness failed him, as he was swept into darkness.

* * *

When he awoke, the first sensation he became aware of was the searing of his shoulder. A moment in the dark had not minimized his pain. He felt himself sweating and, reaching with his good hand to pat his brow, found a damp cloth on his head.

"Father!" Elora flew to his side from across the room when she sensed movement. "Are you okay? I've been so worried!"

"I'm okay. Why have I not healed?"

Sadness shadowed her expression, and her gaze dropped to the floor. "It's because of...what Mother did."

"But—how?"

Darius' mind reeled as he tried to make sense of everything. Besides the pain distracting him, his mind was groggy from the fitful sleep.

"I don't understand, Father, but you're not the only injured one. Others were hurt in the storm too."

The storm. Had it settled? He cocked his ear, listening. Nothing but the sweet chirping of birds against the quiet of the morning sounded outside.

"Father?"

His focus snapped to his daughter, as a tear streamed down her cheek.

"I'm frightened."

His pain slipped into the background as comforting his daughter became the only priority right then. Darius reached for her, but immediately regretted the action as a sharp burn radiated from his shoulder down the length of his arm. Wincing, he grabbed at his shoulder with his good arm as his breath hitched.

"Father, are you okay?"

"Yes, my darling dove. Come." He gestured toward the bed, and Elora climbed in, snuggling up to him on the side of his good arm. "I'm frightened too, but it's going to be okay. Everything will work out. You'll see."

"I do not know, Father. Everyone is talking. Everyone is fearful, and they are saying unkind things about Mother."

This stirred worry in Darius, and he peered around the interior of their dwelling. "Where is your mother?" A start ran through his chest, and panic mounted, but he stuffed it down so as not to alarm Elora.

"She is with the Great Guardian."

As if on cue, the Guardian's voice rang out through the garden, reaching them through the window.

"Come all to the Fountain. Come now!"

"We must go, Father. Can you walk?"

"It is my shoulder that is injured, not my legs."

"Of course, Father." She stood from the bed. "Here, let me help you." With careful maneuvering, she worked to get him to his feet.

Darius winced as he stood, each movement sending a new jolt of agony down the right side of his body. He walked slow steps toward the door and then out into the garden, where the villagers had all gathered. In the center, around the Fountain, the Guardian stood with Amara by his side. She held her hands folded in front of her; her gaze cast to the ground.

Darius glanced around him. Others bore injuries, too. Soft sobs rang through the crowds, and destruction marked the garden area they all stood in. Trees were blown over, whole plants ripped from the ground by the winds, and wilting flowers cast about. Some roofs were torn, weathered by the storm from the night before. He'd never seen anything like the destruction around him, as foreign as these new unpleasant sensations in his body.

He felt a new emotion too—something different and unfamiliar. As he gazed upon his beloved, his love for her dueled with something far bitterer, a feeling that burned him from the inside out, igniting his skin with a fiery heat. Darius's lips curled into a snarl, and he worked to remind himself how much he loved her, how just yesterday he could not imagine himself filled with more bliss.

But then she went and ended all that, didn't she? The thought fed the burgeoning feeling in his chest, his heart racing.

"Thank you for gathering." The Great Guardian swept his hand in front of him, gesturing to the villagers who assembled. "As you know by now, we've experienced a disruption in our way of life."

A murmur rose amidst the crowd, and Darius swore he heard Amara's name muttered.

"Hush, please." The Guardian waved his palm in the air to quiet the crowd.

"Now, Amara has taken a drink from the forbidden Fountain. This is the source of the disruption here. Her decision cannot be undone, but for many of you, it can be reversed. Look around you—everything has changed. You are feeling new pains you've never experienced, both in body and in spirit. And you see the destruction that has befallen our wonderful place. Now that a drink has been taken from the Fountain, one must be offered to all."

Darius' eyes bulged in his head, and he gazed around the crowd. The same shock he experienced registered on the faces, in the postures, of those around him. Everyone talked, questions on their lips, uncertainties lurking in their minds.

In his mind.

"The reason you are injured is because Amara's drink unleashed mortality onto our world. All of you are mortal now, with the exception of Amara. What may seem like a reward is a curse to her. She may never be mortal—she has linked her life with the Fountain—and she will watch those she loves around her die as she continues to live on. Additionally, she will watch the world change as her drink unleashed other kinds of evils among you. But that is her burden to bear."

He met the concerned gazes of those gathered. "For the rest of you, you have a chance to regain your immortality. With one drink. But be advised, as there were consequences for Amara, so shall there be for you if you drink. I have warned you all these years of the danger lurking within the waters, and now I issue my final warning. Drink and pay the consequences. Abstain and live what's left of your mortal existence."

He dropped his head, and his posture sunk, as if he'd been defeated.

Darius watched the Great Guardian, and it occurred to him that this *was* his defeat. He had failed at his job—the most important one. The crowd separated, and voices raised. Tones Darius had never heard saturated the words spoken, and this sent fear coursing through him. He looked down at his daughter, who stood frozen, watching her mother at the front by the Fountain.

"We have to get her," Elora said.

Darius followed her gaze. He knew she was right, because he could hear the hot burn of the new emotion he felt in the words of those around him. They would turn on her; she was not safe.

Darius took Elora's hand and cut through the crowd toward Amara.

"Come," he commanded Amara, ignoring the pain in his shoulder. Guiding his family, Darius weaved through the villagers until they reached the doorstep of their dwelling, shutting the door behind his family when they were safely inside.

"Why?" he demanded.

Amara ignored his question and instead placed her hand on his arm. "You're injured. I'm so sorry. I never meant—"

"*WHY?!*"

This time he yelled, and the volume of his voice surprised even Darius. He'd never raised his voice to her, but he couldn't calm the storm within.

Amara jumped, tears streaming down her cheeks. "I...I had to know."

"And now that you do?"

"I should not have. I should not have taken the drink...But, Darius, we can make it right. You. Elora. All you need to do is drink, too, and all will return to normal."

"What of the consequence the Guardian spoke of?"

"They can't be worse than this."

Darius studied her, and then his glance traveled to their daughter. She sank against the wall, her hands crossed in front of her body. He would give anything to be rid of the pain in his body, and if this was a taste of what mortality had to offer, he wasn't interested. And then he thought of Elora—of her growing old and dying. Of her not recovering from an injury. Gaze returning to Amara's tear-stained face, he thought about when she had drowned and if he had lost her for good to the sea. That was what mortality meant for them.

"Please, Darius. We have to undo this. We have to make it right. We must convince everyone to drink. All of our village, everyone. We must."

Darius' forehead crinkled as he weighed the decision. Never had he encountered such confusion—there was no clear answer. Life had been easy, effortless, wonderful, and now...

"Father, please." Elora came to him now, taking his good hand in both of hers. "Mother is right. We have to return to how we were. We don't know how to do...this." She gestured to his arm, to the hole in their roof.

Her plea was all it took to push Darius' mind over the edge to a decision. "Let's get to work."

First, they approached the Fountain, and dipping their hands in, Darius took a drink and then Elora. The water felt cool and refreshing as it washed down Darius' throat, unlike anything he'd ever sipped before. The taste was sweet, and if he didn't have work to do, he would have desired for more. The moment the water trailed down his throat, his arm righted itself, the bone in his shoulder healing and working into the rightful place. Pain lifted immediately, and the usual vibrancy he experienced from day to day was electrified. A feeling of insurmountable energy coursed through him, and he had never felt more alive.

So they set out, going door to door, home to home, talking to their community, begging for each person to drink. Some, upon seeing Amara, slammed their doors in their faces. Most let them in. Many agreed. But some remained unconvinced, fearful for what new consequences may await.

The day was long, and the work hard, but they made their appeals and then they retired to their dwelling for the night. As they did every night, they tucked their daughter into bed and gave her a kiss on the forehead.

"Everything is going to be alright," Darius promised. "You will see."

"I know it will, Father."

A soft smile touched her lips, but he saw the fear still living in her eyes. With one more kiss, he parted the curtain separating her bed from the main area and retired to his own quarters. Amara lay down next to him, but she was timid, keeping her distance.

With a gulp, she sat up and took a deep breath. "Do you forgive me?"

Darius looked to her, her beauty illuminated by the moonlight streaming in through the window. He reached for her, and she placed her hand in his palm. Something new radiated from her touch. He'd always felt electrified by her touch, but this—this was different. A comfort, a warmth, a desire to extend his forgiveness.

"I do, my love."

Her hand still in his, he yanked her to him so that her body collided onto his. Grabbing both sides of her face, he kissed her, his desire for her taking over. Pushing her garment down onto her shoulders, he kissed each one with quivering lips.

"Ahh!" Amara screamed and fell off of him.

"What? What did I do?"

But she grabbed her head and rocked back and forth on the bed. "No. No, no, no, no. I will not. I will not."

"Amara?" Darius' heart filled with alarm as it beat against his temples.

"Amar—"

He reached for her, but she swatted his hand away. Grasping her head, she looked into his eyes.

"Run," she said. "Run away from me."

Sixteen

Amara and Julia

Julia strolled through the back door of Amara's home and into her kitchen. As she had the night of Julia's arrival, Amara rounded to the far side of the kitchen island and leaned across the granite countertops. Her eyes narrowed as they focused on Julia, but she didn't speak.

Julia tilted her head. "Well? You said you wanted a word. What is it?" She swallowed the rising fury directed toward the other woman. *She* had done this. *She* had set off the chain of events that were slowly killing Charlie.

Amara straightened and walked around the kitchen island tracing the countertops with her fingertip as she approached Julia. She stopped in front of Julia. Her expression had not changed; it held contempt of her own that Julia did not understand.

"Darius tells me you wish to leave."

"Oh does he?"

Julia steeled her posture and held her ground. She didn't like the way Amara looked at her.

"How do you expect to take care of Charlie? My best are on his care."

"You and I both know that won't help."

Now Amara listed her head at an angle. "Since you arrived, I've been nothing but accommodating. I've opened my home to you and enlisted my medical team for Charlie. I thought we were bonding, Julia. Why the sudden ire directed at me? Why do you wish to go?"

Julia gritted her teeth, tension filling her posture. "Something tells me not to trust you after all."

"Would that 'something' go by the name of Darius?" Amara raised her eyebrows at Julia, her expression softening. "He's very handsome. And Charlie is slipping from you. I can imagine how lonely you must feel. I, too, have been lonely for a long time."

She gave Julia a sympathetic look.

"You know, I still don't quite know your history with Darius. But why is that he, who has known you for a veeeerrry long time, does not trust you? Like, at all?" Julia squared her shoulders, a challenge in her stance.

Amara's gaze shifted away, and a humored smiled tugged at the corners of her mouth. "Darius and I"—she began, half turning away from Julia—"have a long and complicated history. He doesn't forgive me for something that happened long ago."

She turned with a sudden jerk back toward Julia, taking her arms in her hands and sending a swath of warmth and belonging through her. "And that is why all of this is so important to me. This is why I can't let you guys go. Charlie needs my help, and I'm eager to give it."

"And why is that?" Julia pushed through the comfort Amara's touch brought, through her desire to just submit and trust her.

"Why is what?"

"Why are you eager to 'help' Charlie?"

Amara tightened her grip on Julia's arms. "I've told you already. He's my Phoenix."

"But you didn't tell me that when he dies it's YOU who will have access to the water again. That you're currently cut off from the source."

The slight crack in Amara's demeanor told Julia she'd hit a nerve. "I see Darius has done more than persuade you to leave." She dropped Julia's arms and traced the pattern on the island counter. "You told me some of your story, so let me tell you a little of mine."

Amara paused and looked up at the ceiling like she was trying to recall details.

"I was the first to take a drink from the water of the Fountain of Youth."

"I know, Darius already told me."

Amara went on, as if Julia hadn't spoken. "And as the first, I not only was forced to carry out the demands of the water like everyone else who drinks"—her voice wavered, and a small shudder echoed through her before she went on—"but there were additional consequences. As I told you before, the whole Fountain lifted up from the earth, the land that is now the island formed around it, and the entire thing disappeared. Only later did I find out that it had moved. And that it moves again every five hundred years." A small laugh escaped. "I, at least, got that much out of Darius."

"What does it mean that the water was hidden from you?"

"Just as it sounds. I could stand in front of the island housing the Fountain and see nothing. It would be invisible to me. If you were to pour some of the invisible water into my hand, it would disintegrate on contact.

"Anyway, I told you before that I knew it was somewhere among the thousand islands. It took me a long time to discover this, and once I did, I erected the research facility there. I knew once I found my Phoenix I would need to confirm he was who I know him to be and that a process like that would need to be handled...discreetly."

Amara cleared her throat and turned back toward Julia, looking her squarely in the eyes. "Darius and I suffered a loss together as a result of everything that happened. It's this loss that keeps him angry with him, that he refuses to forgive. And that's why I need access to the water again. It's my chance to set things right."

"What does that mean?"

Amara exhaled a long sigh, a patient smile on her lips. "Before my drink, life on earth was perfection. There were no wars, no illness, no death, no...loss. I believe if given access to the water again, I can return the natural order of life on earth. I can ensure those things are never a part of the human experience again."

"And...just how will you do this?"

Amara took a deep breath. "By making the water available to everyone." She raised one eyebrow and cocked her head, awaiting Julia's reaction.

"But that would mean—"

Amara lifted her palms. "Only temporarily. Only until the demands are satisfied for everyone who drinks."

"You're talking about genocide. If everyone drinks, everyone will kill."

"Try to reframe how you see this for one second, Julia. You call it genocide; I call it redemption."

"*Redemption?* This—the Fountain—is not just about you and what you've done. There's no redemption in murdering others or being the puppet master pulling the strings so that others kill. I should know. I spent the last hundred years doing just this. If you did this, life would not return to some blissful utopia. People would have to live with the regret of what they did, for an eternity. Not only would this mean the end of life for so many, it would mean having to live with that forever."

"Time heals wounds, dear. No, it will be a redemptive act. Our planet is overpopulated. People go hungry. They get sick. They war.

They die. This would put an end to all of that."

Julia took a step closer to the other woman, their noses inches apart. "But at what cost, Amara?"

Amara nodded, and her eyes crinkled with sympathy. "Think of your regrets. Think of the questions your years murdering other murderers brought up for you. Wouldn't all of that be worth it if you could take part in restoring the world to its intended state? Wouldn't that history serve as a beautiful puzzle piece that fits into the larger picture I'm trying to construct here? As I've said before, you did the world a favor when you took those murderers out. This would be one more favor, and maybe it would help you reach greater acceptance of these parts of yourself."

Julia thought for a moment, and Amara's words almost made sense. *Almost.*

"No," she spat. "Killing more people will only make me weaker. It will only chip away at who I am as a person."

"Julia, you are the same girl you were before your drink, and you are very different. It takes both parts of you to make up who you are. I'm simply asking you to embrace the second part of yourself, the one your drink brought to life. But only for a short time."

"But this is different. If this happens, innocent people will die. Many of them."

Amara was quiet for a moment, and she nodded slowly with a somber expression. "Yes, I can't deny that some innocent people will die. But their sacrifice will pave the way to a better world for everyone else. It won't be in vain."

"I will not kill any more innocent people."

Amara took her hand. "You can do whatever you want while nature sorts itself out, deciding who is fittest to survive. You can lay low, or you can work as an assassin of other immortals, whatever your pleasure."

151

"I take no pleasure in killing other people. Even the vile ones. And for any of this to be possible means Charlie has to die."

Amara took Julia's hand in hers again. "I realize the cost might be greatest to you."

Julia recoiled as Amara's words confirmed what she'd said.

Amara nodded.

Julia snatched her hand from the other woman's grip. "And you're willing to sacrifice him? After what you've already done? I'm sorry, but I can't let that happen."

"*I'm* not sacrificing him. *I* didn't choose him. The water did by his merit and by the decisions he made. It just is what it is, Julia. You and I cannot stop it, but there's still so much time. Almost five hundred years. That's several lifetimes over. You have the freedom to be with him and enjoy that time. His demise isn't imminent."

Julia narrowed her eyes, trying to determine if Amara was bluffing. Did she know more than she let on? Darius was sure she'd figure it out, even if she didn't know already.

"Then you won't care if we leave." Her words came out as a directive.

"Actually, I do."

"What's it to you then? If we have all this time, why keep us here?"

Amara put her hands up in front of her and shook her head. "Oh, I'm not *keeping* you here. No one is a prisoner, Julia. I merely ask you to stay so that I can help look after Charlie."

"We don't need your help," she tested.

Amara smiled. "I have the resources. I have the best medical professionals. I have the magic touch."

She crossed her arms, daring in her gaze. Worse, she wasn't wrong, and if Julia were honest, she'd have to admit her envy over the fact that Amara alone seemed capable to bring Charlie back from the brink of insanity.

"Teach me, then."

"Teach you?"

"Yes, teach me how to administer the kind of warmth and comfort your touch brings. I assume it's related to the water."

"Indeed, and therefore, it's bestowed, not taught."

Julia stared at her in silence, and she made up her mind. "We're leaving. Tonight. I won't stay with someone who is happy to allow my beloved to die. I don't trust that your doctors will do anything to help Charlie, and I won't indulge in your sick waiting game for him to die so you can annihilate what it is to be a human being."

"What you cling to? It's weakness. Imperfection. I can restore everything, don't you see?"

"I see a crazy lady who wants to commit genocide. There's no other view of what you want to do, Amara. You're insane, and even beyond the fact that you are happy to allow Charlie to die, I won't let you use him to carry out your plan."

"Won't *let* me?" Amara stiffened, and darkness overtook her features.

"That's right. I won't let you." Julia glared at the other woman, and their gazes clashed.

Amara snarled, and with a gesture so quick Julia's mind almost didn't register it, she grabbed her by the throat. Amara's two thumbs stacked on top of each other and dug into Julia's neck as a look of utter madness covered Amara's expression, making her almost unrecognizable.

Julia struggled for air and felt a wave of panic. But taking a deep breath, she tucked her chin against Amara's hands. Tears filled her eyes and trailed down her cheeks, and her head began to spin as black specks filled her vision. Julia grabbed each of Amara's arms with each of her hands and, at the same time, pulled them away from her own neck as her knee met Amara's stomach.

Julia heard the wind leave Amara, but the other woman regained her stance. The two circled each other.

"I do not need permission to do anything nor does anyone deny me what I want. You will not stand in my way. If you cannot be on board, you are of no use to me. Charlie is mine now."

"I knew we never should have trusted you." Julia's fingers slid into her boot where the knife strapped on to her leg. She withdrew the blade and pointed it at Amara. "I'm not going to kill you, Amara. But I can't let you continue to harm Charlie."

A million thoughts flashed through her mind at once. The exits. Miniscule flinches in Amara's stance. The question of if she could add one more face to her nightmares.

She could, maybe. If she had to. If it would keep Charlie alive.

Amara lunged, and Julia caught the flesh of her arm with the knife. Amara let out a yelp and drew her arm away. Julia watched as the wound bled and then reclosed, good as new.

"How—"

But there wasn't time to finish the question. Amara lunged a second time and kicked the knife out of Julia's hand. She grabbed her left arm and yanked it backward. A loud "snap!" echoed through her kitchen.

Julia screamed, but the agony would not relent. She couldn't be certain if her arm was broken or dislocated, but a fiery anguish extended down the entirety of the limb. Amara had spontaneously healed when Julia sliced her arm. Why wasn't she?

Doubled over, Julia saw spots. Her stomach filled with nausea and bile climbed up her throat. She glared up at the other woman, who stood there with a satisfied smile.

"I don't want to hurt you, Julia. But I also know you love Charlie and won't stop coming for me. I'm not so worried about that part. As you just witnessed, you can't actually do me any harm. What concerns me is that your existence threatens my plan. And I've been planning this for a very long time. Longer than you can imagine. I've been nothing but good to you, and I'm willing to continue that arrangement if you can get on board. This is your last chance, Julia. You have a choice here."

Julia thought about Amara's words, but the distracting torment in her arm made rational thought tricky. "If what's going to happen is going to happen, just let me take Charlie and go."

"Tsk tsk," Amara waggled her finger back and forth. "It's too late for that. You'll poison him against me, and five hundred years is a long time. I can't run the risk of the two of you mucking things up for me. I don't know how you'd do it, but I can't gamble anything going wrong. It's too bad. I was really growing to like you. I assume that's your answer then?"

Julia's glare only intensified, and she lunged at Amara. With her good arm, she covered Amara's throat, cutting of her air. Amara grabbed the injured arm and yanked, which forced a scream out of Julia's lips and her grip to relent. Amara reached for a knife on the countertop, and Julia defended herself from the blade's swipes with her good hand, resulting in several slashes across her palm and arm.

She swept the interior of Amara's home with her gaze, escape now seeming the only possibility. Amara lunged again and pinned her between the blade she held and the refrigerator.

"I'd so hoped we'd be friends."

Her dark eyes were inches from Julia's own, and Julia snapped her head with all the force she could muster into Amara's face. Amara screamed, and Julia caught a glimpse of broken facial bones putting themselves into place as she dashed through the kitchen, into the front marble encased foyer and out the door. She stopped short when she slammed into Darius, knocking a bag out of his grasp.

"She's trying to kill me!" she screamed.

Darius scrambled, retrieving the bag from the ground and rounding to the corvette that sat parked in the driveway. "Get in!" he yelled, and Julia obeyed, diving through the open window on the passenger side.

Darius didn't check to see if she was buckled, or seated for that matter, before he tore out of Amara's driveway and sped down the road.

He drove her away.

Away from danger.

Away from Charlie.

Seventeen

Amara and Charlie

A mara reached the front door in time to see Darius's corvette peel out of the driveway of her sprawling home. She screamed and pulled at her hair. This was not how everything was supposed to go. Julia was supposed to be her friend, her ally. She was supposed to understand, to see the plan as the world's salvation, maybe even her own. Instead, she had rejected Amara's plan, and now she was gone. *With Darius*, no less. She would worry about that little detail later. Amara knew she had the only insurance plan she needed where Julia was concerned. And when she returned for Charlie, Amara would be forced to make her the first casualty of the new world she was so close to creating.

In the meantime, she shook off the rage building inside of her. First, Darius and now Julia. Why could no one get on board? Why could no one see the flawless beauty in her plan? Amara took a deep breath and closed the front door. She straightened her skirt and cleared her throat. Glancing down she decided to change out of her blood-stained garments before she answered the urgent impulse to check on Charlie.

157

He was still her Phoenix, and she could get control of the situation. First, though, a clean change of clothes so as not to alarm him.

Amara ran upstairs, discarding her outfit quickly and pulling on the first blouse and pants she came to in her closet. White top, black pants. Checking her reflection in the mirror she smoothed her hair and wiped the blood from under her nose with a warm washcloth. She gave herself a soft smile. "Good as new."

Departing her home through the back door she made her way across the courtyard to the guest house. A small breeze kicked up and sent a tiny chill up her body. Otherwise, it was a gorgeous sunny day, and she painted a smile on her face as she rapped a knock on the guest house door.

Charlie whipped the door open seconds later, and he cast a smile at Amara. "Hey, Mara, come on in. I was expecting Julia. Have you seen her?"

Amara strode through the door and took a seat on the sofa. She patted the spot next to her, inviting Charlie to join her.

He sat but angled his body away from her and cast a wary glance in her direction. "You're scaring me, Amara. Where's Julia?"

"She left, Charlie."

His forehead wrinkled into a scowl. "Left? But she…"

Amara reached over and placed her hand on his knee. "I know it's hard to understand, but all of this was too much for her."

He leaned away from Amara and cast her a strange expression. "If you believe that's true, then you don't know Julia at all."

Amara nodded, and her gaze filled with sympathy. She squeezed Charlie's knee in reassurance, but she felt him tense under her grip.

"What's going on?" he said, glancing around with frantic movements. He threw Amara's hand off his knee and pulled his knees into his chest, nestling himself into the corner of the sofa. His eyes held fear and confusion.

"Charlie, you're having an episode."

"Who's Charlie?"

He pulled his knees tighter against his chest and hid his face behind his legs so that only his eyes were visible. Amara stretched her hand out, but she froze inches from touching him.

"You are safe here. You can trust me. I can help. Just take my hand." Her voice was soft and calm, and she flexed her fingers with her invitation.

Mistrust joined the confusion that lived in Charlie's gaze but he reached his hand forward anyway. Amara watched as her calming power washed over him and his whole body relaxed.

"Why does that feel so good? So...familiar?" Charlie closed his eyes and tightened his grip on Amara's hand.

"Because it's supposed to. Because we're connected, Charlie. Because, with me, you're home. We're two sides of a coin. And somewhere inside of your confused brain, you know this to be true," Amara cooed.

She ran her fingers over the top of the hand she held as she spoke.

Charlie came to, and he shook his head. Seeing their joined hands, he withdrew his from Amara's grip.

"I went away again, didn't I?"

"Yes. It's getting more frequent."

"Fewer spaces between, like I'm...like I'm losing myself entirely."

Amara drew away from him, against the sofa. "How long ago did this start for you?"

Charlie rubbed his chin as he thought. "It's tough because I'm so in and out, but probably a few months or so ago. I don't know why it suddenly started."

"Your memories—" she began.

But Charlie interrupted her. "You said Julia is gone?" The volume of his voice raised, and he stood to his feet. "I have to find her."

"Charlie, sit down," Amara said.

"No. She wouldn't leave without me. Before, when she was here…" He glanced at his hands, lost in thought. "She said *we* had to leave, not that she was leaving."

"I guess she changed her mind. I saw her with my own eyes as she sped away in Darius's car. With him."

Charlie clutched his chest and stopped cold where he stood. "But she…she wouldn't."

"You have to consider, Charlie, the toll an illness like yours takes on others. I'm sure she would have liked to take *her* Charlie with her, but you are becoming less and less him. She is better off on her own, away from the stress and the pain of you forgetting her again and again. It isn't fair to her. You do love her, right?"

"Of course," he snapped.

"Then wouldn't you want to spare her from watching your decline?"

Charlie stared off in the distance. "Of course," he said again, his voice dropped by several decibels.

"Then let her go. Let her be free, and spare her the pain."

Charlie fell to seated position into a chair, his gaze lost and full of grief. When he looked in Amara's eyes, his own pooled with tears.

"I don't believe you that she just left without me. Julia would *never* do that." A tear trailed down his cheek. "But you're so right. It's cruel to expect her to watch this. It's cruel that I keep forgetting her over and over again. I don't know where she is right now, but I have to let her go."

"It's best you stay with me. Only my touch seems to ground you."

Charlie gritted his teeth. "*Where* did she go, Mara? She wouldn't abandon me."

"Charlie, you need to focus. You have to face that fact that you are not going to live forever anymore."

"I'd barely gotten used to the idea that I *was* in the first place," he said, his voice flat, his attention elsewhere.

Amara reached for him again, and this time, he didn't resist her touch. Again, she felt the tension ease in his body as she grasped his hand. "I want you to know that I'm here for you. That I will keep you safe."

Charlie turned to her, a sneer on his face. Yanking his hand from her grasp, he said, "And why, Amara? Just why would you be interested in keeping me safe? Julia wanted to leave here *with* me. She didn't trust you. I still believe there's a way I can beat this thing...or...or slow it down or something. But I'm not sure you're the one to help me with that."

He threw his body against the couch and turned away from her, resting his chin in his palm.

"She's gone, and I'm here. Regardless of whom you think Julia is, when things got tough, she ran away."

"No. She wouldn't do that. It's *you* she doesn't trust. You are who she wanted to run from, not me. I need to find her." Charlie stood with a sudden violent movement, looking around frantically and patted his pocket where his phone was. "She knew you'd try to make me heal more, you'd try to speed up my decline..." Charlie stopped short, frozen, and fear filled his eyes. Peering up at Amara, he said, "Who are you?"

"*What* did you say?"

"I said—who are you?"

"No, before that."

But he only stared blankly at her.

Amara's mind reeled. *That's it!*

She turned on her heel and left the guest house, abandoning Charlie in his momentary madness. Eager to get some space, she had to think through what he'd just unwittingly revealed to her and she was unwilling to spend her energy on grounding Charlie.

She approached the small bar in her office, uncorked a bottle of wine, and poured herself a glass. But she didn't drink it just yet. Instead, she proceeded to the basement. At the bottom of the stairs, she fingered the spot on the wall where her safe was and entered the code. The dial glowed red, and a small needle extended from the wall.

Amara pricked her finger against the needle and squeezed, dispensing a droplet of blood onto a small platform underneath the needle. As soon as her blood was detected, the dial glowed blue as it processed her DNA. Ten seconds passed, and it beeped, the color of the dial changing to green. Amara stepped through the opening to her secret vault and approached a padded bench in the middle of the small room. She took a seat and stared at the framed portrait taking up the entire length of the wall in front of the bench.

"To you, my love." Lifting her glass, she toasted the image and took a long draw of the wine. As she stared at the portrait before her, her eyes welled with tears. For a small moment in time, she allowed the pain in, because that grief was such powerful fuel. The suffering ignited in Amara the will to go on with her plan, even when she felt misunderstood by everyone around her. She knew—had known from almost the beginning—that her plan was the only way. And Charlie had just told her how to speed up the timeline even more.

She'd waited millennia, and she'd been patient. Faith kept her strong, kept her forging ahead.

"Good news, my darling. I think I've figured out a way to make it go quicker. All I need now is to test my theory. And then, when all goes according to my plan, they'll all see. Darius. Julia. Everyone. I'm going to make it right. I promise you, Elora."

Amara hummed a soft lullaby to herself, and she polished off her glass of wine. She blew a kiss to the portrait and returned upstairs, heading to the guest house.

Eighteen

Julia and Darius

arius sped down the road with the calm and skill of a seasoned race car driver. "We've got to get you far away from here, where you're safe. We'll regroup and figure out a plan."

Julia ripped her shirt and wrapped her hand so as not to bleed all over the interior of the car. She worked to even her breaths as both her arm and her hand seared with excruciating agony. "But Charlie!" she managed. "I can't leave him there with that woman. She tried to kill me. He's not safe." She tilted her head against the rest, focusing on her breaths to both quiet the rising panic in her mind and the torment from her wounds.

"Long time since you felt pain that enduring, huh?" Darius spared a sympathetic glance before narrowing his eyes on the road ahead.

"Yeah," she sighed. "Long time."

Silence settled between them for a moment. And then Darius's voice broke through the quiet. "I told you my ex was insane."

Julia's head snapped up, and her gaze landed on Darius. "I *knew* it. Too much sexual tension between the two of you. Why the play-boy

163

act then?" Julia asked, resting her head against the seat again.

"Oh, it's no act. I'm quite popular with the ladies." He bobbed his eyebrows toward her.

Julia rolled her eyes. "Handsomeness was wasted on you."

"Ah, so you are attracted to me."

Another eye roll. "Don't flatter yourself. You already think you're more handsome than any of the rest of us."

Julia allowed her gaze to drift to the scenery passing her outside. "It's a good thing you were there," she said in a hushed tone. "She almost killed me."

"I thought you were a badass assassin. How'd she best you?"

Julia pounded her fist into the dash as a wave of fire radiated down her arm. "I don't know. I didn't want to kill her. Plus, I was distracted because she...*healed*."

"Oh yes, that. Another annoying feature of Amara being the-first-to-drink."

Julia's kitchen brawl with Amara played through her mind like a movie. The gash Julia inflicted had closed up before her eyes. Yet, Julia's wounds remained. The throbbing in the torn flesh of her hand served as a reminder. "So make sense of it for me. Why haven't I healed from her attacks but she did from mine? She's immortal. I'm immortal. Should have been a no brainer."

"Yes, well, she isn't just immortal. Her life is linked to the existence of the water. As long as that Fountain flows, she'll keep on living."

"So I've been keeping her alive all this time? By killing the others who have had a drink, replenishing the eternal life stores?"

"In a sense, yes. But she would have continued to exist with or without you because the water still exists."

Darius merged onto the highway.

"Where are we going?"

Julia read the signs as they accelerated.

"Private airport. I'm going to fly us to my beach home, same place we planned to go to anyway. It'll help us get our bearings. Form a plan."

Julia studied him as he drove and mentally weighed her options. She didn't like the thought of going so far from Charlie and, though she *felt* like she could trust Darius, he hadn't proven anything to her yet, aside from whisking her away just now. Julia was struck by the enduring powerlessness this situation drove home. She needed medical attention and a chance to formulate a plan to rescue Charlie. Feeling forced into a decision was becoming a much too occurring norm. Again, she saw no other option before her than to trust Darius. For now, anyway.

Glancing at Darius, Julia found that his posture was relaxed, his expression calm. She consulted her gut, desperate to trust him but unsure if she should. And yet, no warning bells were going off in her head. "Just promise me you're not kidnapping me and taking me to some secret lair somewhere so Amara can have her way with me."

He raised an eyebrow at her, and out of his peripheral, he looked her up and down. "Promise. Though I can't say I haven't thought about having *my* way with you."

"Focus, cowboy. You were telling me how Amara's life is linked to the water."

"Oh yes. I told you Amara was the first one to take a drink from the Fountain."

"Yes, you mentioned that. But how do you know that?"

"Because she and I were among the first people in existence. And things were very, very different then."

"Wait, you said you were among the first to drink as well."

"Yes. I was the second."

Julia lifted her finger into the air. She required one second of silence to absorb all this new information. "Okay. So you and Amara were among the first humans—ever—and were the first to drink…so like, are you Adam and Eve or something?"

"Eh, well, Darius and Amara." He chuckled before adjusting the rear-view mirror.

"I'm being serious." Julia clenched his arm, forgetting for a brief moment that her palm was torn up. The fiery throb that followed reminded her, and she jerked her hand away, cradling it against her body.

"You okay?" Darius's glance shifted between the highway and her hand.

Julia nodded, expelling a tired breath.

"We'll get you all patched up once we're on the plane. Okay?" There was real concern in his voice, and his gaze held pity.

A second nod. "Can you continue with your story? It'll serve as a good distraction from thinking about my arm hurting so much."

Darius returned his attention to the road in earnest. "We were among the first. In our day, there was peace everywhere. The ground grew crops effortlessly. No one became ill, and people lived forever."

"Sounds nice."

"It was, but Amara, in her selfishness, brought an end to it. People have many stories to account for this. Adam and Eve, Pandora's Box, the Mesopotamian's story of Adapa and his god Ea. But regardless of how people try to understand their origins, long ago there was life on this planet, and it was good. And there was the Fountain, and it was forbidden. And even though Amara was a much sweeter version of herself then, she was always relentlessly curious."

"So she drank from it because she was curious."

"Mostly, yes. And because I think she had…*has* a rebellious spirit, and once that woman gets her mind locked on something, she will make it happen. Tell her not to do something, and you've just given her an incentive to do the very thing you wish to keep her from. That's why, I think, she still wants me. Besides my good looks, I refrain from giving her my undeniable charm longer than for a night."

He winked at Julia, who only glared in return. Darius cleared his throat before continuing. "Anyway, she took her drink, and you know well what happens once a person drinks."

Caroline's face flashed through Julia's mind and brought with it a burst of guilt. Which she then stuffed down so she could focus on the story.

"This is us." Darius pulled into a small airport and right up to a hanger.

"I want to hear the rest of the story," Julia objected.

"In time, love."

* * *

When they arrived, the crew was already assembled, the aircraft ready to go. They settled into their seats and waited for the pre-flight checks to finish. As they did so, Darius found the first aid kit.

"Let's get those wounds tended to, shall we?"

He sat down across from Julia and opened up the kit. Sleeves rolled to his elbows, he revealed a tattoo of a dove on his forearm. He donned rubber gloves and laid out the contents of the kit on the small drink table between them. Gauze, tape, band aids, antibacterial ointment, and some nondescript medication.

Darius rubbed his palms together. "Okay, first your arm. Do you think it's broken?"

"I have no clue. I can't really move it at all, and everything makes it hurt."

Darius stood and approached Julia past the table separating them. "Do you mind removing your shirt?"

Julia drew away from him. "Yes! I mind very much!"

A small chuckle escaped his lips. "I just meant the top shirt. I can see your tank top underneath. I just need to see the entirety of your arm."

Julia glared at him before she obliged, but when she tried to pull her top shirt over her injured arm, she let out a cry of pain.

"Shh, shh, no, that's okay. Let me help you." Darius grabbed the edges of her sleeve with gentle hands and pulled with slow, gradual movements. The shirt, already freed from the other arm and from around Julia's neck, slid slowly down her bum arm. She hissed the entire time, but Darius was able to remove it completely.

"Hmm," Julia smirked. "Seems like maybe you have some experience with that."

Darius reared his head and laughed. "I do like you," he said.

His expression sobered as quickly as his laugh had broken out, and his eyes narrowed with concentration. Julia watched as his gentle touch traced up her arm, the sensation not entirely unwelcome. He touched her arm at each intersection of bone, traveling from her wrist up to her shoulder. His hands stopped at her shoulder, and he caressed a lump that had formed there, sending shots of agony down the length of her arm.

Tracing his fingers down her arm, he took her hand in his. "I think you've dislocated your shoulder. I'm going to put it place for you, and it's going to hurt like hell. But then it'll be over."

Julia nodded and braced herself in her seat. Darius took her hand and began to guide it up straight in front of her body. Julia closed her eyes and focused on her breathing as a torrent of pain tore through her arm. Her head swam, and she broke out into a sweat. Up, he raised her arm, and each inch hurt worse than the last until she felt a loud "pop".

"Ahh!" she screamed, but then the pain subsided to a sore hum. Julia expelled a heavy breath.

"Better?" Darius smiled at her and studied her. The crystal blue of his penetrating gaze unnerved Julia.

She cleared her throat and scooted up in her seat, rubbing her shoulder. "Yes, thank you."

"It's going to feel sore for a while. Now let's see that hand."

Julia extended her opposite palm, and Darius examined the slashes. He sorted through the spilled contents of the first aid kit and found the antibacterial cream. Squeezing some onto a gauze, he gently dabbed her palm.

"Hsss," she said, trying to contain her discomfort.

Darius paused and glanced up at her. "Sorry, love."

And then resumed his application of the ointment. He covered her hand in gauze and circled the wounded appendage with tape.

"There, should be good as new before long."

He smiled at her and then began putting the remaining items away in the first aid kit.

"How do you know how to do all that?" Julia asked.

"Well, I've been around for a minute. You pick some things up along the way."

Julia smiled. "Watching you takes me back."

Darius glanced up at her. "To something with Charlie?"

"No, to my father." A soft smile touched Julia's lips. "He was a doctor. So gentle with his patients, like you were with me. I wanted to be just like him."

"And have you? Turned out like him?"

The smile fell from Julia's face. "He saved lives, and I've taken them. You could say I fell a little short."

"Or you could say you followed in his footsteps indeed. He vanquished illness, and so did you. The people you killed were sick. Besides, think of the lives you saved by taking theirs."

"Now you sound like Amara."

"Don't say that," Darius snapped.

Just then a uniformed man approached. "Jet's all fueled up, and we're cleared for takeoff, sir."

Darius gave a nod of his head, and the man disappeared to the front of the plane.

Julia relaxed against the soft white leather of the bucket seat in which she sat as the plane began to roll down the runway toward the departure lane, eyeing Darius whose attention focused out the window of the plane.

"I'm still not sure it's a great idea to just leave Charlie like this," Julia said.

Darius met her gaze. "You aren't leaving him. You're running for your life. There's a difference."

"And he's fighting for his. He just doesn't understand that he is. I tried to tell him that healing will only make it worse, but I don't know what landed before he lost his mind again. If she figures out—"

"It's not a matter of *if* but *when*. You need rest and recovery. *That should* be your focus."

"Why are you helping me?"

Darius sighed. "I like you, Julia. You shouldn't die at a psychopath's hands." He heaved a heavy sigh. "We have a long history together, Amara and me. Let's just say she's done the unforgivable, and I have an inkling of what her plans may be, though I haven't made myself privy to the details. But I know this much—nothing good can come of it."

Julia gulped. Now that she knew from Amara's own lips what that plan was, she had to tell Darius. She opened her mouth to speak when he continued, snapping her attention back to her most urgent concern.

"And now that she's found her Phoenix, she will stop at nothing to see her plans come to fruition."

"You mean once Charlie's lifespan is complete."

"That'll be a part of it, yes."

"I'm not interested in allowing that to happen. So how do we get him? Should we sneak back on the property?"

"Oh no, no, no. We can't do that. She'd see us coming a mile away, and you'll be dead before you set foot on her premises."

I think you underestimate me." Julia centered her glare out at the sky as they took off.

"Do I now? And how is that?"

She closed her eyes, trying to decide if she had the energy for this. But he had been helpful to her, so it was only fair. "Remember how I told you I killed everyone who had a drink of the water? It was my aim to end the curse."

Darius laughed. "You mean the Fountain?"

Her attention snapped to him. "Of course that's what I mean. Why are you laughing?"

"I don't mean to offend. But it's just the preposterous nature of your claim. *You* could not end the curse of that Fountain. And, I'm sorry, love, but you far from exterminated the world of people who have had a drink."

Julia fought down her rising irritation. "Well, I almost did. And then everything went to hell."

"Go ahead and unpack that one for me, love."

"I drank almost a hundred years ago. I was sick, dying. Charlie had a vial of the water he'd taken off a war friend. That friend had heard rumor of it and went in search of the island before he enlisted. Met Rose, the guardian there. Charmed her, seduced her, and made off with the water. He met Charlie during World War I and talked incessantly about the water. Only he was killed on contact without ever having a chance to use it. So Charlie took it as a keepsake. But when I lay dying in a hospital bed, he gave it to me."

The memory put a bitter taste in her mouth.

"After I'd committed my first murder"—She closed her eyes as

171

Caroline's face snapped into her mind—"I wanted to know if I had forever changed or if I'd always be compelled to kill. So we went searching for the source. When we got to the island, we met Rose. She was the guardian there. She wanted off that island, having been tricked by her uncle to take guardianship early and with no one to replace her. So she stabbed Charlie, took him for ransom, and sent me on an errand. In order for her to save his life, I had to kill everyone who had a drink of the water and end the curse. Or so we thought."

Julia dropped her gaze to her hands.

"Woo-whee, that's a story."

"Maybe now you can understand a little better my devotion to Charlie. He never left my side, never gave up believing I could be well, both from what ailed my mortal body and what poisoned my soul."

"And you traveled the world doing what you thought needed to be done to save him. You're both each other's heroes."

Darius glanced out of the window and then at Julia. It was a moment before he spoke again. "I want to say something to you, love, but I don't want you to be angry with me."

His gaze fell on his hands and he studied his palms like something interesting was written on them.

"Only one way to find out if what you have to say will anger me." Julia braced herself, uncertain what would leave his lips next.

Darius met her gaze, and there was warmth in his, sincerity. All the swagger stripped away, he made his appeal. "As much as I hate to think what Amara may have up her sleeve, I'm not sure how to stop her from getting what she wants. I know there's no way to slow Charlie's demise now that it's begun." He paused, cleared his throat, his eye contact wavering. When he looked at her again, she swore there was a mist in his crystal blue eyes. "You have to consider that your time with Charlie is coming to an end and there may be nothing you can

172

do to stop Amara."

"But I have to try! He'd do the same for me."

"To what end, though? You'll likely end up dead in the process, and Charlie's a goner either way."

Silence settled over Julia as she absorbed his words. "You don't know what she has in mind," she said in a low whisper.

"You do?"

Julia nodded. "She told me."

For a moment, interest sparked Darius's face, but then it flickered out. He put his hand up in rejection.

"I don't want to know," he said. "That will only make things worse."

"She's never told you?"

"Not entirely. Oh, she's tried, many times, but I've always asked her to keep me on the outside of it. I haven't wanted to know. I have no interest in her grand ideas of setting straight what she broke. There is no fixing any of it, no matter what she believes."

"So you're saying you won't do anything to stop her? Anything to help?"

Darius smiled at her. "I am helping. I'm whisking you away to safety."

"You know what I mean," Julia pled. "I can't just leave Charlie behind. I can't give up that easily."

"Look, I was willing to get you and Charlie out of there, but now that Amara has turned on you and gone all murderous, there just is nothing left to do. She has him now, and we're powerless to stop any of it from unfolding."

Could she? Was there any truth to what Darius said? Was any battle she thought to fight already lost before it began? She loved Charlie to her core, but the person who held her heart was fading away anyway. And she was so, so tired. Always on the incline, never gaining any ground.

"You could stay with me for a while," Darius offered. "Either at my beach house in Florida or anywhere else of your choosing. We could take a load off, have a good time, and relax for once in a hundred years. I mean you, of course. I relax all the time." He leaned forward, resting his elbows on his knees and piercing her gaze with his crystal blues.

"No one would blame you, least of all me. You have done your part, Julia. You have been a good soldier. I had to let Amara go a long time ago. There is no saving her, and there will be no saving Charlie. Just think about it, okay? We'll be there soon."

His words inflicted a heavy sadness on Julia's heart, the weight of it all bearing down on her. Even if she could get back to Charlie, what chance was there to save him? Amara would be waiting for her, no doubt eager to use Charlie as bait. She couldn't bear the thought of her using him like that, especially if it resulted in Julia's death. Charlie would blame himself forever.

If he knew. Then didn't she deserve death? She was no better than Amara or Darius or Rose or any before her who had killed in the name of the water. She was a murderer, and the guilt she suffered didn't set her apart in any special way as she'd wanted to believe. The reasons she killed didn't make her any more noble a killer than any other child of the Fountain. So even if she died trying to save Charlie, at least maybe there could be some redemption in her sacrifice.

But if she died trying to rescue Charlie and was unable to save him in the end, what gain would that be? Amara would get the water, and she would carry out her plan with or without her.

With or without her.

It all felt so hopeless. Every option she considered, ever decision she mulled over—they all led to the same outcome. Amara was going to win. And Julia was tired. Tired of fighting for Charlie, tired of thinking she was finally able to rest, tired of killing in the name of the water, tired of being defeated at every corner.

Tired.

She closed her eyes and allowed sleep to pull her under for the duration of the flight. She couldn't make a clear decision with her mind so muddled anyway. But sleep only played the same barrage of images in her dreams.

Nineteen

Darius and Amara: Many, Many Years Ago

er skull burned, and the thoughts refused to relent. She ran out into the garden in the dead of night, unable to sleep.

"Guardian!" she cried as she searched. "Where are you?"

"I am here." He emerged from some trees.

"Why are you not guarding the Fountain?"

"It does not need my protection right now. It is available for all to drink, but only for a short time."

"And then what?"

"And then I shall pay my consequence."

"Yours? Why?"

"I failed too."

"I made the choice, Guardian. You did not force me to drink."

"I could not keep you from it, but my job was to ensure no one ever drank. And now many have."

Amara dropped her head, her pain subsided for the moment. This was one more guilt to stack atop the rest. "I am having thoughts,

Guardian. Unpleasant ones."

"And that is your consequence. That and having to live forever."

"Immortality is a gift."

"Until it becomes a curse, and for you, it shall be a curse."

Amara stiffened, not understanding what he meant. "I do not know what to do about these thoughts."

The Guardian gazed up to the sky; the calm midnight speckled with brilliant stars. "There is nothing to do but to listen to them."

Amara grasped his arms. "But Guardian... they are dark, my thoughts. I do not wish to have them or to listen to them."

This time he did look at Amara, his gaze first traveling to her hand on his arm and then returning to her eyes. "Then, my dear, you should have never taken a drink."

Just then, the pain returned, burning her skull from the inside, circulating in her head and down the rest of her body. Amara jumped, the sudden onslaught so intense, so unbearable. She jerked her hand back and clutched her head, falling to the ground.

"It won't relent until you obey."

The Guardian disappeared into the trees, leaving her alone to swallow the pain.

"I...can't..." Amara said to herself. She struggled to her feet, but the pain held her down, the directive playing on torturous repeat in her mind. "No. I will not. I will not end life."

Despite her warnings to Darius to run away from her, she knew he and Elora had been safe. She'd convinced them to drink, and they were returned to their immortal state. But some among them hadn't. Some had chosen to remain mortal rather than face the unnamed consequences of regaining their immortality. And it was for those lives Amara feared.

She fought the searing of her insides and struggled to her feet. She ran away from the Guardian, from the garden and to the sea, falling into the water on the shoreline. Tired, she splashed the cool water on her face, and it offered a split second of relief.

Off to the side, she heard a branch crack, and her head snapped the direction of the sound. A deer stood there munching on some grass, and she heard the directive ring inside her ears again.

"No." Hot tears stung her eyes as she watched the innocent animal eat. "I cannot. He does not deserve it." Still, her body moved without her permission, the command within pulling her to her feet. She fought the compulsion with every step, but her legs moved against her will.

The deer looked up at her, sniffed the air, and took a step toward her. She was friends with the animals, and the thought of carrying out the demands playing in her head on this creature was just as painful as the consideration that she should act on a fellow villager. Still, she could not control her own body as it moved, one step at a time, toward her unsuspecting victim. Her vision was snagged by a sharp rock on the ground. It came to a point on one end, and the voice in her mind told her it'd be the perfect tool.

"No." She resisted, holding her own arm against her side. But she stooped anyway and reached for the rock, clutching it in her hand. As she was down, the deer approached her, nuzzling her face with his.

"Please go," she told it. "Please." The words leaving her lips were weak, her pleas escaping between sobs. "I don't want to. Please, go!"

She pushed at his muzzle, but he only reared and bobbed her head with his nose. He knew she was distraught. He knew, and he tried to comfort her. Even as she fought the compulsion to snuff out his life.

"I cannot!" She screamed into the air as she lifted her hand, rock in her grip. "Please," she cried again, straining her muscles as she tried to hold back, as she failed.

Her hand came down with a forceful strike against the deer's skull. He fell to the ground, disoriented. Her arm raised again.

"Enough, please," she sobbed.

But she struck a second time, and this blow rendered the deer unconscious. But whatever it was inside of her calling the shots was not satisfied. A third blow finished the job, and Amara fell to the ground, her body convulsing with sobs, her white garment soaked in the deer's blood.

She draped her body over the animal's, hugging with all her strength, even as every last ounce of it leeched from her body. Elora sprang into her mind—what would she tell her? Her daughter loved animals, had just been assigned the work of caring for them. And now she had destroyed one. At once, she felt regret and relief. The pain had lifted, the voice had quieted, but her heart had shattered inside her chest.

* * *

Amara stumbled through the doorway of her dwelling, her garment stained crimson, her cheeks smeared with dirt and tears. Her legs wobbled beneath her and struggled to bear her weight. Pulling back the curtain separating her and Darius' bed, she fell on his sleeping body.

"Wake up," she pled, the cry leaving her lips with a whimper.

Darius stirred, and his eyes opened and then bulged as he took in the sight of her.

"Amara, what—?" He didn't finish his question, just stared at the dirt, the blood, the mess.

"I killed him," she sobbed.

Darius patted her, caution in his touch. "What...who?"

She sniffed, burying her face in his chest. "The deer."

Darius shot upright and pulled her body away from his so he could look her in the eye. "You killed a deer? A precious creature? Why? Why would you do that?"

"I couldn't...I didn't mean to. It made me. I had no control."

"Love, you aren't making any sense." Darius drew back the hair from her face, tucking the strands behind her ears. Worry creased his brow, and Amara feared she was scaring him. "I didn't know what else to do, so I came home."

"This is always your home. You are safe here. Come. Let's clean you up."

Darius led Amara to their wash basin, stripped her blood-drenched garment from her body, and moistened a cloth. He washed the blood away from her skin until she was clean and then wrapped a new article around her naked body. "There. Better?"

She nodded, unable to speak. Tears filled her eyes, and she buried her head in Darius' chest. "What will I tell Elora?"

Darius walked her to their bed, and the pair sat down. "You will not speak of this to our daughter. Now, tell me. What happened? Who made you do such a vile deed?"

The weight of his words struck Amara washing a new wave of guilt over her. *Vile deed* played in her mind over and over. When a moment had passed since his question, Darius squeezed her hand.

"Hmm? I think...I think the water did."

Darius scrunched his face. "That makes no sense, love."

"I...I know. But a strange compulsion overtook me, and then something took control. My body acted, but my mind resisted even while it taunted me."

Drawing back from Amara, Darius propped himself against the wall and folded his arms across his middle. Then he raked his fingers through his hair. Worry creased his brow, and confusion lived in his eyes. This was what she feared. That she would terrify him, and he would reject her. Or at least, be unable to accept what she'd done.

"He said there would be consequences," Darius reminded after a long pause. "What if this is what he meant? An end to the harmony

180

between living things…"

"A disruption. That's what he called it."

"My love…" He cupped her face between his palms. "We mustn't tell Elora. Okay? She won't be able to accept it."

"I sent the body out to sea so no one would find it."

Darius gave a curt nod. "Hopefully, that's it, then."

* * *

Once morning arrived, the village set about cleaning and repairing what the storm broke. A clear divide occurred between those who had drank and those who had not. Amara watched everyone with a wary eye—her family. She worried that, at any moment, the same compulsion she was overcome by would call to those around her who had decided to reclaim their immortality with a drink.

Her gaze scanned to Darius and then to Elora, and the question struck her. Amara's heart broke over the possibility of Elora suffering through what she had during the night. She didn't know if her precious daughter would survive striking out against another living creature. At this point, she wasn't sure if *she* would survive what she'd done.

As she considered all this, a reminiscent discomfort started at the base of her neck and crawled up toward her head. *No*, she thought. Already aware of what would follow, Amara braced herself against a tree.

This wasn't happening.

This wasn't happening.

This wasn't happening.

With eyes closed, Amara rubbed her temples.

Someone grabbed her. "Are you okay, love?" Darius' voice grounded her, bringing her back.

She opened her eyes to see his worried expression and tried for a feeble smile. "I'm fine. Thank you."

But he wasn't convinced. "I'm getting Elora, and we're going home. You need to rest. We'll take care of you." He turned to search for their daughter.

While he was distracted, a flash of pain struck Amara, and the call sounded in her head behind it.

Kill.

"No!" She shouted her response, and this earned her some strange looks.

With her palm lifted to the air, she smiled, attempting to assure those around her that she was okay. But she knew she was not. She had to get out of there—no time to wait for Darius. Amara cut through the village, weaving in and out of people as her head burned with pain.

How long would it be before others experienced this? She'd been the first to drink, but those who took a sip were not far behind her.

Kill.

The call came again as she reached her dwelling. She flew through the door and pinned herself to the inside wall.

"I already did!" she screamed, sinking to the floor.

Sobs shuddered through her, and she buried her face in her arms. Intense pain flooded her head, rushed down her spine, and ignited her extremities. With quivering hands, she rubbed her eyes, tried to stay seated. But the command overcame her, raising her to her feet.

"Why is this happening?" she asked the air. "Why?"

Darius dodged through the door with Elora on his heels. "There you are. We could not find you." His face changed, concern crinkling between his eyes. "Are you okay, love? You're pale as the moon." He reached for her, but Amara snatched her arm away.

"Leave me." Her voice shook as did her body. When Darius took a few ginger steps away from her, she kept her eyes on him. "Please. Go."

"Amara, I will not leave you." Darius advanced, but when he did, Amara fell to the ground with a sudden flop and grasped the sides of her head.

She screamed a shrill, agonizing wail.

Darius shielded their daughter by directing her behind his body. "Love—"

"Go. Please."

Her request came out as a weak plea. Amara's face burned hot, and her whole body drenched with sweat. At the same time, she looked around their dwelling, the demon within her asking her to find something to use.

A weapon.

Darius stooped and combed her sweat-soaked hair out of her face. "Love, it is going to be okay. Come. Let's get you to bed." He stood and pulled on her arms in an attempt to bring her to her feet. She held her body limp, but he got her on her feet nonetheless.

Supported on his arm, she whimpered. "The pain is so…"

"I don't understand. You remain immortal. How are you ill?"

"It's another kind of disease." She clutched her forehead as another wave washed over her and lunged toward the wall, out of Darius' arms. From the wall, she plucked the spear, the one they used to pierce fruits in the garden. With the spear held fast in her hands, she faced Darius.

On instinct, his lifted his hands in the air. "What are you doing, Amara?"

"I'm sorry. I cannot help this," she cried, conflict resting in her eyes. "No. I do not want to. Please go, Darius. Please run." Even though she knew he was immortal and so was Elora. They were not at risk for being killed by her. Still, she could not help the compulsion overtaking her, and she did not want them to see her like this.

"I am not leaving you. Just tell me what is happening. Give me the spear, Amara."

183

But instead of listening, she pointed the weapon at him.

* * *

Darius had lost track of Elora, so focused was he on the spear. He allowed his vision to waver an instant from his wife, from the weapon in her hands.

And that was the moment she struck. Lunging for Darius, a growl emerged from Amara's lips.

"Mother, no!" Elora jumped in the way with lifted hands. But instead of halting her mother's attack, she absorbed the tip of the spear. It ran through her chest, and the girl gasped.

"Elora!" Darius caught his daughter as she fell to the floor. A red circle grew from her wound in her chest, and blood wetted her lips. Elora tried to speak, but she could not, the searing penetration of the blade and shock stealing her words. She clasped her father's arm as he held her.

"Be brave, daughter. I will pull it out, and you will heal." With one hard yank, Darius withdrew the spear from his daughter's body, and she let out a wail as he did. "I'm sorry, my dove, but is that better?" He ripped her garment where the wound was, expecting to see it closed. But beneath the material, her flesh was ripped wide open, pooling blood. "How—"

Tears filled Elora's eyes as she sputtered, as she fought for air, her body limp in his arms.

"Elora, no, no, no. Why have you not healed?" Darius quaked with tears.

A final breath left his daughter's lungs, and her eyes glassed over. The hand holding his arm lost its grip and fell to the ground.

Darius scanned her body, not understanding. Not grasping. He shook her body, begging her to wake up, to come back. "My darling daughter, my dove, please return to me. How? You are immortal, how?"

He fell on her form, his body heaving heavy sobs over his deceased daughter.

And then he peered into the face of Amara, the face of the woman he loved, who was one of two reasons he was the happiest man alive. But she'd just taken one of those reasons away.

"What did you do?"

Her body shook in the corner, where she sat huddled. She'd pulled her knees into her chest and buried her face in her arms. She did not speak, only quaked there as Darius' eyes narrowed on her. As he stared in disbelief. She couldn't meet his eyes. The shame forced her to keep her head concealed.

"What did you do?!" he screamed at her.

She jumped but otherwise did not move.

With gentle effort, Darius picked his daughter up. Then he walked to Amara and, with one hand, hoisted her to her feet and dragged her out the garden where everyone worked. In the center, by the Fountain, he threw her down.

"Guardian!" he screamed.

The Great Guardian appeared. His gaze traveled among them, first to Elora's bloody corpse then to Amara, huddled in shame. Last, he turned to Darius.

"I see the full consequence has been dealt."

"*This*? She is immortal!"

"Indeed, she was. But Amara unleashed the waters by dipping her hand in. She threw off the balance and, because of that, owed a debt." He paused and waved his hand toward Elora. "She has now paid it. You are only immortal now so long as another immortal does not strike you down."

Amara shuddered at his words.

185

"So, that's it?"

"Not quite." The Guardian folded his hands in front of his tunic, eyes sad and cast to the ground. "Each of you will be awakened with the same compulsion, and many will die, leaving only the immortals who have had a drink and then killed another immortal. And I...I have my own price to pay."

With those words, the world began the sway. The Fountain shook where it stood until it lifted off the ground and floated in the sky, sweeping up the Guardian with it.

"The Fountain shall now be hidden, and I along with it. It will go to a far corner of the earth and will be safe from the rest of humanity." Man and Fountain swirled in the sky until, with a blast, they vanished altogether.

Amara did not budge from where Darius had cast her to the ground. She could feel nothing but the many shards in her chest that were the shattered remains of her heart. Sneaking a gaze to Darius' face, she found his fixed on her. Disdain housed within his expression.

"You took her. You tried to take me. Why?"

She opened her mouth to speak, but no words escaped her lips. She wanted to explain, to tell him she was at the mercy of whatever raged inside of her. But then she knew he'd understand soon enough. And she wanted to scream and wail, except she could not understand that her daughter was gone. Even though she desired to go to her, to touch her, she feared such an act.

Elora would wake up any minute.

Amara knew it. All she had to do was wait.

She was immortal after all.

They all were.

They all *were*.

As Darius glared down at her, grief and hatred swirling in his gaze, she swore she would make this right. No matter the cost, Amara would repair what she had broken.

Twenty

Darius and Julia

⚜

*T*he jolt of the jet's wheels touching down startled Julia awake. She opened her eyes, immediately registering how groggy her short nap had left her. With a big yawn that forced her body to stretch, she caught Darius's eye. His gaze roved over her body, leaving her feeling both flattered and violated. They disembarked the plane in silence, and Julia took one more glance at the small but beautiful aircraft as Darius held a car door open for her. She climbed inside, eyes still glued to the plane.

"This must have cost you a fortune."

"When you've had as long as I have to build up your wealth, this baby is a drop in the bucket." Darius blew the plane a kiss. "She's so beautiful."

He closed the car door behind Julia and rounded to the driver's side. She inspected the interior of the car, not having noticed what she'd even climbed into. Red leather upholstery hugged her body and she realized she was sitting in a Porsche. Darius climbed in on his side and pressed the ignition button.

Julia shook her head at him. "You sure do love your toys. I've never understood people's love for inanimate objects."

"That's because you've never owned a private jet."

With another wink, he shifted the car into drive and tore out of the small, private airport. Julia scanned her surroundings out of the car window and caught a glimpse of a row of palm trees lining the street.

"Florida," she said. She tried to recall the last time she'd been to this state. It had been many years. "You make your home in the U.S.?"

She turned to Darius, who leaned against the driver's seat relaxed.

"I have many homes, but one of them in the U.S. in Florida. I like beaches. And warmth."

"And being far from Amara?"

"And that."

Darius drove in silence until they were on a road that ran adjacent to the ocean. Blue and green stretched out of the car window as far as Julia could see. She rolled her window down, allowing in the scent of the ocean. Inhaling deeply, she closed her eyes, enjoying one solitary moment of serenity.

Before long, they arrived to a property right on the sand. Stepping out of the vehicle, Julia took in the scene greeting her. They had pulled onto a large cement slab underneath a beach house. Milk white stilts held the house up, and when Julia's gaze traveled the height of the dwelling, she saw that it extended several stories into the air. Out before them, the ocean roared as waves lapped the sand.

Darius walked up a flight of stairs, and Julia trailed behind. When they entered the house, she found herself standing in the main living area. A gourmet kitchen painted in blues and greens opened to a sitting room. The side of the house facing the ocean was all sliding doors, and they stood open, allowing the ocean air to permeate the interior, filling the room with scents of salt and surf. She crossed the space and went outside to the balcony overlooking the beach. The balcony was covered, and several ceiling fans whirred slowly overhead. Cushioned chairs lined the length of the deck.

Julia approached the railing and took in the ocean view. It was a calm morning, and the waves came and went with a whisper. The warm breeze carried with it the scent of salt, and Julia closed her eyes, absorbing everything.

"Peaceful, isn't it?"

When she opened her eyes, she found Darius standing next to her. She hadn't even heard him come outside.

"It was." She'd tried not to sound rude, but in truth, he'd interrupted her one moment of tranquility in days.

"Sorry, my lady. Would you like a moment alone?"

When she gazed at Darius's face, she didn't find jest in his eyes, only sincerity, which nagged at her conscience and made her feel bad.

"I'm sorry. I'm just so exhausted."

"Well…" He ran his fingertips down the length of her arm, leaving a path of confusing chills behind. "You can have your pick of the rooms. The only one that's not open is on the very top level, and that's mine. Of course, you are welcome to stay there. Just know you wouldn't be alone." He winked at her and bobbed his eyebrows.

"Thank you, but I'd rather be alone." She angled her body back toward the serene scene in front of her.

"It's tempting, isn't it?" Darius's voice cut through her thoughts.

"What's that?"

"To want to hole up here and forget everything beckoning you in the big, wide world."

She turned her body toward him. "Is that what you've done? Holed up in places? Tried to forget what Amara is? What she's doing?"

He interlocked his fingers over the railing. "Somewhat. I've wanted to forget her, forget our past together."

"So enjoying the company of a different woman every night helps with that."

He gave her a light smack on the arm. "Hey now, not *every* night!" His laughter died and he sobered. "I do want to forget her, and yes, keeping company helps. As does the travel and substances and keeping busy. But this place—when I'm here—it transcends me, if even for a moment. I can get pulled into the allure of the ocean and the warmth of the air and disconnect from all my other realities."

"You still love her, don't you?" The question was pointed, but Julia wanted to know.

"Amara?" Darius recoiled, drawing his posture away from Julia, and then he shrugged and draped himself over the railing. "I did love her once. Deeply. But that woman is gone. She wears her face, but she's gone."

Julia didn't miss the sadness in his tone, the grief hidden among years of running around and trying to forget a woman who lived but died long ago. Soulless, but remaining in physical form. In some ways, she felt the same way in recent weeks. Even when she looked into the face of Charlie, he wasn't really there. Still, she didn't miss the fondness hiding beneath Darius's sad tone.

"I was thinking about what you said on the plane," she began. "And yes, it is tempting. I want to run away. I want to be done with it all. I don't mean to sound like a baby, but it's hard, and I'm just so tired."

Darius angled himself toward Julia and inched closer to her. He covered her hand with his on the railing, and she didn't pull away. "I get that. I do. And I wasn't kidding when I said you're welcome to stay. I promise, no funny business on my part."

Julia laughed. Noticing the blue of the water—a blue that almost paled in comparison to the color of Darius's eyes—she wondered if she could just put it all out of her mind. She'd been consumed by everything for so long—she couldn't remember a reality where Charlie, the water, and death did not rule her thoughts, day and night. She breathed, ate, slept, *was* those things. She had to admit she was ready for a break from it all.

And now, in this moment, mesmerized by the gentle lap of the ocean's waves, the humid kiss of moisture in the air, and the smell of salt from the water, Julia wanted nothing more than to stay right there. Darius's offer was tempting, and he understood in a way no one had for a very long time. Not even Charlie.

That last thought was accompanied by a current of guilt. But she had to admit the truth therein. Charlie didn't know what it was to kill others, other than what he experienced in the war. But to Julia that felt entirely different. Charlie had never experienced the water's call to kill, and though he forgave her for her actions, though he stuck by her and never left her, he could never fully comprehend just how powerful the water's demands were, how much Julia fought against them, and how it felt to be overcome—betrayed—by your own mind and body. Charlie had little time to get used to his own immortality, had only known life in their Iowa town a hundred years ago and life in solitude on the island, while Julia had been all over the globe. Julia hadn't realized how alone she'd felt until now, until the soft sighs of the ocean whispered the truth to her.

She'd tried to convince herself that she'd grown accustomed to being alone, but the real truth was that she was tired of the solitude. As much as she adored Charlie and was grateful for their time together on the island, that kind of isolation forced her to face everything she'd done. Those months were very different than the ninety-five years before where there was always a focus, something for her to lose herself in so that she didn't have to deal with what she was becoming—had become. And all of Amara's and Darius's justifications for her actions were things she'd told herself over that time, to get through. Only now, she wasn't so convinced that there was any justification for the lives she took.

She glanced out of the corner of her eye at Darius, draped in silence as he took in the scenery before them. He hadn't lifted his hand from hers, and her gaze traveled to their two hands, his covering hers. He got her in ways no one Julia had ever met could. Though she wasn't sure what his experience was, Julia knew Darius understood the loss caused by the water. He knew the pain of watching the person you loved more than life itself lose herself, to feel helpless and frightened and confused. Sudden understanding struck Julia for Darius's actions over the years. Their experiences were so similar, yet the way they chose to deal with them so different. Julia had embraced what she was becoming and tried to put an end to the Fountain's curse. Darius had run to anything and everything in order to forget.

"I get it now," she said, turning toward him. This forced their hands apart.

Darius gave her his attention, folding his hands together. "What's that now, love?"

"I get why you ran. Why you have drowned yourself in women and God knows what else. It's easier to forget than it is to acknowledge what's happening to you, what needs to be done. I don't mean that in a judgmental way. I see the appeal. I feel the pull to that now."

"Hmm..." Darius grunted. "I haven't met anyone like you, Julia..." He raised his eyebrows for her to complete her name.

"Franklin. Julia Franklin."

"Julia Franklin," he repeated, and somehow her name sounded sweeter when spoken with his buttery voice. "And I've met a lot of people."

Julia smiled and looked back toward the beach. "Have you managed to accept all parts of yourself? Like we were talking about before? Reconciled to yourself whom you were before and what the water made you?"

"I think so, yes. Despite the fact that I, as you astutely put it, 'ran' from it all, I do accept what happened. And that acceptance is what convinces me I have to stay away from Amara. I can't pretend like none of that happened. I know I'm not the man I was before we drank, and I will never be him again. I'm okay with that. But I don't need reminders of what he suffered. Those are what I aim to drown out. It's not a lack of acceptance that drives me. It's accepting that what's happened is behind me. I can't change it so I aim to enjoy my eternal years."

"But is that enough? I feel overwhelmed by the grief of what I've done, and I can't stop blaming myself for what's happening to Charlie, for my friend Rose's death…"

"I don't think grief is possible without a side portion of guilt and regret." Darius rested his elbows on the railing and nudged Julia. "None of any of this is your fault. Like all of us, you've done the best you can with the cards you've been dealt. If you choose to allow Charlie and Amara to go on, their stories unfolding as they will—without your intercession—I think you've earned it. There's no weakness in admitting defeat. This thing is just bigger than all of us."

Julia wasn't sure she agreed with that assessment, but she was exhausted from trying to sort it all out. She stretched as a huge yawn hit her.

"You must be tuckered beyond compare. Come. I'll show you to a room."

Julia followed him into the beach house and up the stairs. On the next floor up, she had her choice of rooms and decided on the first one they came to. A mermaid theme overtook the decor, displayed all over the room. Darius drew dark blinds, making the room almost pitch black, and left her alone. She washed her face and brushed her teeth in the adjoining bathroom with the toiletries Darius provided and then sprawled out on the king-sized bed. Sleep came in an instant to the soundtrack of the waves outside.

Her slumber was quiet at first, but then the dreams began. They were not the usual bombardment of faces most nights brought but dreams of her romance with Charlie, almost as if she watched her memories play out in a movie. Happiness morphed to anger as Amara's face infiltrated her sleep, and then her dreams grew dark.

Amara stood on the island at the Fountain. She took a drink, and when she turned to look at Julia, blood trailed down her chin. Suddenly, the Fountain burst from the ground with Amara. Both woman and land rotated in the air until they disappeared with a burst of radiant light.

In her dream, Julia was transported, and now they stood among crowds of people. Amara stood by the Fountain and handed out drinks of the water to everyone who came with a smile that could not be trusted. Julia lunged for her, running her through with a sword, but she didn't bleed. She only cackled mockingly and offered the next person a drink of the cursed water.

"Nooo!" Julia shot upright in bed, sweat soaked through her pajamas.

She panted, trying to catch her bearings. The soothing sound of waves outside grounded her, reminded her of where she was. As she focused on the ebbing and flowing of the ocean outside, her breathing calmed, and she climbed out of bed. Approaching the bedroom door, she pushed it open and stepped into the dark night. She had no idea how long she'd been sleeping, but the moon hung high in the sky above and over the water. The dark sky was clear and lit with millions of fiery pinpricks. Even in the middle of the night, the air was warm and humid, but the breeze soothed her skin.

"Just forget it all," she told herself.

She closed her eyes and sniffed in the aroma, working to drown the still vivid images of her dream. Amara was not her problem, not her mission. She wouldn't be able to stop her if she tried, so why exert the effort?

Charlie.

As if in answer to the question posed by her own thoughts, his name sprang into her mind, and she engaged in a mental debate. The voice of reason, as it had so often since her death, sounded like Rose's.

Don't you want to save him?

Of course I do!

Then what are you doing here shacked up with Darius?

I had to run. Amara tried to kill me.

That's not us. That's not what we do. We run toward fights, not away.

I'm tired of the fight.

The voice in her head morphed into her own. *Shut up! You are weak. You are a baby, a coward.*

It's not weak to admit defeat.

Darius's words popped into her head, and they sounded more appealing than the first time she heard them.

Charlie would never leave you behind.

I'm not leaving him behind. He can't be saved.

But you don't KNOW that...

"Ugh!"

Julia growled, pushing herself away from the balcony railing. She strolled to the end of the covered deck that spanned the entire level and down the stairs onto the beach. Barefoot, she ambled through the sand, allowing the cool grains to infiltrate her toes, sticking to her feet with a delightful grit. She lingered near the ocean shore, where the volume of the waves was loudest. Standing still for a moment, she looked out over the black water and wondered about a new life for herself. Would her mind ever allow her to be free to leave it if she never went back? If she just moved on from here, maybe with Darius, maybe alone, without even a glance over her shoulder?

She longed to let go of it all. To throw it out into the waves and allow the infinite waters of the ocean to carry it all away so that she could forget. So that she could be free.

It was all too much for her. Before she registered the burgeoning emotions, her cheeks stained with tears, and she fell into the sand and sobbed. Wails came from deep inside her belly and racked her entire body with convulsive heaves. Her hands in the sand, the grains under her nails in between her fingers, the waves crashing just feet from her, she wished the ocean would carry *her* away. She cried and cried, her face burning under the force of her tears, the explosion of pent up emotion long overdue.

Warm arms wrapped around her from behind, and she jumped. Looking up, she found the face of Darius gazing at her with a pained expression. He pulled her into his embrace as they both knelt in the sand. His arms circled her shoulders, and he rocked her back and forth as he held her. Julia reached out and grasped his arms, holding them tightly against her, happy for the comfort, happy to allow herself to be weak for this moment and to be supported, even if it was by an almost stranger.

Darius held her, not uttering a word, and she wailed into the night until her tears ran out and her body shuddered with dry sobs. Despite her many hours of sleep, the cry had left her exhausted, devoid of energy.

"I don't think I can do this," she whispered at last.

"Do what, love?" He nuzzled her hair with his lips.

"Any of this."

"No one is asking you to do anything."

"Someone is. Some voice deep inside of me. But I don't have what it takes."

Darius lifted her chin with his finger until their gazes locked. "Whatever it is you feel like you have to do? I have no doubt that if anyone has what it takes, that person is you."

She stared into his eyes for a moment, mesmerized by their beauty.

She could give in and just forget. She could give herself to him and be done with the rest. But that annoying voice inside would not be quieted.

"I know you don't want to know what Amara has in mind, but I have to tell you. It's too much to carry alone."

Darius's gaze darted away, and when he looked back at Julia, a darkness had taken up residence. "I—I don't know. Ignorance is bliss?"

Julia gulped. "Except when your ignorance is chosen. Then that makes you culpable."

Darius let out a low whistle. "You know how to bring the heat, don't you?" He moved a strand of hair out of her face. "Are you okay now?"

She wasn't sure what her answer was, but she nodded anyway. "I will be. But first I need to tell you. I need you to know, and then we need to stop her."

Darius sighed. "Okay, love, tell me what you know."

Twenty-One

Darius and Julia

*T*he dark night sky brightened to pale pinks and oranges as the sun crawled upon the horizon. Darius stared at it, still awestruck by what Julia had just revealed to him.

"So she thinks she's going to get everyone to drink, let them duke it out in some survival of the fittest fashion, and then the earth will be full of immortals again?"

"That about sums it up." Julia dug a seashell from the sand and cast it into the water.

"That woman is a sociopath."

"Like you didn't know that about her."

"I mean, I knew, but I guess...this is just more malicious that I'd even credit to her. I underestimated her insanity, her drive to undo what she did. She's really so delusional to believe that this will make it like it was?" He shook his head, and his eyes narrowed. Swearing, he punched the sand.

"What happened anyway? Why are you so angry with her?"

Darius glanced at Julia and then out at the ocean. "Take a walk with me?"

He stood and extended his hand to Julia, helping her to her feet. They strolled along the sand in silence. Julia's eyes were puffy after her earlier sob fest, and the night's events had exhausted her. She waited for him to continue, too spent to prod the topic along.

Darius took his time, but when he finally spoke, he said, "Obviously, you know that when you drink of the water it demands life from you. No one knew this when we first drank. I mentioned before that there was someone who watched over the water, the Great Guardian. His only job was to protect the Fountain, to make sure no one took a drink."

"Do you know where the Fountain came from?"

"No one does. It just always...*was* to our knowledge. Amara couldn't bear the curiosity, and against all wisdom, she drank. When she first felt the urge to kill, she took the life of a deer. Back then that was a big deal. All life was sacred, valued, respected. Of course, the water wasn't satisfied for long." He broke off, a shaky sigh shuddering through him. Julia reached over and squeezed his arm, and he gave her an appreciative smile.

"When it took over again, I was there in front of her trying to calm her, trying to talk her down. But you can't reason with the water's demands. They're too loud, too overwhelming. Amara lunged for me, and I should have died that day."

He gulped and heaved a heavy sigh before continuing. "Instead, our daughter, our Elora, thirteen years of age, jumped in front of me just as the spear was meant to meet my flesh."

He stopped walking and closed his eyes, lifting his face toward the sun. With his right hand, he rubbed the dove on his arm. And when he opened his eyes, tears had welled.

Looking down at his arm, he said, "My Elora, my dove, died that day. Before this, we had no concept of death or loss, and it was too much to bear. I stayed with Amara for a while. I tried to grieve with her, but I couldn't forgive her. And she just grew more and more obsessed with the idea of making it right.

"And now, this plan of hers… It doesn't rectify anything. It just ensures more death. At the end of the day, nothing she does can bring Elora back. Which means she can *never* right her wrong."

He picked up his pace again and wiped his eyes on his rolled sleeves. Julia stopped short and grabbed his arm, halting his tracks. Sadness overwhelmed her, and she felt the tears sting her eyes. Colliding her body against Darius's, she pulled him into an embrace and held him. She squeezed as tight as she could.

"I'm so sorry. That's awful. I'm so sorry."

She thought about her remorse over killing Caroline, a girl she barely knew. And though she often felt like she knew her other victims—those who drank from the Fountain—not one victim she claimed came close to killing a family member. She wondered how Amara lived with herself, how she wasn't consumed by her loss. But then it occurred to her that she was, and Darius's story made sense of Amara's plan, insane as it may be.

As if he read her mind, Darius, still in her embrace, said "Amara quieted her grief with the delusion that she's going to undo it. If it were me, I'd beg for death rather than live with myself after I'd killed our beautiful child."

Julia released him, and they held gazes with a mixture of sadness and understanding in each pair of eyes. Acceptance lived here between them, resonance of each pair of experiences. Darius grasped both sides of Julia's face and brushed her cheeks with his thumbs. He gave her a sweet smile. She could tell what was on his mind, what he wanted to do and, in this moment, she had no ambition to stop him.

Darius leaned in, laying a soft peck on her lips. The kiss felt warm on her mouth and his lips lingered on hers before parting. He drew away, still holding her face between his palms and looked her in the eyes. "Thank you," he said.

"For what?"

"For asking. For listening. For the epic hug."

Julia brushed her lips with her fingertips. "Why'd you kiss me?"

"I wanted to. Have wanted to. And it seemed like the moment. I'd take it further, but it's apparent there are no vacancies in your heart."

Heat filled Julia's cheeks, but she ignored the sensation and began walking again. The kiss was nice, a welcomed retreat from the confusion and torment of her mind, a sweet comfort and expression of understanding and belonging, but Darius read her correctly. Only one man held her heart. She cleared her throat and decided to change the subject. "So you've been running from your grief all these years."

"Not entirely. I dealt with my grief. Got this tattoo." He flashed his arm along with a grin. "Amara and I were on-again/off-again for a very long time. But after a while, I just couldn't be around her anymore. It wasn't the same, wasn't complete. I tried telling her that, short of raising Elora from the dead, there was nothing she could do to change how I felt. But Amara is accustomed to getting what she wants."

"What ever happened to the Great Guardian—the one whose sole job it was to ensure no one ever drank from the Fountain?"

"Ah, yes. He was murdered."

"By whom?"

"That long line of descendants your friend Rose was the last of? That lovely family tradition started with good 'ol Benedict Smith."

"Who was that?"

"One of Amara's minions from long ago. She grew restless with chasing the water, and when she was close, when she'd narrowed the location of it down, she came up with a new plan. She told Benedict Smith—one of her recruits—that the water was the Fountain of Youth mankind had sought. That he should find it and drink it, knowing full well what it would make him do, and since the Great Guardian still protected the Fountain, she also knew who his victim would become. Only, she didn't count on Benedict taking matters into his own hands once he committed his murder. When he killed the Great Guardian, the guardianship passed to him and he was then bound to the water, to the island. When the Great Guardian perished, the island rose from where it was and moved one last time, finding its final resting place, and you know where that was."

He smirked. "Any information Amara had on the water's whereabouts was lost, and her search had to start over. Benedict was angry at Amara for using him, for knowingly turning him into a murderer, and he determined never to let her get her hands on the spring again now that he knew what it made people into. He established the order of guardianship and tasked his bloodline with minimizing casualties."

Julia stared out over the ocean, thinking of the life power found within the spring. Of the destruction. "So the water has been cut off from Amara since the beginning. The guardians were only protecting it from other people."

"Precisely."

"You've kept tabs, huh?"

Darius smiled. "I had to. I had to know where it was, and more importantly, that it was safely hidden from Amara."

Julia felt a bitter sting and huffed. "I can't believe I was so stupid as to think that I could end the curse by taking out everyone who ever drank. And now, come to find out, there are more of you. Who knows how many?" She kicked the sand. "And now I have to live with the fact that, not only am I a serial killer, but that those deaths did nothing toward the end of ensuring no one would be poisoned by those waters again. Once Amara has her way..."

"What's more is that she'll have influence over those who drank, much like she has over you, over me, over Charlie..."

"You mean her touch? The way she's able to exude warmth and comfort? What is that about?"

"The magic touch." He smiled. "That's what she calls it. Much like everything else that distinguishes Amara from other immortals as the first to drink, she is gifted with the ability to influence other immortals. That's how she got so many, who were angry at her for taking the drink, to follow suit."

"So, like, she can bend our wills?"

Darius laughed. "Not exactly, love."

"Then what is it?"

"My theory? Has to do with the Phoenix. Though the warmth of her touch extends to all immortals and you might find yourself comforted by it or even swayed a little bit,"—He spat into the ocean at this— "you noticed before that she alone could help Charlie when he was losing his mind. That as long as she could put her hands on him, he would calm and eventually be able to return to himself."

"Yes indeed, I am aware of that. You might recall it bothered me quite a bit."

Darius elbowed her as they continued their stroll. "Oh, I remember. I suspect that's intentional, in the...design of all of this. That it's her one defense against the threat the Phoenix poses to her. If he's losing himself and he's confused, then she can ground him, manipulate him even."

Worry creased between Julia's brows. "I don't like the sound of that. But what do you mean threat? I thought the Phoenix helped her by revealing the Fountain to her at last."

"He does. According to the Great Guardian, the Phoenix also has the capability of ending the water, of ending her. And the two are not mutually exclusive. She can't die, as you've learned, and that's because the water still flows."

"So if you can figure out a way to destroy the water, Amara will be vulnerable?"

"Bingo. Only trouble is that I have no idea how to make that happen. But it all goes back to the Phoenix. It has to do with his ability to absorb things from people, but I just don't know how it all connects. To be honest, it's been such a long time that I figured those things the Guardian told me were either inaccurate or that no one was noble enough to become the Phoenix he spoke of."

Julia smiled at this. "Noble. That's a good word for Charlie. But why didn't you mention this before?"

"Two reasons. One, I didn't think it would matter. Charlie is deteriorating so quickly anyway. There really isn't any way to stop that from happening, and I figured he'd complete his life cycle before there was any opportunity to figure out how he might be able to make Amara vulnerable. And two, I had no interest in any of it anyway. As I've been clear about, I never wanted to know Amara's plan."

"Sorry," she responded.

"I'm glad you told me. And I don't want it to happen. I think genocide is evil, of course, but selfishly, I can't exist the way we were before without Elora. It hurts too much, and I need to continue to move on from that. If Amara gets her way, she forces me into the very thing I've most dreaded. The only thing I can't figure out is why it's happening so quickly or came on so suddenly."

"I thought you said it had to do with how many sick people Amara made him heal."

"That's definitely part of it, but to my knowledge, this process of losing his mind never started while he was still there with Amara. Am I right about that?"

"Yes. We lived for three months together on the island before it began. And then one morning, he just woke up with someone else's memory."

Julia stopped in her tracks and grabbed Darius's arm. Her gaze drifted as she thought about the events leading up to his first memory.

"The night before he woke with the first memory, he healed me."

"You?" Darius snapped. "But why should you require healing?"

"A silly accident." Her expression was serious as a start ran through her. "He cut me with a knife, and then he wanted to show me how his ability worked. So I allowed him to heal me."

"His ability is not meant for immortals."

Julia's attention snapped to Darius's face. "What does that mean?"

"The Great Guardian warned he should not heal an immortal. He didn't say what would happen, just warned that there would be dire consequences. That the immortal had already benefited from the water. If you were injured or if you were dying as an immortal, that means another immortal inflicted something upon you. The water would want your eternal life stores. You can't double dip in the Fountain. Balance, remember?"

"*I* did this," Julia whispered, and the weight that had become her steady companion bore down on her heart again. "This is my fault. Healing me accelerated his condition. The consequence is that his lifespan was cut into a fraction of what it should be. We could have gone on together. We could have had our five hundred years, but my stupid cut killed Charlie."

She covered her mouth and nose with her hands as two waves, grief and guilt, crashed inside her heart. Julia fell to her knees. "I can't stop hurting the people I love."

She thought she'd emptied the reserve of tears earlier, but now, in the sand, with the knowledge that it was *her* fault Charlie was so sick, a fresh supply fell.

Darius kneeled and took her in his arms again. "This isn't your fault," he whispered, nuzzling his nose in her hair. His voice took on a dark tone. "This is on *Amara* and *her* choices. You didn't know what you were walking into, and neither of you chose for all of this to happen."

"I just wanted to stop Charlie's pain, to reinforce the hope he clung to that I could get better. I never thought I would. It would have been better if I just died in that sanitorium."

An ache filled her chest and spread to her extremities. All of this was too painful, too heavy, more than she could bear.

Darius tipped her face so their eyes met. "Listen to me, Julia. I would argue that things have transpired precisely as they were meant to. And despite my earlier resistance, it's clear that we have to stop Amara. I won't return to an immortal world, you can't let Charlie die for nothing, and we can't allow Amara to make another disastrous choice for humanity. I don't know how to fix all of this, but we have to try. And, Julia, there's one more thing. But you won't like it."

Her face tear-stained, she lifted her red and puffy gaze to meet his. "What's that?"

"You're going to have commit one more murder. You're going to have to kill Amara."

Twenty-Two

Darius and Julia

B ack at the beach house, Julia showered and dressed as she considered what was ahead. She would have to face Amara again and, in so doing, the possibility of her own death should Amara best her. The task would require her to stay at arm's length, just long enough to finagle Charlie away from the woman. This whole ordeal gave Julia anxiety, a feeling that was foreign to her.

Until she had returned to the island expecting to find Charlie, she'd become an expert in knowing her plan and almost always in control. But the events that unfolded—continued to unfold—left her feeling out of control, at the mercy of everyone and everything around her. Such a feeling was uncomfortable for Julia, and she didn't quite know what to do with it all.

She held up the skinny jeans and black t-shirt Darius had provided her with. *Of course* he had women's clothes at his place. It worked in Julia's favor that he happened to have brought someone else here before that was approximately her size. She had none of her possessions with her other than her phone when Amara chased her away with her murder attempt. Glancing at her phone, she resisted the urge to call Charlie and instead pulled up the app that tracked his phone. It blinked, making it appear that Charlie was still at Amara's estate, but she couldn't be sure. He could have left his phone by now in a moment of confusion. Somehow, though, looking at the little blinking dot on her phone made Julia feel a little closer to Charlie, and she stroked the screen.

"I'm coming back for you," she whispered into the air.

Returning the phone to the charger Darius had picked up for her, she grabbed the brush that another someone had left behind and ran the bristles through her wet strands of hair. She mulled over Darius's words from earlier.

You're going to have commit one more murder.

Could she kill again? After everything she'd been feeling about those she'd already murdered, did she have it in her to take another life? That is, if they could even figure out how to destroy the water and make her vulnerable.

"It's not my problem," she said allowed.

Her concern was to rescue Charlie, not save mankind. She never asked to be a savior. She only wanted to live her life and give her love with Charlie the true chance it deserved. But things had gotten so complicated now. Still, though it was clear she wanted—needed—to get Charlie back, Julia didn't know if she had anything beyond that inside of her.

Her mind shifted to Darius, to the story about his daughter, his insistence that eventually returning to an immortal world without her would be his personal hell. Still, was it Julia's responsibility to keep him out of that hell? That was not her story, and she was tired of righting other people's wrongs, the water's wrongs. And if she was going to lose Charlie anyway, wouldn't her time and energy be better served taking care of him? Being with him?

Julia longed for the days when her biggest problem was an antiquated view of women in medicine and her dream to become a doctor anyway. Falling in love with Charlie had so fundamentally redirected the path of her life in ways that left Julia's head spinning when she stopped to think about it. And they believed, like naive children, that their love could save anything. Her life, his life, others from the water's control, its demands. But *this*? This felt too big. Darius asked too much.

"Julia! Get down here!" Darius' voice reached her up the stairs from a level down with a hint of panic on the edges of his words.

Julia's heart raced, and she snatched her phone from the charger and flew down the stairs. She found Darius glued to the floor, staring at the TV, which was playing the news. A headline scrolled across the bottom of the screen:

Breaking News: Eden Pharmaceuticals introduces modern day Jesus.

The words scrolled on repeat across the bottom of the screen, and the picture revealed the horror they referred to. A line of people as far as the eye could see collected outside of a building. There were obvious indications that many in the line were sick or disabled in some way. Julia's heart dropped to her stomach. On the building was a simple logo for Eden Pharmaceuticals with the 's' curling into a green leaf on the end. Julia knew as soon as she took in the picture what the people stood in line for.

Or for whom. The camera scanned the scene and then narrowed in on a news anchor. She spoke into the microphone. "This is Malia Stargrove reporting for news channel 8. I have here with me Lyla Snyder, who claims to have been a test subject for Eden Pharmaceuticals. Lyla, did this man heal you?"

A young blonde woman gazed at the reporter and then the camera before her eyes darted away. "He did. I suffered from Cystic Fibrosis for many, many years, and he just took it away with a touch of his hand."

"Amazing, amazing. And did it hurt?"

"No, it felt amazing. He touched me, and it was like the illness left my body in a burst. And I've never felt better."

"So from that day you haven't had any symptoms of your old disease?"

"None, whatsoever. I do submit to blood tests monthly as follow up with Eden Pharma but I'm told my results haven't wavered."

The news anchor thanked the girl, and then the scene panned to a studio where a colleague sat on one side of a desk with Amara on the other. She was dressed in a fitted black two-piece suit, her hair and makeup done to perfection. Stunning, she smiled at the camera.

"Thank you, Malia. I'm Thomas Edgar reporting from the studio, and I have with me the founder and CEO of Eden Pharmaceuticals, Ms. Amara Martin, to comment. Ms. Martin, is it true that this 'modern day Jesus' can heal any ailment?"

"Yes, it is true. Any at all. He is a miracle, and he performs miracles. And as a member of the Eden Pharmaceuticals team, he invites any and all to come to our headquarters here in New York to be recipients of his gift."

"And is there a charge to the public?"

"No, free of charge! This gift doesn't discriminate, and we don't either. We want everyone to experience freedom from whatever they are afflicted by. Anyone anywhere."

"And does your 'modern day Jesus' have any comments to share?"

"It was his idea to open up his abilities to whoever wants to receive them, but he himself is a humble man, and he wishes to not be named or interviewed. We at Eden Pharma back him and what he can do with everything we are. We have run tests, and his ability has shown unwaveringly to take anything anyone suffers with. And the results hold. So bring your cancers, bring your chronic illness, bring anything and everything, and we will help you. We want to help you. As always,

Eden Pharma is about bringing healing to the world." Amara flashed her warmest, most beautiful smile into the camera.

"I want to rip those perfect teeth out!" Julia growled. "She knows, Darius. She knows it'll bring his end so she's making sure of it. I have to get to him." She clutched Darius's arm with her plea.

"Of course. But we can't just march in there. We need to have a plan."

"Do you think she still has him at her house? I have tracking on his phone, and it's showing him there."

"Well, aren't you a little spy genius?" Darius smiled.

"I just didn't want him to wander off in confusion and be lost to me. But yeah, I am a genius."

"Okay, so assuming she takes him to her place when he's done healing, we may have a chance to grab him there. You may remember there are woods on Amara's property. Her cameras don't extend into the woods. I have the perfect place in mind that we can hide out and surveil their comings and goings. We'll wait until we can be sure Charlie is at the guest house, and then we'll go take him."

"Do you think he'll be guarded?"

"I don't know, but I'm armed with an assassin, so I'm not too worried about that. We'll have to evaluate once we're there."

"Ha, Darius. How good of a fighter are you?"

"Love, please."

Julia rolled her eyes. "Listen, Darius, I've been thinking about what you said. About Charlie's ability being one that can also destroy the water and make Amara vulnerable. I know you want me to kill her—"

"Let me stop you there. I don't want Amara dead, but I know that the only way to ensure the Fountain is gone forever is to destroy them both. Julia, you asked me before if I still love Amara, and I told you that the woman I loved is gone. She is, but that woman"—he pointed with an aggressive motion toward the TV screen—"wears the face of the one I loved. And because of that, I can't kill her. She's the mother of my daughter, and I know, if push comes to shove, that I would not be able to carry out what needs to be done. And that's why I need you to when the time comes."

"And what time is that? How would I even know?"

Darius looked down at his hands with a sad expression and answered in a quiet tone, "I'm not sure. I wish I knew. But I think it'll be clear if and when it happens."

Julia shook her head and bit her lip, pacing the space between them. "That's what I'm trying to get at. I don't think I can. It's not my job to clean up her mess, to end this curse. I thought I'd done that once before, and now I have a lot of guilt to sort through. I got Charlie back but not really. And now I *will* save him, because I love him. I thought our love was enough, that it could preserve who we were. He thought he rescued me from death, and then he thought he prevented me from becoming a monster, and then I thought I saved him from dying and from being experimented on, and now I'm going to get him away from Amara and her plan too."

She took a deep breath before continuing. "But I can't save the world. And my love isn't enough to protect him from being destroyed by what's happening to him. I have to accept that. I have to so I can move on and live with myself. I'm going to get Charlie out of there, but beyond that I make no promises." She stopped in her tracks and eyed Darius. "I understand if you don't want to help me. Charlie isn't yours to rescue."

Darius crossed the space between them and took Julia in his arms, the crystal blue of his eyes penetrating her gaze with sincerity. "I'm helping you. I'm inspired by your love for your man, and he's so lucky to have you. You should get him and keep him safe and spend whatever moments the two of you have left together. And you're right—it's not your job to clean up Amara's mess. And it's not your job to ensure she's ended. That's what I want. I want that damned water to be destroyed so it can't ruin anyone else's lives. I've run for a long time, and I've evaded my part in all of this. I'll work to rectify that by helping you get Charlie back. But promise me one thing, Julia—"

He ran his finger down the length of her nose.

"What?"

"I'm sorry if this is inappropriate to say, but promise me that once your boy's days are lived that you will find me."

Julia gulped, a mixture of anger at his mention of Charlie dying and of a desire to comply with his request. "Only time will tell, Darius, but I'm sure we'll meet again. Someday."

Darius smiled and gave her a squeeze. "Let's go get your man."

Twenty-Three

Amara and Charlie

*T*he turnout had been better than she imagined, almost overwhelming. And if people responded to this—to Charlie's healing ability—so enthusiastically, imagine how eagerly they'd take the drink once offered. Of course, she'd have to work with her team to figure out a way to distribute enmasse, but she had her ideas. Whether they made an injection of it, capsulized the water, or offered a straight drink, she would have the trust of people and government alike when she offered it after the world had seen what Charlie could do. And for those who refused, well, they were mortal anyway. Death was inevitable for them one way or another.

Gaining the trust of the public was the brilliant side effect of offering Charlie's healing ability free of charge to any and all. If the public could embrace a miraculous healing, then the Fountain of Youth would be an easy sell. Through her testing process, she'd gained witness testimonies as to what he could do, and those served her and this process well now too. Amara smiled, impressed with herself for having the idea of bringing in Lyla to give a testimony of her healing.

She pushed Charlie through the door of the guest house in a wheelchair. The two men she'd hired to help her transport him and guard him held the door, and once she wheeled the chair to the bedroom, they worked together to heave Charlie's limp body into the bed. She tucked the covers around him and kissed his forehead.

"Rest now, my Phoenix. You've earned yourself a nap."

Charlie moaned, and a deep sigh echoed through him.

"Will you need us for transport in the morning, ma'am?" one of the men asked as he stored the wheelchair in a corner of the room.

"No, he requires twenty-four hours of rest, and then we'll offer his help again. So tomorrow evening, be ready to go."

The man who had asked the question gave a curt nod and disappeared.

Amara pushed a piece of Charlie's hair out of his eye. "Thank you for your gift to the world, Phoenix. You are a blessing. And I promise to let you rest in between. A day of healing rotated with a day of rest and recovery, just like we did back at the lab. I know this is hard for you, but your sacrifice is going to save so many..."

She kissed his forehead again and ran her fingers through the locks of his hair, now matted with sweat. She stood from his bedside and closed the door as she exited the bedroom.

Amara jumped at the sight of Lucy, the nurse she'd hired to tend to Charlie overnight. She grasped her chest and let out a sigh. "You startled me."

"So, sorry ma'am. Any special instructions?"

"If there is anything he needs to increase his comfort, don't hesitate to give it. If he awakes and knows where he is, please chart it so we can keep track. And if you need resources or supplies, simply ask me."

"You've got it." Lucy waved her cell in the air. "I'll call if anything arises, but you get some rest now."

Amara smiled and gave a nod of her head. "Thank you."

Back in her bedroom, she removed her earrings one at a time and changed into her silk pajamas. Tonight, she would give herself the luxury of sleeping in her own bed, and she anticipated a slumber so deep and restful, one unlike any she'd had since taking her own drink. Because she knew she was close, so close, that everything she'd worked for and waited for was almost within her grasp. She drifted off with a smile still painted on her lips.

* * *

Amara regarded her reflection. Face painted, every strand of hair in the rightful place, and a smart teal button down blouse hugging her curves stared back at her. The perfect attire for another round of interviews and healings. Well rested from her night of sleep, she breathed in her victory and pushed down the nagging question of when Julia would return. As much as Amara wanted to revel in her current wins she knew Julia remained as a last standing obstacle. One that required removal.

The loud ring of her phone made her jump and disrupted her musings. Glancing at the time on her cell it read 3:17 p.m. It had been almost a full 24 hours. She rolled her eyes to see that it was the nurse phone and hit the button to answer. "This is Amara."

A panicked voice responded. "It's Lucy. Charlie's awake, and I'm not sure what to do. He's become violent!"

"I'll be right down." Amara hung up and gave herself one last look. She blew a kiss to her reflection in the mirror, slipped on her shoes, and descended the stairs.

Lucy huddled behind a chair while Charlie threw mugs and silverware at her. This scene reminded Amara of a few days ago, when Julia found herself the victim of Charlie's tantrum. Amara marched through the door, past flying forks and dishware and up to Charlie.

She reached for his arm without hesitation, laying her hands on him.

"Relax now," she said.

His opposite arm was posed to through his next weapon, and he dropped the appendage, mug still gripped in his palm, to his side. Tension left his body, and he gulped.

Turning a fearful gaze on Amara, Charlie said, "I'm so lost."

"Shh, I know, I know. But you're safe."

Amara took the mug from his hand and massaged each of his arms with her hands. As she did this, she guided him to the nearest chair at a table, and they both sat down. Amara continued her massage, and Charlie closed his eyes as her comfort washed over him.

"That feels good," he murmured. "Why is that helping so much?"

"We're special to each other, Charlie." She smiled. "That's your name."

His gaze wandered across the room, and he mouthed his name over and over. He turned back to Amara.

"Why is my body sore?" He closed his eyes as her massage moved up his arm.

"Because, Charlie, you've done a wonderful thing. You've helped many people. You're healing now, almost recovered to your full capacity, and you'll only continue to feel better the more time passes."

She gave him a reassuring smile, but he stared at her with a confused scowl on his face.

"How are we special to each other?" he blurted.

"We're connected, and we both have special gifts. Yours helps the world, Charlie. And mine helps you." She emphasized her point by squeezing his hands in hers, drawing Charlie's gaze to them.

"But…" Confusion covered Charlie's expression. "No, this isn't right."

"What isn't right?"

"This. Something is missing."

Amara cocked her head. "What do you mean? What is missing?"

"I don't know. Just...something." Charlie glanced around the room like he was looking for something. Or someone...

Amara cleared her throat. "Charlie, listen. You're very special, very gifted, and I'm here to keep you safe and comfortable. Is there anything you need right now?"

He shook his head. "Nothing and a million things. Can *she* go?" He gestured with his head toward Lucy, who had only just peeked from behind the chair hiding her.

Amara didn't even spare a glance the nurse's direction. "Lucy, you're dismissed."

The nurse jumped up and grabbed her belongings, scurrying out of the door without so much as a farewell.

"Anything else you need?"

"I—I wish I could remember..." He trailed off. "Wh—what's the important job I did?"

Amara scooted her body closer to Charlie's until she sat knee to knee with him. She grasped both of his arms in her hands. "You are my Phoenix, and you have an extraordinary ability to heal other people. And the more you heal, Charlie, the closer you get to fulfilling your role as Phoenix."

"And then what happens?"

"And then the whole world will be saved from their mortality and from illness and death and loss. You are singlehandedly ushering in a time of redemption, of liberation from the mortal chains that keep humanity bound."

Charlie frowned at her and then closed his eyes. "I don't know what that all means, but it's a lot."

"I know. No one has ever been worthy to do what you're doing, Charlie. You are one of a kind."

Charlie's eyes popped open and awareness filled his gaze.

"Mm—Mara?" he asked.

Amara smiled on the outside while frustration bloomed inside her. It had been over a day since Charlie had returned to his right mind, and she was finding it quite easy to control him when it was out of it.

"You're back," she said. "How do you feel?"

"Tired. Sore." He slid his hands out of her grip and rose to his feet, helping to stabilize himself against the wall. "Where's Julia?"

Amara stood too as a barrier between the door and Charlie. "I told you, remember? She left."

"And I told you I didn't buy that. How long was I gone?"

"Gone? I—"

"From my mind. How long?"

Amara twirled her fingers, caught herself, and straightened her posture. "It was the longest stretch yet, over a day."

"A day!" Charlie yelled. "Where is she, Amara? There's no way she would stay away this long. What did you do with her?"

"*Do* with her? What do you think of me, Charlie?"

"I don't know, Mara. You seem eager to tell me what I should think about what's happening to me, what my purpose is, don't you? What would you like me to think of you?"

"I—Charlie, I'm here to help."

"Help whom, Mara? The last I saw Julia she wanted to leave here, to go with Darius. And not alone. *With me.*"

Amara saw her chance. "Oh, Charlie, you don't know."

"Know what?"

She glanced at the floor, and when she looked up at Charlie, she had summoned tears to well in her eyes. "It seems your Julia, in her fear of never being quite good enough for someone so noble and pure of heart as you, has run off with Darius. I'm sorry to tell you this way."

Charlie's scowl etched deeper into his face. "I don't believe you."

"I know it's hard to understand—"

"No. Not this time, Mara. You can talk a good game to me, but not this time. There's nothing you can say to convince me that Julia just, on her own, abandoned me. She would not do that. No, she had to be driven away."

Charlie gazed off, like he was concentrating hard on something. Still staring at the floor, he said, "She said we weren't safe anymore. I remember. She said it was life and death." His gaze snapped to Amara's face. "I have to get out of here."

He snatched the phone Julia had given him off the charger and stuffed it in his pocket. Charlie advanced toward Amara, but she blocked his path and put her hand to Charlie's chest.

"And go where? You'll forget who you are before you even get off the property."

"I don't care," Charlie spat.

He tried to push past her, but she planted her feet and pushed against him.

"I can't let you do that. It's not safe for you."

"Since when have you cared about my safety?"

Amara gasped, and her mouth fell open. She covered her heart with her hand. "How can you say that? You are precious to me. Every measure I have taken was to keep you safe."

"And to what end, huh? Not because you care about me beyond what I can do for you. And I'm not going to do it anymore. Whatever time I have left, I want to spend it with Julia, not holed up here with *you*."

Charlie pushed past Amara, but she grabbed on to him arm and pulled on him. "YOU CAN'T GO," she thundered.

Charlie shook her off with almost no effort and shoved her onto the couch. "YOU can't make me stay."

Amara fell into the cushions, shock on her face. "You can't go, Charlie! You can't—"

But no sooner were the words out of her mouth than he disappeared through the door. He dashed off. Amara jumped to her feet and ran after him, but he'd already disappeared around the front of the house. By the time she rounded the massive expanse of home, Charlie was a streak in the distance. She saw him waving his hands wildly to a car, which pulled over. Charlie climbed inside and the car took off, carrying him away, out of sight.

"NOOOO!!"

She fell to her knees on the pavement and tore at her hair as rage and anguish shuddered through her. Hot tears streamed down her cheeks, and she pounded the road with her fists, screaming into the night.

Her Phoenix was gone.

Twenty-Four

Darius, Julia & Charlie

⁂

harlie didn't even bother looking at the person whose car he'd jumped into until he saw Amara's form disappear behind them, having fallen to the pavement in defeat. Even now, he struggled to tear his gaze from the road, one minute passing and then two.

"You okay, there, son?"

Charlie's attention was torn from the road behind him by the question. He looked at the man behind the steering wheel, giving him a quick once over. Nothing stood out about him—he was an older gentleman with a head full of white hair and glasses perched on his nose. He kept his eyes on the road, glancing Charlie's direction out of his periphery every few seconds.

Probably questioning his decision to stop. "Fine." Charlie cleared his throat, tapping his fingers on his thigh. His mind reeled. He was free from Amara for the moment, but Julia was gone. He knew she was. Otherwise, she'd have been there with him as he huddled in the corner terrified.

"Where ya headed?"

"Anywhere. Just get me away from here." Charlie peeked out each of the windows of the car.

"I have a spare sweatshirt in the backseat if you want it." The older man nodded toward the rear of his vehicle.

Charlie glanced down at his body. Shirtless, he'd hardly registered the cool air hitting his skin until right then. He still wore sweat pants, but his feet were bare. He was almost entirely recovered from whatever illness Amara had earlier made him absorb, but the remaining weakness echoed through his body. Shivering off a chill, he turned and reached behind him for the old man's sweatshirt. Slipping it over his head the fleece lined shirt covered his arms and chest with warmth. Nervous, he tapped both his legs and his hand landed on something hard against his thigh. He paused, and patted the pocket of his pants, his face brightening with a smile. Reaching his hand into his pocket, he withdrew the cell phone Julia had given him.

The phone! Now, if he could just remember how to call her. With the screen lit up, Charlie paused. His mind went black. Where was he? Gripping his seat on either side, fear coursed through him with a sudden surge.

"You okay there, boy?"

Charlie followed the voice to his left and saw it came from a man, a stranger. Panting, he shut his eyes, trying to quell the fear, to remember something...anything. But the only thing that filled his mind was black. Nothing. With terror written into his expression, he turned to the man—a stranger— driving. "Where am I?" His heart thrashed against his ribs. Panic tore through him, and he had a sudden and urgent impulse to flee. "Let me out of here!" Charlie screamed at the old man behind the wheel.

The poor chap only stared blankly with dumbfounded confusion. He jerked the car to the side of the road. "There you go, son. I was just trying to help you." He watched Charlie, who sat, hand poised on the door handle. "Well, aren't you going to go?"

Charlie froze, his chest heaving as he panted, his eyes wide with fear. Where was he? What was he in? Squeezing his eyes shut, he tried to remember. And with that effort, he was met with an onslaught of memories. They rushed through his brain like an angry cyclone, and he gripped his head in an attempt to make them stop. "Ahh!"

"Are you okay, boy?" The man reached his arm toward Charlie, only to yank it back as he watched the insanity unravel before his eyes. "Can I do anything for you?"

"I don't....I can't..." Charlie tried to make sense of the images swirling inside his mind, but nothing would come together...There! A familiar flash of red hair danced through his memory, and that one felt different from the rest. From the murdered sister, the lost child, the heroic fire rescue, the death of his mother. Those memories lived in his mind, but they differentiated themselves from the red hair, somehow. Still, it was only a head of hair.

Charlie looked with desperation at the old man gawking at him, but try as he may he could recall no memory of him. *Who was he? Could he be trusted?* A sinking feeling filled Charlie's gut, as if he should be scared, as if..."Sir, where are we?"

"New York, son." The old man's face twisted into a mixed expression of concern and caution, but he didn't ask Charlie anything.

"New York. New York. New....York." Nothing. Not even a glimmer. It was as if, besides the images floating in his mind, his brain had been completely washed clean. He had no reference for who he was, no indication.

"What do you want to do, son? Shall I keep driving?"

Should he? Why were they even in this vehicle? A creeping feeling of danger crawled through Charlie's insides, but he didn't know why. If this man were trying to abduct him, he wouldn't be pulled over to the side of the road. No, he was trying to help. But how could he help?

What did Charlie even need?

"I...I'm sorry. I don't know."

The man sat up against the back of the driver's seat and waited. A few beats passed before either of them said another word.

"I think I should get out," Charlie said at last. "I should go."

"Okay. Where are you headed?"

"I—I don't know." He reached for the door handle and pulled.

"Well, are ya sure? I can drop you wherever you like."

Charlie climbed out of the car and bent his head through the window. "Thank you, but I don't have a destination." And he slammed the door.

* * *

Darius hung up his call. "Well, you'll never guess who that was." He threw his

leather weekender into the car and climbed into the driver's seat.

"What did she want?"

"Seems Charlie came to. Was asking for you."

"And?"

"And he ran away. Got out of there so fast she couldn't catch him and climbed

into someone's car."

Julia closed her eyes and huffed a sigh. "Tell me you are joking."

Darius glared at her from the corner of his eye. "And why would I jest about

something like that?"

Julia grabbed Darius' arm as panic rippled through her. "Who knows who picked him up? What if Charlie got into the car of some crazy person? What if the person discovers he's out of his mind and..."She broke off, a million scenarios polluting her worried mind.

Darius reached across to take Julia's hand. "You have to trust he's going to be okay. You must trust you'll find him. Your love has guided you all along, and it will lead you to him."

She huffed. "And you see where it keeps taking us, our love. Let's hope it does a better job of charting our path this time."

Darius accelerated, and they left the small, private airport.

"Okay," said Julia, regaining her wits. "She doesn't know we're already here so that buys us some time."

She turned around and suspended her body between the front and rear seats. She dug around in her bag until she found her phone. Flipping her body around, she plopped into the passenger seat once again and pulled up the tracking function.

"I'm so glad I installed this thing on Charlie's phone. Let's just hope he has it on him still." She tapped her phone's screen. "Okay, the phone tracker indicates Charlie is definitely not at Amara's mansion, but he's not too far."

"You're a pretty good little stalker with that thing." Darius scanned the area in front of them as he drove.

"Please, what do you think I did for the last hundred years? Let me tell you: it's waaaay easier now with technology." She laughed, and the release felt good, easing some of the tension from her body. "Besides, not stalking. I told you before. It was for his protection."

"Mmm hmm." Darius flashed a coy grin.

Julia punched him in the arm. "Shut up and head north."

Darius obeyed, directing the car north in a slow crawl as Julia regarded her phone. Her body trembled with anticipation, her stomach turned flips. She hoped against hope that Charlie was okay, that he hadn't fallen at the mercy of some stranger who was looking to take advantage. He didn't know this world the way Julia did. He was still so trusting—that was, when he was lucid. If he was out of his mind, well, that raised a host of other concerns. She shook those out of her head.

"Why did Charlie run away?"

Darius drummed the steering wheel with his fingertips. "She said he was asking her questions, and then he wanted to see you. Somehow, he didn't believe that you wouldn't be right by his side." He glanced at her out of the corner of his eye. "Even a half-insane man can see what a gem you are."

"Charlie's the gem. He's the one who never left *my* side."

Julia's heart lurched with guilt as she recalled her earlier impulse to run. She thought back to the first time she and Charlie set foot on the island, to her request that Charlie kill her if need be, to the fact that he had taken a drink to become immortal so that one of them could kill the other. To stop her. To free her from the curse. The act *was* purely selfless, arising out of his love for her, out of his desire for her to be well. Everything Charlie did came from such a place. Out of love, setting himself aside.

"It seems like for this whole Phoenix thing to work out that an awful lot of conditions had to line up."

"Why do you suppose it's taken all these millions of years for them to be met? It's true. An immortal born of selfless motives, never having killed in the name of the water, and at the right time."

"What do you mean, the right time?"

"The bird always returned to the island—to the source of the water—to burn up and reincarnate. For Charlie to become the Phoenix reborn, the one the Guardian spoke of who could end the curse and Amara, the Phoenix had to finish his life span and return to die while he was on the island after having taken a drink for selfless motives and blah blah blah. Charlie was there at the right time under the right circumstances. And he made all the right choices."

Julia fell silent. Charlie did always seem to know what to do. This was one of his many appeals for her. She focused on the tracker on her phone.

"We're almost on him. Our blue arrow is catching up to his red dot."

Her heart raced with anticipation as much as with worry. She glanced back and forth between the map on her phone and their surroundings. And then their blue arrow was on top of the red dot. "Pull over."

Darius did as told, coming to park on the side of the road. On the side they'd pulled over, there was a small gas station, lit up from within. The parking lot was completely empty. On the other side of the road, fields stretched beyond, and Julia made out a form stumbling through the grasses spread before them.

"Charlie!" His name came out in a whisper, and she flew from the car, crossed the road, and jogged in pursuit of him.

Julia approached Charlie, who wandered the field aimlessly, looking as lost and confused as she was sure he felt. He seemed to be plagued with indecision, dodging first to the left then to the right. Julia cased the surroundings. There was nowhere for him to go. The field they stood in was small and empty, with nothing but a sign sticking out of it. True, he could make a run for the gas station across the street, but Julia stood between him and the road. The wind kicked up, and Julia watched Charlie cradle his arms against himself, shivering. He froze as she came near and then took off at a dead sprint.

"Wait!" she cried.

She expected he'd keep going, that she'd have to chase him down, but that didn't happen. Instead, his steps halted. She caught up to where he was frozen in place, and as she reached him, he turned to face her. Bent at the waist, she put her finger up to ask for a second to catch her breath.

Julia stood up straight and panted. "Thank you for waiting."

Charlie looked her up and down, from her hoodie to the black leather jacket to her jeans and boots. Julia took the hood off her head, her red locks cascading down her shoulders.

Charlie shook his head with a violent movement. "Red," he said. With a suspicious glance her direction, he motioned toward her hair.

"Charlie." She reached for him, but he drew his hand away. "You're Charlie. I'm Julia. We love each other, and you're safe with me."

He reached for her with a tentative hand but then drew back, uncertainty in his gaze. She could see the war waging within him. He wanted to take her hand, but he was scared, uncertain if he could trust her.

"Come on. We need to go. I don't want to alarm you, but you may be in danger. I can help you. I can keep you safe, but you have to come with me." She flexed her hand with her invitation.

"I—" His gaze darted, and he flexed various directions, like he was trying to figure out if he wanted to run or not.

Helplessness threatened to tear Julia apart, but then a thought occurred to her. And some of Charlie's earlier words rang in her memory. She made a decision, and without hesitation or giving herself a chance to change her mind, she closed the gap between them, locked her fingers around his neck, and drew his mouth to hers. Her gentle kisses didn't find resistance, so they became more bold. Julia's lips tingled as Charlie wrapped his arms around her, gripping her, holding her to his body.

Charlie drew away, looking into her eyes. "I know you. I don't know who you are, but I know you." He kissed her again, his hands reaching up and touching her hair. When he pulled away, he ran a strand between his fingertips and then let go, watching it fall.

"Your hair. I keep having memories of a faceless red-haired woman. And the kiss—" He reached up and touched his fingers to his lips. "I know you in that kiss."

"Yes. Yes, Charlie. I just...I hadn't tried that before to bring you back."

Both of them panted, the intensity of the moment stealing breaths and stopping time.

Charlie stared at her, lifting his palm into the air. Julia rested her hand against his, and Charlie interlocked his fingers with hers. "I don't know who I am, where I am. But..." He closed his eyes and squeezed them tight. "Nope! Nothing! I can't remember anything but a flash of red hair." When he opened his eyes, Julia hadn't moved but watched him intently.

"Are you okay?" she asked.

"Yes, I think so."

"You don't remember anything else at all?"

"No." Still, their bodies were glued together, neither of them having moved. "But I want to."

"Okay, good enough for me. Just so long as you don't throw things at me."

"What?" He reared away from her.

She chuckled, and her body shook with her laughter in his embrace. "Nothing. Are you ready to go, though? Will you trust me?"

"I want to," he repeated.

"Okay." She didn't pull her body away from his, but she pointed to the road, to the car she'd jumped out of. "We have to get in that car, and then I'm going to take you someplace safe. Okay?"

Charlie nodded. Hand in hand, they jogged to the car and climbed in.

Twenty-Five

Julia and Charlie

D arius pulled into a marina.

"Of course you have a boat nearby too." Julia raised her eyebrows at him.

"What do you want me to say? When you've lived as long—"

"Yeah, yeah, amassing wealth, well-traveled, many homes. I got it. I have to admit that it is convenient to know someone with unlimited resources when on the run."

"Glad to be of service." Darius tipped an imaginary hat at Julia before glancing back at Charlie. "Is he okay?"

Julia turned her gaze on Charlie, who had not said a word the entire ride over.

He stared out the window with a sad frown on his face. Seeing him this way made her heart lurch, and she wished she could ease his suffering. "I don't know."

Darius snuck a second wary glance at the helpless Charlie. Lowering his voice, he asked Julia, "Are you sure you'll be okay without me?"

Julia huffed. "I'll have to find a way to soldier on." And she gave him a smile.

"You make jokes, but I think you fear a future without Darius." He winked at Julia.

"I fear a reality where you speak of yourself in third person." Julia made a face at Darius. "But I do appreciate your concern."

Julia's gaze traveled out to the dock ahead with endless boats parked against wood and concrete. She turned back to Darius. "What's your plan?"

"Go to Amara, I guess. Distract her. Divert her. Not that she could find you where you're going if she tried."

"And she will try. It's the only place I can think of to take him where he'll be safe from her."

"It's a good plan. But know this: Amara gets what she wants. And she doesn't quit until she does."

"Well, if anyone can keep her distracted, it's you."

"You're not wrong there." A silence lingered between them. And then Darius angled his body toward Julia. "I guess this is it then."

"For now. Take care, Darius. And thank you for everything." With a flick of her wrist, she opened the car door and climbed out. She took a deep breath before she pulled Charlie's door open. "Ready?"

He glanced around her, out to the marina, with mistrust in his eyes. "As I'll ever be."

Climbing from the vehicle, Charlie wandered behind Julia, following her to Darius's craft, 'No Regrets,' which she found to be an ironic name.

"I don't know why it can't ever be summertime when we're traveling to the island."

She climbed into the boat and opened a small hatch. Tossing the contents about, she landed on a couple of blankets. She threw one to Charlie and wrapped herself in the second as she took the wheel.

"Listen, it's going to take a little time in the boat, but I'm taking you somewhere safe."

Charlie's gaze searched her, and she could tell he was trying to remember. Still, emptiness lived in his eyes. As much as he was here with her, he was also gone. She dismissed her disappointment, the concern about his demise, the weighty responsibility he didn't even know he bore in this whole thing. She just had to get him to the island, to the only place Amara couldn't reach him. Then they'd have some time. She blazed over the dark water and, with the help of the boat's navigation system, forged a trail through the river toward the island.

The cursed island, and now their refuge.

"Is this your boat?" Charlie shouted over the wind and engine.

"It's Darius's."

"Who's Darius? Never mind...It's nice." Even as he said so, he tightened the blanket around himself, the cool wind sending shivers down the both of them.

"Thanks. Darius drove us here. You've met before."

"We have?"

"Yup. I wasn't sure about him at first, but turns out, he's good people."

"Oh…" Charlie's face contorted as he searched the recesses of his mind for any indication of a memory of what she talked about. "Why didn't he come with us?"

"He has another job to do. And ours is to stay safe."

Charlie's question gave Julia pause. It was a reasonable one, but how did she answer that? She didn't know how long he'd remain in this state before returning to her. What if his mind was gone permanently? She had to face that possibility, and so she made a decision.

"You know what, Charlie? I promise I'll tell you everything when we get where we're going."

He nodded and peered out over the water, silence settling between them for the remainder of the trip.

When the island finally rose out of the water before them, an undeniable sense of relief washed over Julia. They were almost there, almost to safety. She sidled the boat up to the side of the land and hopped out. Extending her hand, she pulled Charlie onto land, and they worked together to secure the vessel.

Charlie stood up tall, studying everything. "Where are we?"

"This, Charlie, is home. At least it was for a little while. Maybe being here will help you remember."

She took off through the trees toward their cabin with Charlie trailing behind. Every few feet, Julia glanced behind her, and each time, Charlie scanned their surroundings with questions in his gaze as he stumbled in her shadow. When they reached the small dwelling, Julia opened the door, gesturing Charlie inside.

He walked through and looked around as Julia stocked the fireplace with wood and then set it aflame. On her knees, she stoked the fire until it roared to life. Turning, she watched Charlie, fear and longing dueling within her.

"Anything?" she asked him.

Sadness filled his expression as he shook his head. "I wish I could say 'yes.'"

"Why'd you come with me? Other than the fact I'm a good kisser." She laughed in an effort to ease the heavy mood.

"That definitely helped." A smile spread across Charlie's lips and almost reached his eyes. "My mind is like a white sheet of paper. Blank. Except for a few repeating images that feel like memories. I can't be sure if they're mine, though. They seem unrelated, but they're all I have."

"What are they?"

"Mostly sad ones. A woman who is supposed to be my mother dying, walking in on a girl who hung herself, losing a baby...they don't feel like mine."

"That's good, at least, that they don't feel like yours."

His head snapped up. "Why?"

"Because they aren't yours. But you... acquired them...and when you do remember who you are, they feel like your memories even though they aren't."

"That makes no sense."

"I know." Julia tapped her fingers on her knee and stared at the floor, trying to decide how much to tell him.

"But then there's one image that feels a little closer to belonging to my memories. Your hair."

On impulse, Julia reached up and touched her head. "You mentioned that before."

"Yeah. Sounds strange, I know. But wild red waves run through my mind. And then when you called my name in the field, your voice sounded familiar, and when you kissed me..."

At the mention of their kiss, Charlie looked into Julia's eyes from across the room, the space between them filling with a thick tension.

Julia stood, unsure why. She crossed the room to Charlie and took his hand. With both their hands lifted, she placed her palm flat against his. Heat circulated between their fingertips, which traveled down the length of Julia's arm, overtaking her body an inch at a time.

Charlie watched her, his eyes fixed on her face. Neither of them broke eye contact, searching each other's gazes with mutual curiosity, hesitation, desire even. In some ways, to Julia, it felt like the first time she touched him.

As her heart drummed inside her ears and her stomach fluttered, she was taken back to the night he'd first told her of his feelings. Almost a hundred years ago, and yet in this moment, it felt like yesterday. She wanted to hear him say those words again, to sweep her up in his arms and kiss her with all the pent-up emotion they'd been saving.

But she knew she couldn't ask that of him. That, to him, she was a stranger. Because of that, this one moment of intensity, the heat between them as they stood there palm to palm, was more than she could ask or expect. Here time stood still. Here the current realities they faced ceased to exist. And as their fingers touched and her body lit with sensations, Julia forgot about everything.

The magic water which made her immortal.

Her murdering mission.

Charlie's declining health and impending death.

The fact it wouldn't be long before Amara came for them.

But in that moment, only two people existed in the entire world—her and Charlie. It was as if the cabin swirled around them, blurring until it disappeared and only the two of them remained. She couldn't believe she'd given any consideration to running away, and a pang of guilt struck her. So consumed was she by her love for Charlie, her desire for him, all else faded.

And then Charlie did the unthinkable. He laced his fingers between hers, yanked her arm toward his body, and swept her up. Wrapping his free hand around her waist, he collided his body into hers and crushed his mouth against her lips, kissing her with every ounce of desire and passion she'd been wishing for.

His lips interlocking with hers, their tongues doing the same, Charlie pressed her against the wall. His hands gripped her neck beneath her waves, squeezing at her skin like his life depended on keeping his mouth glued to hers.

Julia's body filled with electricity, each of his touches shocking her skin, her body, like this was their first time. She dug her fingers into his flesh as Charlie's hands gripped her with iron force. Any timidity from before was gone. He commanded their kisses with strength, with desire, with familiarity. Leaving her lips, his mouth found her neck, a trail of soft pecks cascaded down the length of it and roamed across the landscape of her collarbone, her shoulder. She giggled when his lips traced her collarbone, tickling her on their journey. His mouth returned to hers, the kisses slowing to soft, sensual lingering ones. Julia swore she felt his love in this expression, if it were possible.

When their lips parted, Julia's eyes remained closed as the effect of what had just happened lingered. When she opened her eyes, she found Charlie gazing at her, but the same vacancy lived in his expression. Julia glanced at the ground, undone. Thrilled at what they'd just shared and devastated by the reminder in Charlie's face that he didn't know her.

Even so, Charlie's gaze intensified as he drank her in. He brushed a piece of hair out of her face. "I don't know what it is about you. Why I don't remember you but there are things familiar about you to me. And I don't understand the passion, the draw I feel between the two of us when you're a stranger to me. But it's there, and I can't deny it. When we were necking there in the field, it's like it ignited something familiar inside of me, and now I can't shake the feeling.

"That's why I kissed you just now. Because I wanted to. Because I feel a connection to you that goes deeper than any amnesia and is stronger than my fear. And so…" He lifted his gaze to meet hers. "If you say I can trust you, I will. I don't know what's happening or where I am. Hell, I don't know *who* I am. But everything inside of me tells me I'm safe with you."

He paused. "You said you'd tell me what's been going on, and I want to know. I don't know if it'll make any sense to me, but I will believe whatever it is you tell me."

Relief filled every recess of Julia's heart, and she exhaled a long breath. She opened her palm toward Charlie, inviting him to take her hand.

"Come on. Let's sit down, and I'll tell you everything."

Twenty-Six

Amara and Darius: Present Day

As Amara approached her mansion, the usually quiet road in front was filled with news vehicles. So saturated was the road she could hardly pull up to her own home, but she managed to carve a path through the line of vehicles.

"What is this?" Stopping her vehicle, she took in the scene around her.

She sat in her car for a moment, unsure what to do, what this was about. She didn't have time to answer questions—there was a Phoenix to find! Turning in circles down the country roads around her had done nothing to turn him up. She'd lost the trail of the car he jumped into and eventually gave up, coming home to *this*.

What terrible timing. Besides, she already had a press conference scheduled for the next day to answer any and all questions about Charlie's abilities and Eden Pharma's offer to heal people.

Amara growled as she opened the door of her vehicle and climbed out, watching with a wary eye. Reporters surrounded her and blocked her path from the car to her half-circle drive. As soon as she closed the car door, the onslaught of questions thundered in a chorus from the crowd before her.

"Is it true you kept your 'modern- day Jesus' trapped and bound?"

"Witnesses say your modern-day Jesus not only heals but becomes sick when he does. What are your comments on this?"

"Does your modern-day Jesus consent to healing?"

"It seems activist groups are rising up to protest Eden Pharma in its attempts to use a person against his will in the ways you have. Do you have a statement?"

Amara raised her hand, confused and eager to stop the barrage of questions flying at her. In the short amount of time since returning home from Charlie's healing escapade and his escape, something had erupted on the scene without her awareness. She fingered her cell in her jacket pocket. She'd turned the ringer off when the incoming calls wouldn't relent—they were a distraction to her pursuit of Charlie. Now, it seemed, she should have taken those calls.

"Tomorrow, folks. Tomorrow I will answer questions at the press conference." She pushed past a couple of the reporters but more blocked her path. She tried to weave through them, her hand in the air dismissing their endless blitz of questions. Tension mounted in her chest and frustration built. No one understood what she was working to accomplish! Her plans promised salvation, freedom from modern illness and even death. She didn't have time for this, didn't have time for ignorance and questions and distraction. She felt herself losing control, and a scream rose in her throat.

"The lady said she'll address all of your questions tomorrow at the press conference. Kindly leave her property before we have to call the authorities." The smooth voice cut through the others like silk and stopped Amara dead in her tracks. She turned to find Darius with his hand outstretched and a mischievous grin on his face. "Shall we, my lady?"

The world went quiet around her. He'd come back not only to help her find Charlie, but he rescued her now. She slid her fingers into his hand, and he covered her like he was shielding her from the verbal attacks of the reporters surrounding them. With Darius in the lead, they cut through the line of reporters and made an easy entry into Amara's home. A calm overcame Amara, and she closed her eyes as Darius led her through the crowd, shutting them out, focusing on the touch of his hand around hers.

When he slammed the door once inside, she woke from her blissful serenity.

"And just what the hell was all of that?" Darius demanded.

"I have no idea." Amara woke her phone up and viewed the multiple visual voicemails lighting up in her inbox. "Oh no, no no…"

Darius was also on his phone. "Yup, word's out. Someone cracked about Charlie."

Amara growled. "We had a confidentiality contract!"

She grabbed at her hair and paced as she scrolled through her own phone.

Darius read, "Brandon Chesterson, of York, Maine spoke up about Eden Pharmaceutical's "modern-day Jesus." He was one of Eden Pharmaceutical's test subjects before they made the healing abilities of a man known only as Charlie available to the public. According to Mr. Chesterson, the man who healed him was "bound" against a wall, a prisoner forced to carry out the healing. 'I almost turned and left. He looked so pathetic. There was defeat in him, and I have to live with the fact that I still let him heal me. Don't trust Eden Pharmaceuticals. They aren't who they claim to be.'"

Darius expelled a low whistle. "You've done it now."

Amara stopped in her tracks, and her attention snapped to Darius. "We can come back from this!"

"Can you? Do you see the quantity of press out there? They aren't going to leave, Mar. It's over."

"Don't. Say. That!" she screamed through gritted teeth. She raked her hands through her hair. "I just need to think. I will figure it out."

"Face it, darling. Charlie's gone. The press is on to you…"

Amara stopped inches from Darius's face. "The press will love me again when I can give them the Fountain of Youth!" she spat.

Darius shook his head. "I'm an idiot for coming." He stared into her eyes, saw the desperation there, and wasn't moved. "You know, you almost had me all those years ago. After I'd ignored you for hundreds of them and then you called me with pleas and promises, I returned to you, and you just about convinced me I could have a life with you again, even without Elora."

He sighed. "But that drink changed you, Amara. Seeing your face pains me because I see the woman I once loved, the woman I would have given anything for, died for…" He cut off, unexpected emotion choking him.

Amara reached for him, her touch both unwanted and desired. She ran her fingers down his cheek and then across his mouth. "We can still pick up where we left off, Darius. YOU are what I've been fighting for."

She watched as he closed his eyes, as he turned his face into her palm, breathing her skin in. She knew he still fell under her spell, that a small part of him could not resist her.

"It is easy to forget when I'm with you, Mara." He nuzzled his face against her hand on his cheek and opened his eyes. "But every time I leave, I hate myself after because all the reminders flood my mind."

"Then don't leave this time." There was a desperation in her voice, but she didn't care. She meant every word.

"I hate you. I hate how you make me ache with desire for you, how your touch on my skin makes it so difficult to say no to you."

Amara smiled, delighted. Her own body ignited with sensation, with desire, but she waited for Darius to make his move. She would not force his hand. If he wanted her, he would have to come and get her.

Darius narrowed his eyes, and Amara could see the conflict in them. He licked his lips and drew Amara into his arms. With his body pressed against hers, he kissed her with longing and desire. She draped her arms around his neck, her body going limp in his grasp. But just as she expected things to kick up a notch and meld into deeper expressions of their eternity long love, Darius released her mouth, stepped from her arms.

"I can't do this. You're a siren, Mara, and your call will never stop tempting me." He turned from her as he tried to even his breathing, to calm his heartbeat. "I thought I could handle one kiss, but I can't open that door to you."

"What happened?..." Amara touched her lips where Darius's mouth had been as she trailed.

"Nothing happened. Nothing's changed, Mara. You? Me? We're old history, and it needs to stay that way."

With tears in her eyes, she clung to his arm. "Are you ever going to be able to look at me and not see her face? Don't you think I've been punished enough? That I haven't lived every day condemning my own actions? Why do you think I've worked so hard and so long to find the water again? And why do you think that once I did find it, I've kept tabs on it?"

Darius shook himself free from her grasp. "Because, Amara! Because you can't accept what you've done any more than I can! You can't bring her back...you can't—" Now tears stung his eyes, too, at the memory of their daughter, at the brutal image flashing through his mind. Blood and screaming and disbelief. And he kicked himself for allowing his heart to go there, for being vulnerable to her.

"I know." Amara touched him again, and he didn't resist. "That's the one thing I can't do. I know that." She searched his gaze as tears blurred both visions. "I'm sorry, Darius. I'm sorry for what happened to her."

"What *happened?*" He tore his arm from her grip. "How can you make it sound like she was just some bystander in an accident, Mara?"

He clutched his chest and stumbled, as if his heart were breaking within. His face burned red, and he seemed to light with a sudden energy, bouncing in his steps, advancing on her. He pointed his finger into her face and spit as he said, "What happened to her, Amara, is that you killed her. *You.*" He turned away. "I can't even *look* at you when I think about it."

"I know," she whispered. And then her hand was on his shoulder again. "But it wasn't really me. You know that, right? It was the water."

"It should have been me…You were coming for me, and I should have died that day instead of *her.*"

From behind him, Amara wrapped her arms around his waist. "It shouldn't have been anyone. I'm sorry the water tried to take your life through my hands. And I'm sorry it took her instead. I wish things had played out differently. I wish she were here with us now too."

"*Now?*" he snapped, tearing from her hands. He spun and stared her in the eyes. "If none of that had happened, we wouldn't be here now, Amara. Not like this. Tell me, do you also wish you hadn't taken that drink?"

A beat passed between them, Amara holding Darius's gaze without waver. "We cannot change what was."

"That's not what I asked you."

She gulped and knew Darius read the waver in her expression. She wanted to satisfy him with her answer, but she couldn't both tell the truth and tell him what he wanted to hear. "We cannot change what was," she repeated.

Darius bobbed his head in an exaggerated nod. "So then, that's your answer. You wouldn't, Mara, would you? Even with the death of our daughter, even with our estrangement, with how you single-handedly brought death and destruction into the world, even all those who have died because of the water. You would still take that drink, wouldn't you?"

"Look, Darius. Taking that drink made me into who I am. And soon, once Charlie finishes his life cycle, I'm going to revert everything back to how it was."

"Yeah? Can you resurrect *her* too?" Darius clashed his gaze against Amara's. "You are not the same woman I loved in the beginning. She would have done anything she could to prevent these things from happening, to save her precious girl. But you..."

Mara lunged for him, gripping his shoulders. "No, you don't understand. You don't know what I have in mind, Darius. Of course I'd change what happened if I could. Why do you think I've been waiting for the Phoenix instead of running around and living my life like it's some big party, as some people do?" She stiffened at her own words and loosened her grip around him.

"No. You are not going to turn this around on me. I didn't leave you. You left me by making the choice to drink, by poisoning yourself and anyone else who would join you in your rebellion. No, you left me first. You chose yourself, your curiosity. Couldn't just listen to the Great Guardian and let things be. *You* did all that."

"Everything you say is true, and now I'm going to fix it! That's what I'm telling you, D. I'm going to turn this around and undo what I've done." She tightened her grip around his waist. "Can I show you something?"

Darius spun around, forcing her arms to unwind from around him. "What?"

"Just, follow me." She led him to the basement stairs and descended them. After performing the several steps of her security protocol, her secret vault door slid open, and she led Darius inside. When they walked through the door, Darius' knees went weak, and he almost fell down. Before him, on the wall, hung a life-sized portrait of their daughter. His feet refused to move, as if the concrete had enclosed around them, trapping him.

"I had it painted centuries ago. As best I could from memory. There were many, many drafts, but this final likeness of her bears close resemblance, don't you think?"

Finally, his feet unstuck, and Darius took a step toward the portrait. And then another and another until he stood before the painted image, looking almost into the eyes of his lost daughter. Frozen in time at the age of thirteen, her beauty had only just begun to blossom. He ran his fingertips down her face and then the painted strands of hair as his chest caved in. Only in his memories had he seen her face since she took her last breath and died in his arms. A dry sob shuddered through him, but no tears fell.

"Such a beauty. I miss her every day." Amara placed her hand on his shoulder.

Darius growled at the sound of Amara's voice. He turned from the portrait and glared at the woman, tearing himself from her touch.

"Is this supposed to endear me to you? I haven't seen her face in literal millions of years, and I'm supposed to thank you?" He stepped closer, his handsome features taking on a dark and threatening appearance.

"No, Darius I—I just thought you might like to see your daughter again. I can't bring her back to life, but I can do this for you."

"And I'm to have gratitude, am I? That you would allow me to gaze upon the face of my dead daughter, whom you killed, whom I will never see again. I'm supposed to be convinced that your insane plan to get your hands on the water and offer the world over a drink is a *good* idea?"

"She told you?"

"Of course she told me! It's worse than I anticipated. You can't willingly give the water to everyone and let them duke it out survival of the fittest style. The very fact that those are your intentions tells me you've learned nothing."

"Oh, but you're wrong. I've learned that the way things were before I drank is the natural order of things. The way they are now—with sickness and war and violence and overpopulation—that is not what was intended for humanity. I know of my mistakes, and this is why I am so desperate to rectify them. And the only way to do that is to even the playing field, let everyone drink. Why can you not see the logic in this, Darius? I *KNOW* I can't change the fact that I killed Elora, and I know you are fearful of living in a perfect world without her—"

"There is no such thing as a perfect world *without her!*"

Amara jumped at his outburst, and his words echoed through the room. She tensed her jaw and exhaled. She wasn't getting through to him. He would just have to see when it all happened. "In time you'll come to understand."

They stared at each other, a furious silence settling between them. And when Amara's phone rang, breaking the silence, they both jumped. She glanced at the screen and rolled her eyes, clicking the green button.

"What *is it?!*"

She sobered, listening to whomever was on the other end. "I see. Five minutes, then?"

She nodded and ended the call. "We have to go. There are crowds of protestors both at Eden Pharma's headquarters and outside my home. We aren't secure here and my people are sending a chopper. Unless you want to fight those crowds, you're with me."

Twenty-Seven

Julia and Charlie

Washcloth in hand, Julia wiped her face and expelled a heavy sigh. She had to tell Charlie everything, which meant she had to tell him everything-everything. Confess to being a murderer after he'd stated his trust in her, tell him that all of this, every last bit of what's happened to him, was her fault. She preferred just to go back to their making out until his days were lived. But she was done running now, and she had to face everything ahead.

She dried her face on a towel and left the bathroom, finding Charlie sitting in front of the fire he'd stoked to life.

"Not bad, wouldn't you say?" He pointed to the fire with a smirk on his face. "Some things you just can't forget, I guess."

"I guess." She sank into the chair next to him, her smile fading. "Are you doing okay?"

"I'm fine. You saved me from some fate I do not yet know. I have a feeling that wasn't the first time, either."

"Truth is, Charlie, you've saved me more than I have you. In bigger ways."

"I'd love to know how."

Julia slouched in the chair, the warmth of the fire bringing comfort to the outside of her body, the memories of their love story warming her from within. "You served in a war." She turned her head to look at him. "Did you know that?"

"Nope." Charlie's gaze got lost in the flames.

Julia watched him, his dark eyes blinking, a little lost as he worked to recall the memory. He pursed his lips, and that action made his dimples sink deep into his cheeks, which sent a shiver of satisfaction through her. She shook her head, trying to free herself from her desire for him, if even for a moment, so she could tell him their story.

"Well, you did. We grew up together, and we were the best of friends. And then one day, when we were nineteen, you decided to enlist in the Great War, now called World War I. I was so angry at you. It wasn't until you returned that I understood why. I loved you even then, Charlie. But I was too focused on myself. On what I wanted."

"What did you want?"

Julia smiled, recalling how deep those dreams went for her so long ago. "To become a doctor. To prove that women could do what men do and more."

"A doctor. That's progressive."

When she looked up at Charlie, there was admiration in the eyes returning her gaze. "Not anymore. Turns out women *can* do anything men can. And sometimes more." She laughed. "But I was focused on that, and if I'm really honest, I took our friendship for granted. I think I knew somewhere in the recesses of my mind that you were more than my friend, but I figured I'd get to that one day. Once I safely achieved my goals. But when you returned from the war, you messed all that up." Julia paused, stealing a glance at Charlie. His expression had settled into a frown, the one he always wore when deep in thought. "What's on your mind?"

"I'm just trying to remember something, anything, from what you're telling me. Nothing yet, but keep going. Tell me what a mess I made of things."

"You did too!" She laughed. "Truth was, I knew the moment I saw you. And probably before then. There was this girl—" Julia's memory of Caroline's face cut her story off, and she sobered. She hadn't intended on bringing her up, at least not yet.

"What?" Charlie looked at her now, his expression morphed into curiosity and maybe a hint of concern.

"Nothing. Just...I was jealous is all. A few nights later, you told me you'd grown to love me, that thoughts of me were what saved your life when you almost couldn't go on at war."

Glancing at Charlie, Julia's fingers traveled to her lips as she thought about their first kiss. And then about the one they'd shared earlier, when Charlie surprised her by whisking her up in his arms.

"I didn't realize until that night how much I'd wanted to kiss you. How much I'd grown to love you. But just as our love story started, it threatened to end. I became ill. Very ill. With a life-threatening disease that seemed determined to kill me. But you were not okay with that. And this, Charlie, is where our story gets a little strange."

He waved his hand for her to continue.

"No. First, I need to know you're ready to hear what I have to say. It defies any reason or logic. You're not going to believe it, even, and you may hate me once I finish telling it to you."

Charlie stood suddenly from his chair and came to kneel at Julia's feet. He braced her knees with his hands and looked her in the eyes. "Please. I need to know everything."

"Promise me you won't freak out."

"What's that mean?"

"That you won't panic or run away or hide from me."

"Good glory. How bad is it?" He settled on his knees and rested his hands in his lap.

"The story is pretty spectacular, but it brings us to why we're here. Why you're in danger—well, we both are, actually…"

"I can handle it. Tell me the story. Help me understand what's happening here."

Julia huffed, sizing him up with her gaze.

"What?"

"It's just…every time before when you haven't remembered who you are, you've been so erratic. I get it's scary, but you seem so reasonable right now."

"I was terrified. Out in that field. But you calmed me with your lips." He winked at her.

"Really? All I needed to do all along was make out with you?"

"Pretty much. What made you decide to kiss me anyway?"

"It was something you told me during one of your lucid moments. You said, 'Everything I need to know I've found in your kiss.' I had to try, to see if somehow that helped the situation."

"It was the right choice. I can tell you're a good person."

"Hmm. Well, that opinion may change once you hear the rest of what I have to tell you."

One side of his mouth twitched. "We'll see."

"This is the longest you've been gone, Charlie. I mean, in your mind. Usually it doesn't last this long, which is why I'm going to tell you everything. I'm worried…I'm worried you aren't coming back to me. But if at any point during this story you remember anything, tell me. Okay?"

"Deal. Now keep talking, lady."

"When I got sick and it looked like I was going to die, you brought me a vial of water. You'd taken it off a buddy from war who always swore it could miraculously heal anything. But not death. He died, and you kept it as a memento, only remembering you had it when I was on my death bed. And I drank it to satisfy you, never believing it was more than common water.

"But it was so much more. Not only did it make me well, it filled me with an inexplicable energy, like I could do anything. But that energy had a purpose, and soon, the water came calling."

"What do you mean?"

"There were side effects. I didn't just recover and then get to move on." Julia leaned forward and reached for Charlie's hands. Clutching them in her own, she continued. "The water you gave me came from the true Fountain of Youth. That Fountain flows outside." She nodded her head toward the door behind her. "But it doesn't just make you better and endow you with immortality. It must get the life-giving power from somewhere. So it awakens something inside of those who drink it…"

She looked Charlie in the eyes as she held his hands in hers. "The water demands lives for the life it gives. It turns those who drink from it into killers so that life power can be returned to it. And that's what I became."

Charlie yanked his hands from hers, drawing them to his lap. "You—you've murdered?"

"Yes."

His gaze dropped to the floor, shuffling at the ground in front of him, trying to process, to make sense. "Couldn't you just resist it?"

"No. Not the first time anyway. I killed someone, and you watched me do it. And rather than turning me in to the authorities or writing me off, you helped me because you felt responsible. I never blamed you, Charlie. I wielded the knife. But you gave me the drink, so you blamed yourself. We went on a journey then, to try and find answers, and it led us to this island."

She took a deep breath, steeling herself for what was left of the story.

"You okay?" she asked Charlie, whose face had gone white.

"I think so."

"Remember, don't freak out. Okay? This is bigger than either of us."

He nodded, but Julia could have sworn he inched away from her by a miniscule amount.

"We encountered someone here whose job it was to guard the water. To make sure no one got off the island with it. She failed, of course, as your war friend stole some. She told us that I would kill over and over, as long as I existed. And that the only way to get out of it was to kill another person who had a drink of water. She wanted it to be her, but I refused.

"So you took matters into your own hands, and you took a drink, too. Seeing her opportunity, Rose—who guarded the island—stabbed you, held you for ransom, and sent me on an errand to kill all the other people who had ever had a drink from the water. She just wanted it all to be over. Turns out, none of us knew how far back the story really goes."

"What?" Charlie patted his body as if his wounds would be fresh.

"Open your shirt."

"I don't think now's really the time—"

"Just do it."

Charlie unbuttoned his shirt and pulled it off.

"Look at your torso."

He glanced down and saw the imprints of the flowering plant branded on his skin. The design was beautiful, and it was evidence that the story Julia told was true. Charlie traced the lines. "What is this?" he asked in a breathy voice.

"There is a plant that grows around the water, from it. And it can heal. The girl who was here—Rose—took care of you while I was gone doing what she assigned me to. And when she dressed your wound with the flower, they left an imprint."

Charlie's eyes were wide, and he scanned the room as he absentmindedly traced the design on his skin with his fingers. Julia waited, watching him absorb what she told him. When his eyes traveled up to meet hers, they narrowed. "How long were you gone?"

With a gulp, Julia cleared her throat and puffed out air. "Almost a hundred years."

If Charlie was shocked before, he was in total denial now. Shaking his head, he murmured. "No, no, no, no."

Julia reached for him, planting her hands on his shoulders. "Charlie, look at me!"

He did, eyes full of fear.

"I know this is a lot, but you're kind of freaking out. And you promised you wouldn't, remember? There's more I need to tell you, okay?"

He nodded, even as his hands trembled.

"Okay. You and I? We're immortal. We haven't aged a day beyond when we drank from the spring outside. But that was just the beginning of the story."

"The beginning?" He rubbed his eyelid with his finger, his hands shaky. "Am I a murderer, too? I feel like I might faint." He waved his reddening face with his hands.

"You're okay, Charlie. Just keep your eyes on me, listen to what I'm telling you. You have never killed anyone, okay? But there is a woman, and her name is Amara. She took you, Charlie, because she suspected you were special. And she was right. What you are is unlike what I am. Turns out, you're the only one who can stop her. I just don't know how yet."

"Stop her from doing what?"

"Something very, very bad..."

"Well, who is she? What does she want?"

"She is the first one who ever drank from the water. The water is, essentially, Pandora's box, the proverbial tree of the Knowledge of

Good and Evil."

"I don't know what those are."

"When she drank, she ushered illness and mortality into a world that was basically perfect. And she wants to make it right. But she can't get to the water. Not while you're alive."

Charlie froze. "You didn't bring me here to kill me, did you?"

"No! No, I brought you here to keep you safe from her. She doesn't want to kill you, either. But she does want you dead, because then she'll have access to the water again. She's been cut off since she drank. But she plans to give everyone a drink as soon as she can get to the water."

"But then won't everyone become killers? Wiping each other out until only the immortal who survived remain?"

Julia nodded her head slowly.

"Ohhhh...that *is* bad. But I don't understand. How can she want me dead but not want to kill me?"

"Remember a moment ago when I said what you are is unlike what I am and that you're special? Well, every person before you drank from the water for their own gain. To satisfy curiosity or to get well or to see if they'd live forever. You drank to save me, and then you paid your debt to the water with your own immortal life. And now you can heal like the water does. But the more you heal, the more you forget who you are. The more you absorb the memories of those you make better, the blurrier your identity becomes. Until, finally, you'll run out of healing juice, and you'll die. And when that happens, Amara will be able to see, touch, and have access to the water. And then the world is in danger."

"Wait...I can heal people?"

Julia squeezed her eyes shut so she wouldn't roll them. She scolded herself for her impatience. Charlie was not focusing on the things she needed him to. "Yes, Charlie, you can heal people. But as I said, it's

255

making you weak, making you forget."

"How do I heal?"

"I'm sorry. I know this is all daunting, but we need to focus on the bigger issue here."

He put his hand up. "Just—how do I heal?"

"You touch people. You can sense where in their bodies they're sick, and then you will yourself to absorb their illnesses or injuries. You get sick for a short time with whatever you took from them, but then you recover. And they're well."

"Not a bad deal, I guess."

"Not for them. But for you…"

"I know. I heard that part. So what then? Sounds like no matter what, I'm going to die. It's just a matter of when." The words sounded mechanical leaving his lips.

Julia dropped her head, her chin meeting her chest. Thinking about Charlie dying threatened to tear her apart. "I'd like to figure out a way to prevent that."

Charlie huffed. "Yeah, me too. But what if there isn't one?"

Julia shrugged, while Charlie stood to his feet and paced in front of her.

"Why have I lost my memory? You said healing made it worse, but what does it have to do with all of this?"

Julia's gaze dropped to her hands, and a wave of guilt rushed through her. "Darius said you would lose yourself so it would be easy for you to do what needed done to end the water's curse. Whatever that is. I'm sorry, Charlie, you should have more time but it's—it's my fault your deterioration started so early."

A single tear fell down each of her cheeks.

Charlie stopped in his tracks and came to Julia, taking her in his arms. "Don't cry," he said in a soft, gentle tone. "How could any of this be your fault?"

Julia managed a laugh through her tears. "Didn't you hear my story? Arguably, I am to blame for so much of this." She looked up into his deep brown eyes. "But you healed me, Charlie. Your touch healed me, and I was never meant to be a recipient of it. Your gift isn't meant for immortals—it's just that, a gift. It's meant to give the world all the goodness of the water, a time of peace before Amara gains access again. But healing me, an immortal, upped that timeline. It's like an abuse of that gift. And I'm sorry."

"Listen, I heard your story like an outsider since I don't remember it. But it sounds to me that everything each of us did was because of our love for each other. If I healed you, I wanted to, and that's not your fault. But that's interesting that you say it's not meant for immortals and that healing you sped up the timeline of the end of my life." He released her and tapped his chin with his finger, thinking. "You said I'm the only one who can stop her?"

"Yes, I just don't know how."

"And you said I can absorb things from people."

"Yes."

"Can I absorb other things?"

"Like what?"

He walked in slow circles, gripping his chin with his forefinger and thumb.

"Like...anything?"

"I don't know. We haven't tried."

Charlie nodded, his eyes moving back and forth in his head as he processed. "Okay. You say the water is here on the island? And it's what she's after?"

"Yes."

He halted, snapping his attention to Julia. "Why don't you just kill her? Aren't you experienced in that? Wouldn't one death be better than what she has in store?"

"I agree, yes, but I can't. There's something binding her to the water. Because she first drank it. I can't kill her as long as those waters flow."

Charlie's face brightened, and his finger shot up into the air. "And she doesn't have access as long as I'm around. And I can absorb things.... Show me the water."

"Why?"

"Because I have an idea."

Julia remembered Darius's words to her earlier. That Charlie had managed to make all the right choices along their journey together. Darius's assessment was right, and she knew she could trust whatever Charlie was thinking, even if this 2.0 version of him wasn't exactly *her* Charlie.

"Follow me. It's right outside."

Twenty-Eight

Julia and Charlie/Darius and Amara

ulia and Charlie stood over the rock wall that surrounded the Fountain of Youth.

"I did this?" Charlie splayed his fingers on the stone surrounding the water before tracing the lines. "This is good work."

"You're very talented." Julia watched him, but his expression remained blank. "You still don't remember anything?"

His fingers froze in their tracks along the stone and he turned to look at Julia. "Still just your hair."

Instinctively, Julia reached up and ran her fingers through the red strands. "You did always love my hair." A certain sadness fell over her, over them. "Nothing else, though?"

Charlie shook his head. "I'm sorry. I wish I could say 'yes' but..." He broke off, gaze searching their surroundings until it circled back around to lock on Julia. "Maybe we should try necking again." He bobbed his eyebrows up and down at her.

Julia laughed, relieved at the release of tension Charlie's flirtatious joke provided. As much as she wanted to pick up from where they left

The Killing Cure: Redeem

off before, she was too distracted now. "What's your idea? Why did you want to see the water?"

"So I have an ability to absorb things, correct?"

"Yes."

"But we don't know what the limitations are to my abilities."

"I hadn't thought of the potential that you could absorb anything other than illness or injuries from other people. I guess I'm not sure beyond that." Julia didn't like where this was going, and a feeling of dread creeped over her.

Charlie bent, fingering the antidotal leaf.

"That leaf is an antidote to the water's effects. If you eat the leaf, you'll regain your mortality."

He looked up at her. "This just keeps getting stranger and stranger. So why haven't you taken it?"

A wave of realization washed over Julia, and she jumped. "Charlie, why don't you?! I can't take it because I was nearly dead before I drank from the water. I'd go right back to that. But you—if you took it, you'd just be human again." Her eyes bulged with excitement.

"O...Okay. I—I could try, I guess. But what about everything you just told me?"

"What about it?"

"If I'm truly the only one who can stop her...?"

"Oh, that. Well, if you're human, you're no longer the one who can end the curse. They call you the Phoenix, by the way—don't ask. And if you regain your mortality, then you're not the Phoenix, and everything that's supposed to happen won't, which means Amara never gets access to the water!"

Julia covered her lips with her hand, kicking herself for not thinking of this before now.

Charlie's gaze broke from Julia's, and he traced a pattern in the dirt in front of him. "If I don't take the antidote, I will definitely die but might be able to stop an evil villain from world domination. But if I eat this leaf—"

He held the green plant in the air, turning it around and allowing the sunlight to filter through.

"Then, Charlie, you'll come back to me. To yourself. You'll live."

"Hm." Charlie glanced at the plant and drew it to his nose to sniff. "Worth a shot, I guess," and he stuffed the leaf in his mouth, swallowing it down.

* * *

Darius trailed Amara out the door, away from the growing crowds of reporters and protesters in front of her home and into her chopper.

"Where are we going?" he asked.

"We'll fly to the Thousand Islands, out to my research facility there. It's not well known, and it's remote so it's secure. But from there, I need to find my Phoenix."

Amara frowned, done trying to explain herself to Darius, frustrated that someone broke their contract. The messes were compiling one on top of each other, and she could feel her own hysteria rising. But as the chopper rose into the air, she gazed down over her house at the masses of people, and she was grateful to have an escape.

"He's not *your* Phoenix," Darius hissed.

She rolled her eyes and ignored his statement. He'd see soon enough. She watched him, brooding as he peered out of the window, deep in thought. She couldn't resist asking. "What's on your mind, D?"

When he turned his crystal blue gaze on her, malice lived in his eyes. "Trying to decide if I should cut and run. Leave you to your devices."

"You do what you want, D. I'm getting my way no matter what."

"That's what I'm afraid of."

"People die all the time, every day. I'm just accelerating the process.

Remember how precious the earth was to us once? It's nearly ruined now. I know my choice threw off that balance, but we can restore it all."

Darius shook his head with furious motion. "If you get your way as you say you will, someone is going to have to kill me. There is no redemption in this plan of yours." He rested his chin on his palm, skulking out the window.

The pair endured the remainder of the ride in silence. Before long, they touched down on the little helicopter pad at Eden Pharma. Darius and Amara stretched their legs when they climbed out and looked around. Amara watched as he scoped out the area, taking in every detail. She resisted the urge to show him around, to invite him inside. Instead, she walked straight from the helicopter pad down to the dock and climbed on to one of the smaller vessels tied there. When Darius hesitated, she said, "Well, aren't you coming?"

"Where?" he snapped.

"We're going to get my Phoenix back. You and I both know where he is."

"You can't go there."

"I can't, but I have mapped coordinates from when my men found the island and guess what, Darius? You can."

"Why would I help you?"

"Because I know you care what happens to *her*. So get in."

Darius's gaze traveled out over the water for a moment, and he seemed to be deep in thought. Amara half-expected him to refuse, but instead, he followed her on board without another word.

* * *

Charlie clawed at his throat, the burning sensation so intense he could have sworn the antidote set a fire in his mouth that climbed down his throat and into his stomach. The leaf he'd eaten became lodged in his windpipe choking him as the fire raged down his esophagus. He hacked and coughed and sputtered until he threw the leaf up. Falling back on the ground, he rubbed his throat, receiving relief at last.

Panting, beads of sweat formed along his brow line, and he glared at Julia. "That was a cruel trick."

She was by his side and extended her hand to him. "Why would I trick you?" She clutched her chest, hurt by the assertion. "I thought it might save you."

Thoughtful, Charlie's glare of contempt traveled to the plant. "Then *what* was that?"

Julia plopped down on the ground, disappointment hitting her as understanding dawned. "Because, Charlie, you really are the Phoenix. You can't un-become him. You have a role to play in all of this. I just hoped...I hoped it would work."

Charlie picked at some rocks on the ground, tossing them aside once they were unearthed. His expression looked thoughtful, and Julia wondered what was going through his mind.

"I'm the only one who can stop her," he said. "But we don't quite know how."

"That's right."

"In addition to all of that, I have a supernatural ability to absorb illness and injuries from other people."

"We've been over this, yes."

"Just like the flowering part of the plant I just tried to eat."

"Mmm hmm. What are you getting at?"

"What if my ability isn't a coincidence? What if being able to absorb illnesses and injuries and the like *is* what defeats her?"

"I don't follow." Julia tensed, uneasy about what conclusion Charlie might be building to.

"I don't know who I am anymore. There's no sign of my memory returning. It makes sense that losing myself is by design, that it makes it easier for me to do what needs done."

"Charlie...?"

"You said the Phoenix was made when someone drank of the water for completely selfless motives, while Amara's drink was taken out of purely selfish ones. What if—more than just the symmetry, the balance in it all—what if that's by design too? Someone who drank because they wanted to be young forever or they needed to get well from a disease might not be inclined to defeat Amara in the way she needs to be defeated."

"I don't know what you're driving at, but I'm not liking the sound of all of this, Charlie. You may not remember who you are, but I do. And I have fought *really* hard so we can be together. I'm not ready to give up on you—on us—that easily."

His gaze met hers, and there was warmth in his dark eyes, softness in his expression. "I know, and though I have no recollection of everything we've been through together, I thank you for what you've done. But that's all been a part of it, too, see?"

Julia shook her head as fear mounted in her chest. "What do you mean?"

"Every step of the way, you and I have acted from our love, and each of those steps have carved the path to bring us here. If I'm this...Phoenix, you ultimately play a role in ending the curse because I couldn't be the Phoenix without you. You are central to all of this. You couldn't be what you are, do what you've done without me, and I wouldn't be in a position to end this without you." His eyes filled with excitement, and his expression set with resolve. "I know what I need to do."

"What and also...how?"

"I just know. I can't explain how I know but I do. I know how to beat Amara."

Julia gripped her knee, digging her fingernails into her own skin to stop her hands from trembling. Her whole body shook, and she felt like she was going to puke. "How?" she asked again, her voice leaving her lips with a squeak.

Charlie stood and approached Julia, pulling her to her feet. He looked into her eyes, and she could have sworn in that moment that he'd returned to his right mind. Licking his lips, Charlie tilted Julia's chin toward his face and laid a soft kiss on her mouth. When he pulled away, he rubbed her chin with his thumb, gripping her face in his hands. "I understand why I loved you once."

Those words—meant to be comforting, to be a compliment—cut Julia to the quick. Those were words spoken by someone who didn't love her now, and they were words used in the midst of a farewell.

Charlie was saying good-bye.

He released her face and turned toward the water. Her feet refused to move, glued to the ground beneath her, her body quaking with dreaded anticipation. "Charlie, what are you going to do?"

He disappeared behind the cottage and returned with one of his tools, a pick, in hand. Turning away from Julia, Charlie went to work on the barrier around the water, disassembling it piece by piece.

"Charlie, please, tell me." Emotion choked Julia and sent tears spilling down her cheeks.

He paused, mid-strike and turned toward her. "I'm going to set the world right."

* * *

Amara made it inside the covering just as it started to rain and fired up the boat. Darius clutched her arm. "What exactly is your plan here?"

She glanced at his hand holding her arm then returned her gaze to his. "I have the coordinates. You need only to accompany me."

Darius bared his teeth at her and hissed through them. "That's not what I asked you."

Amara rolled her eyes and sighed. "We're headed to the island—I told you, it's time to get the plan on track." She yanked her arm from his grip, turning her attention to the window beyond.

"And how do you see this playing out?"

"Since the land will be invisible to my eyes, you will be my eyes. My hands."

Darius gripped both sides of his head. "I will not help you take Charlie."

Amara shrugged. "We'll see."

She approached a nearby spread of counter, uncorked a bottle of wine, and poured herself a glass. "Fancy a drink?" She gestured with the bottle.

Darius's only response was a grunt and he turned away from her.

They set out, and the boat made way toward the island. A hush fell over the pair as they rode along the river, as the sun broke over the clouds and illuminated the day through the soft rain. Darius paced the interior of the boat with tension in his posture, and Amara took slow sips of her wine.

"There's no use resisting, D. Just like when it all began. It's going to play out how it's supposed to."

He stopped, his shoulders easing, and nodded as he looked Amara up and down. "Yes, I hope that's true."

Amara didn't like the way he uttered those words, and she had the impression they held different meaning from hers. She followed the map with the coordinates that were punched in, reveling in how close she was to Charlie. She closed her eyes for a moment and felt the air for the water, for the others. Despite the fact she could see nothing out before her, she *felt* the presence of the Fountain and the two inhabitants nearby, and the feeling was comforting, indulgent, affirming. This was the right plan. The water called her home, invited her to reunite with it, to set everyone free with just one taste.

Opening her eyes, she saw on the screen that they were nearly upon the island. The trip felt so quick, though it had passed in silence. She squealed with delight. "It's here!" she exclaimed, her red nail clicking against the screen.

"How do you know?" Darius narrowed his eyes at her, and that seemed to quell her excitement for the moment.

"I'm watching the read-out." She gestured to the screen she stood over. A little dot approached a small mass on the map, the coordinates around the land matching those in the corner.

"What do you see when you look out the window?" Darius's gaze landed right on the land, the one their little dot made its way toward on the screen.

"Just the river spreading before us. I can see other islands up ahead of us in the distance, but nothing immediately in front of us...wait..." Amara dropped the wine she held and ran to the window, splaying her fingers on the glass.

"What? What is it?" Darius ran to her side.

"I can...I see something..."

* * *

With the wall deconstructed most of the way, Charlie gazed down into the small spring. "It's not much, is it?"

"Not to look at, though it is pretty."

"Peaceful, even." He squatted down and ran his fingertips along the surface of the water.

Julia kneeled by his side, fear for what he intended coursing through her. "You still haven't told me what you're thinking."

"I know. Because I know you'll try and stop me."

He lunged for her, landing on top of her, knocking the both of them to the ground. With Julia pinned down, Charlie gave her one last, lingering kiss. She was so stunned by his sudden movement she didn't have time to process what happened next.

Not until it was too late.

Charlie sprung up off Julia and dove for the spring. Hand outstretched, he submerged his palm into the water and closed his eyes.

Julia jumped to her feet. "What are you doing, Charlie?!"

"It's the only way!"

He screamed, agony constricting his face. Blue light emanated from his palm, and as he willed his hand to absorb the Fountain, the water rose up into a cyclone and poured into Charlie's palm, disappearing as it met his touch.

Julia yanked on him as tears streamed down her cheeks. "Stop, Charlie, please!!"

She tried to pull his arm, his body, but she couldn't move him. He was rooted to the ground.

Tears fell down Charlie's cheeks, and he screamed, his body writhing but his hand remaining steady as he absorbed the deadly Fountain.

"I see it all! I see every last injury, illness, life this water took. I see the life it restored and the death it caused. It so painful...too...much."

Julia watched, helpless, as Charlie fought against the water, trying to pull his own hand free, trying to make it stop. But he appeared powerless over his own limb.

"I'm trying...to...stop..."

Julia wrapped her arms around his body, yanking with all of her might, her feet anchoring into the earth, her forehead sweaty and rain-soaked as a shower fell. Together, she and Charlie fought to retrieve his arm, but it would not be moved.

Charlie turned, looking at Julia's face.

"Jul..." Recognition lit in his eyes as tears filled them.

"Charlie, stay with me. Stop. Please. Please, don't go!" She stroked his cheek with one hand and continued attempting to draw his arm out of the water with the other.

"I can't. It's too late."

He sniffed, turning his gaze to the spring as the last few drops of water absorbed into his palm, leaving the earth beneath dry.

"I love you, Jul."

The water was gone.

And Charlie fell to the side.

Dead.

Twenty-Nine

Amara and Darius/Julia and Charlie

A smile broke over Amara's face. "Darius, I can see the island!"

"No." The word came out in a whisper, his dark skin turning pale as his gaze traveled back and forth between the mass of land before them and the look of pure ecstasy on Amara's face. "But that means…"

"He did it. He's gone." She finished the sentence for him. Turning from the window, she paced with excitement. "Which means the water is all mine. Which means we are *this* close to starting our lives over, to restoring our world how it once was." Her voice rose to a shrill pitch as her hands waved wildly in the air. Then she froze, gripping Darius by the shoulders. "Don't you see now? The pain we've suffered, the losses...I can set all that right. With you by my side."

"Don't *you* see, Amara?

She returned to the window, smashing her palm to the glass, reveling in the fact she could see the land. The anchor now dropped, their boat sat just yards in front of the island. Amara closed her eyes, took a deep breath, and searched the air for the water. She wanted to feel it since this was the first time she'd been this close to the Fountain since the beginning.

But something was wrong.

She opened her eyes, cut a glare at Darius, and tried again.

"What?" he asked.

"I can't feel it." Eyes shut, worry creased her forehead.

"Can't feel what?"

"The water, Darius. I can't feel it. I should be able to this close, with Charlie out of the way. But I can't. Can you?"

Darius sighed and closed his eyes. After a moment, he opened them again, looking into the concerned gaze of Amara.

"Nothing."

"Something's wrong. We're going to find out just what." She stormed away from the window, making her way off the boat. The soft rain from earlier had intensified, and angry clouds dumped from the sky.

On land, she took the lead, crashing through bush and tree until they reached a small cottage. There, on the ground in front of the dwelling, was Julia. She draped herself over Charlie's still body.

"What is this?" Amara's tone was harsh. Hand on her hip, she planted her feet just paces in front of Julia and Charlie.

When Julia turned toward them, she revealed a red, blotchy face. Her eyes swelled from tears, and her chin trembled. Her gaze clashed against Amara's as she spat, "He's dead. Because of you."

Amara clucked her tongue. "Nuh, uh, uh, I didn't make him the Phoenix."

Julia sprung to her feet and dove at Amara, driving her body up against a tree and pinning her there. She held her arm against Amara's throat. "This is on you! You were the one in the beginning. You created this whole mess, and now Charlie's dead!" She spat as fresh tears stung her eyes.

Amara choked against Julia's arm, but her laughter broke over until she overtook Julia with one easy move and pushed her arm away as if she swatted a fly. Feeble, Julia stumbled to the ground, her strength sapped by grief.

"You want to blame me, but you two made your own choices. I didn't handpick Charlie to be the Phoenix. I'm sorry for your loss, but it was inevitable. He's fulfilled his role, and I'm going to set the world free. Now, show me to the Fountain. It's been so long..."

Julia's sadness was replaced by a moment of satisfaction—the one small glimmer of hope spurred on by Charlie's death. The corner of her mouth twitched into a half-smile.

"It's gone."

Mara's face turned to stone. *"What?"*

Julia stood, her legs weak beneath her. Her chest ached, sending pain through the rest of her body. "That's why Charlie's dead, you idiot. He used his ability to absorb all the water. All of it. It's gone. It's over."

Amara's body trembled, and she threw her gaze in every direction around them. "Liar! Where is it?"

She rushed forward, frantically searching amidst the bushes and trees. She dropped to her knees and felt along the ground. "Where is it?" With a flushed face, her eyes bulged in her head, insanity etched into every detail of her expression.

Julia swallowed down her grief for a moment, enjoying the rise the water's absence got out of Amara. "What's the matter? Isn't this how you saw things playing out?"

Amara stood up, her chest heaving with rapid, angry pulses of breath. She closed her eyes and evened her breathing, fisting her hands at her sides.

"Fine," she said, and when she opened her eyes, her usual calm demeanor had returned. "I will figure this out."

"There's nothing to figure out anymore." Darius cut Julia a look. "Julia, the Fountain is gone, and Amara's life is linked to it."

Recognition lit in Julia's expression. "No," she said.

"You're the only one who can. This is the only way to really make sure the curse is ended. For good." He took a step closer. "This is what you've fought so hard for...what Charlie sacrificed himself for. So it can be over."

Amara's gaze roamed from Julia to Darius. "You want her to kill me, D?"

She grasped her chest, tears welling, betrayal working its way into her expression.

Darius's gaze landed on Amara's face, locking on hers, narrowing. "You've never been able to see anything but what *you* want, Amara. This isn't about what I *want*. It's about what needs to happen."

He sniffed.

Julia's body ached with grief, and her heart ignited with anger. She glared at Amara, distracted by her interaction with Darius. She knew her moment, if she wanted to take one, was now. She lunged at Amara and bowled her over, knocking her to the ground.

"You killed Charlie!" she screamed. "He's gone and you took him!"

Julia threw a punch.

Stunned, Amara spit blood. She narrowed her eyes, malice in her gaze.

Julia punched her again and scrambled on top of the other woman, securing her fingers around Amara's neck.

Strangling her.

Julia dug her fingers and thumbs into her skin, cutting off her windpipe. Rage and grief overcame her, and she squeezed tighter, looking into Amara's wide eyes.

A rogue tear fell down Amara's cheek, her mouth gaped open as she tried for breath, and she clawed at Julia's arms, inflicting scratches

Julia couldn't feel.

It wouldn't be long now. Now that Amara was just another immortal because of the water's destruction, Julia could sense the life draining out of her. Amara kicked, fighting with everything in her, but nothing could tear Julia's fingertips from their grip.

This was the end. A few more seconds, and Julia would be free of the curse that ruled her life for a century.

That stole her childhood.

Snatched her dreams from her fingers.

Smudged her soul.

Took Charlie.

Her entire history flashed before her as she steadily snuffed out Amara's life. Julia snarled as anger and grief mixed within her, pushing her forward, energizing her for this one, last murderous task.

She locked her gaze on Amara, on her struggle, on her pleading eyes. But then, in Julia's mind's eye, she saw the face of Rose. Caroline. Each of Julia's ten other murder victims. One by one, their faces flashed before Julia, and she felt her fingers loosen with each passing countenance, each reminder of her pain or her regret, her longing and loss and grief. Last of all, Amara's image transfigured into Charlie's face, his deep dimples sinking into his cheeks with a wink and a smile.

Julia released Amara, falling to the ground as convulsive sobs racked through her body.

Amara wheezed, desperate for air. She rubbed her throat and lay there stunned.

"Why'd you stop?!" Darius screamed.

Julia turned to find him, crouched on the ground, tears in his eyes.

Julia sniffed, shuddering with her cries. "Charlie's sacrifice has to mean something." She closed her eyes, tears burning down her cheeks. "He never wanted this for me. He became the Phoenix because he drank to save me from this fate. I can't add any more ghosts to my haunting. And I can't dishonor his sacrifice by adding more to the death toll."

She gulped, her gaze roaming to Amara, who continued to rub her throat and stare ahead with eyes.

Amara looked to Darius, and he stood from his crouched position and crossed to her. She reached for him, and he took her hand. Kneeling, he said, "Hey, the magic touch is gone too."

"I'm sorry," she said. "I'm sorry."

Darius nodded and ran his lips across her knuckles. "Me too." They stared at each other, both eyes filled with tears.

"You wanted her to kill me. I never knew you hated me that much. I always thought we'd be together again, that our love was eternal, fated."

"Darius' and Amara's love was eternal. But we're no longer them, are we, darling?"

Silence settled but was almost as quickly interrupted by a sudden burst of flames. Defying the rain that fell, Charlie's body was on fire.

"No, no!" Julia screamed, and she scrambled through the mud to his corpse. She grabbed at his face as the flame etched up his body, toes to head. She kissed his cheeks, the hot flame licking her arm as it engulfed the whole of Charlie. The fire blazed tall and wide into the air, and Julia was forced away from him, the light of the fire blinding her, the heat scorching her skin.

Amara cried out, clawing at her throat. Before their eyes, she transformed in earnest. Her skin changed, second by second, with different maladies, one by one. She was a monster, changing in quick succession from one horror to the next. Any and every affliction imaginable sprung up on the surface of her skin, contorting her body grotesquely one at a time. Her throat split open and then closed. A stab wound appeared in her stomach and disappeared. She clutched her throat, some invisible force choking her. As if she experienced every pain the water itself had absorbed. Every murder committed at its command. Then she transformed into Elora, her own victim, her daughter, the one who had set her free from her the curse to kill.

Darius fell to the ground, mouth open wide, words failing him. He reached for the face of his daughter, palming her cheek, and she nestled into his hand, her misty eyes meeting his. And then her face changed again, and Amara looked at him.

"Darius. I've seen it all. Everything the water did. It's my fault. Please know I would have chosen differently."

She cried out and clutched her stomach. Screaming, she rose to her feet, some invisible agony tearing through her body. Her skin glowed, and then the light broke through her flesh, casting rays of illumination in every direction. They reached from every corner of her body, and her scream intensified. Julia and Darius stood back, watching in horror, helpless.

The rays expanded until they exploded in a bright burst. When the air cleared, Amara was gone.

Two piles of ash lay side by side.

Without warning, Julia's chest closed up. She gasped for breath, her lungs refusing to fill and crushing pain echoed through her entire body and reached from her chest down her spine, her groin, every extremity. Extending her hand, she grasped for Darius, as if he could do anything to help. She'd never forget this agony—it was too familiar, too marked in her memories. But before she had a chance to speak, she too fell to the ground, unconscious.

Thirty

Julia

⚜

J ulia tried to move, to wiggle her fingers, but her body was pinned to a bed. Or so it felt. Every inch of her ached, but the dull throb in her chest and ribs was the most intense, even if it wasn't as severe as she'd remembered. Struggling to blink her eyes open, bright lights blinded her, forcing her to squeeze them shut again. She tried a second time, squinting until her pupils adjusted minimally, and all she saw was white around her. White walls, a white curtain hanging to the side.

Horror overcame her.

This was too familiar, too sterile, too…

Where was she?

With great exertion, she lifted her hands and felt her ribs, her chest. Bones protruded from her thin form, and the reality dawned on her. She'd returned. Somehow, some way, she was just a sick girl back at the sanitorium. Before she knew it, her breaths had accelerated, and she was having trouble catching them. It was then she noticed the thin tube under her nose, the ease of air flowing from it. At that moment, she heard her heart beating with a rapid sound, and the noise snagged her attention to the right of her bed, where all her vitals were on display.

On the one hand, relief fell over Julia. This was not the sanitorium. But on the heels of that relief, confusion soared. The last thing she'd remembered was Amara turning to ash and then...all went black.

"Well hello, love," a buttery voice greeted her, and when he came around the curtain, Darius stood before her.

Julia opened her mouth to speak but found her voice to be hoarse. "What—"

"Shh shh shh." Darius covered her lips with his fingertips. "You conserve your energy." With a wink and a smile, he pulled a stool to her bedside. "It's finished."

Julia's mind reeled. "She's really gone? And the Fountain too?" she asked, ignoring Darius's command to rest.

"Yes, for good."

Julia let the news absorb. She wanted to feel happy about Amara's demise, relieved the water was, once and for all, destroyed. But there wasn't nearly enough joy to fill the void of Charlie's death. It wasn't a worthwhile price, in her opinion.

She squeezed her eyes shut as the memory of his body bursting into flames played on repeat in her mind.

"Are you alright, love?" Darius took her hand in his.

She nodded. "Where am I?"

"Well, the curse has finally ended."

"Okay, but what happened to me?"

"When the curse was lifted, it seems, you were restored to your former state—the way you were before you ever took a drink. We all were."

A start jumped through Julia's body. "I have consumption again?"

Her mind ran a million directions as his confirmation sunk in, even if she already knew the truth. Knowing Charlie was gone had her wishing for her own death. But never did she imagine she'd regain her mortality. "Am I going to—?

"—Die?" Darius finished for her. "See, the great thing about having tuberculosis in the twenty-first century is that it's a treatable disease now. You've been in the hospital for two days, and you're responding well to the medication. They've got you on pain meds to ease your symptoms, but they can always give you more if you wish. In the meantime, the doctor expects a long but full recovery."

A strange hybrid of relief and grief dueled in Julia's heart. She'd wanted to die, and she'd wanted to be human again. But she didn't want the latter without Charlie. Tears welled in her eyes at the thought of him. Here she was, with a chance to finally live a normal life—one devoid of magic water or murder or isolation—but it was without him.

Darius reached over and swiped the tear falling down her cheek. "I forgot to tell you. I have a surprise for you." When he stood, he pulled the dividing curtain all the way open, revealing another patient in the room. Julia lifted her head, straining to see.

Her eyes grew wide as she watched the even rise and fall of his chest, as she took in the dark strands of hair on his head, matching the overgrown stubble on his face. He stirred, his mouth flinching, and dimples displayed themselves in his cheeks through his facial hair.

Charlie...

Was alive?

"Now, I hesitated showing him to you, really I did, before you promised to run away with me." Darius winked again and plopped down on the stool.

"But he...he..." Julia's words came out in a whisper.

"Died? Technically, yes. Charlie the Phoenix died. Charlie the man

279

lives."

"How—?"

"When the curse ended, everything was set right for all those it impacted. He did perish as the Phoenix, but that was his role. His reward is regaining his humanity. From the ashes of Charlie the Phoenix, Charlie the man was reborn."

"Did you know this would happen?" Now both of her eyes filled with tears, and they spilled down her cheeks.

"No. I didn't know *what* would happen."

"Is he okay?"

"Yes. He's just resting. They've run tests, and everything looks healthy and normal."

"And your daughter—?"

All the mischief and jest fell from Darius's expression and was replaced with his own grief. "I'm afraid those who have died stay dead."

He took her hand and laid a kiss across her knuckles. With a sniff, he switched his charm back on. "So I take it you like my surprise then?"

Julia gave an emphatic nod of her head as she stared in disbelief at Charlie. He was there, alive. She was alive and would get well. They could start again.

Charlie mumbled something in his sleep.

"That's my cue." Darius stood from the stool. "I'll leave the two of you."

Julia squeezed his hand. "What about you?"

"Love, I was immortal before the drink, and I shall remain as I was."

"What will you do?"

"I'll live life, as I always have. I'll be around. If you get sick of that guy over there," he waggled his eyebrows toward Charlie, "come find me."

With a wink, he turned his back and left the room.

Julia waited, the heart rate monitor betraying her anticipation to the room as Charlie woke.

His eyes fluttered open, and he lifted his arms into a stretch before turning his gaze to Julia. But when his eyes met hers, he sprung to his feet, pulled out the IV line hydrating him, and ran to her bedside.

"Jul!" His voice fell to a whisper as his eyes welled. "You're awake. How do you feel?"

"Pretty terrible, but…human."

His eyes crinkled with his smile, and his dimples sank into his cheeks. "I told you we'd figure out a way. That we would make it back to each other."

"You kind of saved the world, Charlie." She laughed, combing her fingers through his hair. "You are the bravest, kindest, most selfless man I have ever met. And trust me, I've met a lot of people over the years. And still—with all I've seen, the things I've had to do—I've never met anyone like you, Charlie. You are one of a kind."

She paused, emotion getting the better of her, and Charlie squeezed her hand.

"Well, Jul, I happen to think you're pretty swell too. You're stuck with me. Somehow, together, we're going to get you well…again…and then we're going to figure this life out until we grow old and die."

Julia sniffed. "Maybe in Colorado?"

Charlie smiled. "I'd like that. And once you're up to it, you're going to give me oodles of children."

"Oodles?"

"Gaggles. Hoards. Flocks of children. Scores of infants. A whole herd of little people. A murder of babies. Wait…nope."

Julia laughed again and immediately regretted this as it sent a shot of discomfort through her. "Why don't I focus on regaining my lung capacity first?"

"One thing at a time. I can get behind that." Charlie brushed her forehead with his lips. "Finally, we're free."

The same images of those she'd killed over the years scanned through her mind in a second, like a slideshow on speed. Squeezing her eyes, she resolved to put those out of her head, accepting her past as a part of her story, one she had begun to redeem by refusing to add any more faces to her litany of regrets. Everything she'd always wanted—the life with Charlie she'd imagined—could at last be hers.

Her last mission was to get well, and she felt confident she could succeed at this one. She looked at Charlie, the smile on his lips reaching his eyes as his dark, tousled hair stood up all over his head. His strong hands held hers, and contentment crashed over her like a wave.

"Free at last," she said.

Julia knew that whatever her mortal life might bring her way, she and Charlie would figure it out.

Together.

THE END.

Need a little more? I have a gift for you! I was intrigued by the story of Charlie's friend Arnold who originally ventured to the island, met Rose, and broke her heart when he took off with the water. I figured there was more to his story, so I wrote it! If you're equally as curious or you just need more Killing Cure world in your life, go grab your free copy here: https://dl.bookfunnel.com/623cagq73c

About the Author

Thank you for reading The Killing Cure Series! I'm so grateful you took the time to invest in Julia's and Charlie's story and I hope you enjoyed every step of the way! If you did, I would sincerely appreciate it if you took the time to post a review on Amazon or Goodreads. And if you put up a review, please let me know so I can personally thank you! Reviews are such powerful tools in getting books you love in front of more readers and it's a simple way you can help me in that process. I love connecting with readers, so look me up on the following:

You can connect with me on:

🌐 http://www.cskendall.com

[f] http://www.facebook.com/cskendallbooks

Subscribe to my newsletter:

✉ https://mailchi.mp/8b049e9c7c20/booknews

www.ingramcontent.com/pod-product-compliance
Lightning Source LLC
Chambersburg PA
CBHW052028240626
47153CB00006B/2002